Escaping Victoria

A Townsend Crime Novel

N. L. Blandford

ALSO AVAILABLE

Dark Psychological Thriller

The Perilous Road To Her (Book 1)

The Perilous Road to Freedom (Book 2)

The Perilous Road To Him (Book 3)

On The Perilous Road (Book 4) – Coming Soon

Comedic Thriller

The Great Bloody North – Hillford Holiday Series – Book 1

For Dad
The person I get most of my quirks from.

Trigger Warning

This book is an organized crime novel and contains violence, emotional, and physical abuse, as well as references to child abuse, and perceived incest.

CHAPTER ONE

NOW

THE MESSAGE COULD REFER to one of two men in Victoria's life. One, she'll feel relief, albeit complicated relief. The other, she'll be devastated.

With the constant discarding of burner phones, to avoid law enforcement or enemies encroaching on the strict confines of The Family, Victoria doesn't recognize who sent the text message. It definitely wasn't a member of her security team.

The unknown sends her on a roller-coaster of emotions. A fog masks her vision and she falls back on the bed.

Her training kicks in, and she heaves methodical inhales and exhales to bring her heartbeat back to a normal range. The fog dissipates. She raises her phone. The four words burrow into her eyes. Her future changed, for better or for worse, with one message.

Victoria's shaking finger hovers over the call button. Her stomach is in a vise, and with each breath, it tightens. She decides it's better to lock the phone than make the call. The dreadful message disappears, but is not forgotten.

Her surroundings back in focus, she pushes herself off the bed, grabs her smooth plastic room key and heads for a place of refuge. The hotel bar.

Victoria grips her phone, as though letting it go would unleash whatever secret it holds. She has become a professional at avoidance. Avoidance of feelings. Avoidance of reality. She doesn't want to know if white satin will cushion the one person she can't bear to see in a coffin.

Before leaving her room, Victoria leans her ear against the adjoining door to room 1204. The cool metal against her cheek does little to soothe her. She hears her client, Mr. Conrad, reassuring his wife of his safety and imminent return home.

Her protection detail finished for the night, and confident in the high-level security of The Bellamy Hotel, Victoria heads to what little solace she might be able to find downstairs.

Scoping the hall, she positions herself to the side of three elevators; to avoid a direct hit should danger erupt upon a door opening. Her toes tap as the number above one of the golden elevators counts down. When it reaches twelve, she focuses on the door with the arrow alight.

A wave of floral perfume smacks Victoria in the face. The source is a woman in her thirties in a white bathrobe with the hotel's monogram B on the chest, surrounded by her 'perfect family'. Victoria fights the urge to roll her eyes.

Normally, she would wait for the next elevator. It's safer to be alone. Today, she's grateful for the company. The distraction.

"We're goin' swimming!" The young girl pulls down the goggles from the top of her head. She reaches her arms out like a zombie. Her brother imitates her. The woman removes the goggles, much to the girl's dismay.

Victoria nods, stares forward, and moves her phone to her left hand. The hand closest to a potential threat should always remain free. Her peripheral vision detects the adults' glance at each other. Each places a hand on a child's shoulder. As if that one touch could protect them from the world. From Victoria. Her work excludes harming children, but if it didn't, no parent could stop her.

The elevator bounces as it settles on the first floor. The children's noses are as close to the door as possible without touching it, their reflections distorted by the golden sheen. Tiny feet are dancing in excitement. The parents move between Victoria and the children. They're gone within a millisecond of the door opening. The woman's floral perfume lingers behind and Victoria's temples pulse.

Outside of the elevator, reality regains its grip on Victoria's thoughts. The unknown hanging in the air like a heavy mist. Victoria tries to shake it off before entering the hotel bar. The sheen of the dark oak bar-top hides centuries of secrets. Will Victoria add another tonight?

The bartender, Brad, smiles and uncorks a bottle of whiskey Victoria hasn't bothered to learn the name of. He positions the crystal glass with the honey liquid in front of the seat on the farthest side of the bar, and returns the bottle to its spot on the glass wall behind him, with gold shelves holds the finest and most expensive liquor a guest could ever ask for.

Victoria takes her place on a high-top chair where she has lived most nights, for the past three months. It is a prime spot where she can watch the exits and entrances without being obtrusive.

Leaning against the bar-top, she assesses the room. In the dining area, two couples occupy blue suede booths, the occupants engrossed with their partner. An older man, mid-sixties, wearing a tailored light grey, double-breasted suit, takes refuge from the cool April night in a large leather lounge chair by the blazing stone fireplace. She notes his face is in full view above his half-folded newspaper.

The man is new here, unlike the couples. She'll keep an eye on him.

Victoria swirls the amber liquid in the glass. The drink goes down like water. She doesn't notice the waves of honey and vanilla fudge, or its cinnamon and toffee flavours. Without a word, Brad pours her another.

Victoria caresses the worn Peter Rabbit sticker on the back of her cell phone case. The one piece of her childhood she refuses to let go of. Rather than bringing her comfort, it taunts her.

Could this text be a ruse? Someone trying to unsettle her. Pull her back to Nova Scotia and away from the high-profile businessman she's been protecting? The one for whom a bullet grazed her shoulder only a month-and-a-half ago.

Communication from The Family was usually initiated by Nathan, her father. Their monthly, unemotional calls, focused on business updates from both sides of the Atlantic Ocean. Not knowing who might be listening, the calls were brief and cryptic. When an emergency arose, or a longer conversation was necessary, Victoria would steal an unsuspecting person's phone and contact Nathan on that month's predetermined emergency number.

Ever since Victoria's departure from the compound, Nicholas, her brother, has kept his distance. He only calls when Nathan cannot. Which is rare. She hurt him when she left the Townsend compound, and the country, without telling him. She regrets the hurt she caused, but for her own sanity it was necessary. If Nicholas had the opportunity, he would have convinced her to stay, and she would be miserable. Or dead.

Neither Nathan nor Nicholas have ever contacted her with such an ominous tone.

Victoria considers it atypical for Irving McKinnon, the head of the multi-layered criminal organization, to reach out to her. He would use Nathan or Nicholas as the middlemen. Unless something had happened to both of them.

Victoria reassures herself that the message said 'he's dead', not 'they'.

If it was a trick to pull her Mr. Conrad, the organization faced a bigger issue than a possibly deceased client. It could mean that they have an infiltrator.

Victoria vows swift punishment if anything unnatural has happened to Nicholas.

She glances at her phone but cannot bring herself to make the call.

The man by the fire closes his newspaper, folds it over the arm of the chair, and leaves the bar. He nods to Brad. Victoria watches as the elevator he rides stops on the twelfth floor. Her chest tightens.

"Brad, who was that man?" she asks.

"Oh, that's Mr. Singer," he answers, topping up her glass. "I heard he used to come here for years with his wife. In memory of her, he returns on their anniversary."

"Right." Her gut twinges. She pushes the feeling aside. Not everyone has ill intentions towards her. *Just let the man grieve,* she thinks.

After three drinks, a courage Victoria rarely requires pushes her to unlock her phone. The generic blue swirled background taunts her. She brings up the text message. With teeth clenched, she hits the call button beside the phone number.

Whose voice will she never hear again?

Chapter Two

Then: November 2003

Taco Tuesdays are Emily's favourite day of the week. Not because of the tacos. Her mother isn't the best cook, maybe the meat was supposed to smell like sweaty feet, but what does Emily know? She's only six. What she loves about Tuesday is that her dad isn't working, so they have uninterrupted family time.

The Tuesdays when Emily is alone with her dad are the days, she feels the most loved. Even without his arms around her, Emily feels her dad's adoration. Emily always wears a big smile when friends of her parents comment on how alike daughter and father are. "A mini-Rodney," they'd say as Emily mimicked his body language, words, and interests.

She may not want to be a surgeon like him when she grows up, as the thought of looking at the inside of a person makes her queasy, but she hopes to be as caring and devoted to her family as he is. Sure, a bigger house with beautiful things would be nice, but Emily's dad reminds her that possessions don't make a person, their heart does. As long as hers is in the right place, she'll rarely go wrong.

Emily wishes her mom's heart was in the right place more often. She doesn't believe her mother hates her, per se. She treats her well enough; home-schools her, hugs her when she asks, and plays with her, if not reluctantly, at least once a day. What Emily hopes for is to not feel like she's a chore that her mom has to check off a list.

Tonight, Mom, Dad, and daughter are together. Tacos finished; the game of Candyland is spread out over the dining room table. Emily's on a mission to win the mountainous pile of leftover Halloween candy across from her. With fewer ghosts and goblins visiting their home this year, Emily dreams of adding to the haul she brought home. Her mouth waters at the thought of the hoard that would last her until Christmas. Someone else could have the Tootsie Rolls. It was the milk chocolate and wafer crunch of the Kit-Kat's she was after.

Emily rubs her hands together. She's made it through the Molasses Swamp and can win it all if she makes it to the Candy Castle before Mom, who is two spots behind her. On the purple square six spaces from the castle, Emily needs to pull a purple card to win.

The prospect of the prize excites her. She tears the top card away from the pile. Her arms fly into the air. "Yes!" She leans over the dinner table, knees lifted off her chair, and moves her player six places. She reaches for the pile of candy, but before she captures her winnings, the front door crashes open.

Her dad bolts to his feet. Emily and her mom whip around towards the disturbance. Losing her balance, Emily falls off her chair, banging her chin on the edge of the table. The taste of iron fills her mouth. Drops of blood and tears paint her rainbow striped dress. Her mother screams something and grabs her daughter's hand. Emily's blood throbs in her ears, almost as loud as the surrounding commotion.

Dragged like a rag doll up the stairs, Emily's feet trip over the steps, but she keeps up as best as she can. Through the wooden stair rails, she sees three figures covered head to toe in black enter the dining room. Her dad braces himself in the arched doorway between the strangers and the living room, barricading the quickest way to the stairs.

Emily is up the stairs and shoved into her parents' bedroom closet before she knows what is happening.

"Stay here until I come get you. Okay?" Her mom's voice quivers as do her hands.

Wide-eyed, Emily nods.

A hanger teeters back and forth as her mother holds out a grey sweater with the face of Mickey Mouse on it, "use this to help stop the bleeding. Daddy will fix you up soon."

Emily listens but can't make out what is going on downstairs. She wishes she had her favourite stuffed animal, but grips her mother's sweater instead. The remnants of her lilac and orange perfume bring her some comfort.

She hears three loud bangs and covers her ears with her hands. They don't drown out her mother's scream. Two more bangs. Silence.

Emily scrunches her eyes closed and listens as hard as she can. The yelling and fighting have stopped. Her eyes dart through the slats of the closet door and around the bedroom. She thinks, maybe everything is okay but decides she'll wait for her parents to come get her. As her mom told her to.

Heavy footsteps pummel the stairs. The copper door handle turns slowly and something black pokes into the room.

She stuffs the soft sweater into her mouth to muffle her breathing, as three strangers stand in the middle of her parents' room. All three turn and face the closet.

Emily's mind races in circles. Can they see her through the door? Has she been too loud? She tries to curl up into a ball and bury herself under a pile of dirty laundry, her arms over her head for added protection. She squeezes her eyes as tight as possible. Maybe they won't find her?

The wooden doors creak, and her heartbeat quickens. Her throat swells with trapped screams. Silent prayers of *Daddy, please come find me*, and *make the bad people go away*, travel towards heaven.

Despite the pile of sweaters and shirts on top of her, she's getting colder. She can't feel the weight of them anymore. She doesn't want to open her eyes. Maybe they'll just leave her here.

"Hello there, young lady." A gruff yet gentle voice dances above her.

She keeps her eyes closed. Whoever it is, isn't Daddy, so she doesn't want to see them.

"It's okay. We won't hurt you. Why don't you come out here and meet some new friends?"

Emily shakes her head under her arms.

"In that case, I'll just sit out here until you're ready and my friends will wait outside."

The springs in the mattress screech in protest as the unknown figure sits.

For Emily, it feels like an eternity, huddled in the closet's corner. Why won't he just leave?

As if the stranger hears her thoughts, the bed creaks and the carpeting whispers the man's farewell.

Emily counts to one hundred and creeps to sitting, but keeps her eyes closed. Maybe he's just playing a game with her. She peels one eye open, as it refuses to do so on its own. No one's there. Reassured, her other eye pops open. She refuses to release the grey sweater her mom gave her. She crawls out of her hiding place, ducking under the low hanging clothing to avoid the bad man hearing her. She shuffles her feet towards the bedroom door and grips the door frame.

Her heart stops when she pokes her head into the hallway.

On the top step, the scary man sits holding Peter Rabbit, whose fur is worn from years of play and companionship. Every muscle in Emily tightens as she watches the man flop her favourite stuffed animal's ears back and forth.

If he hurts Peter...

"Nice rabbit you have here. What's his name?" The man says without looking at her.

"P...P...Peter."

"Peter's a good name for a rabbit."

The man's not wearing the black hood anymore. His brown hair perfectly brushed back. He reminds her of the actor her dad likes from those old black and white movies. He had a funny name, like the egg on the wall the king's men couldn't put together, Hum... something. Distracted by thoughts of snuggling up on the couch with her dad, the name sticks to the tip of her injured tongue. Emily squints away her tears. She needs to find her parents.

The man swivels towards Emily, she turtles behind her mother's sweater at the sight of his dark, hollow eyes. "Where's my Daddy?"

A small smile emerges from the corner of the man's mouth, held there by his square jaw. "Well, sweetheart, your Daddy's going to be gone for a really long time. Your mother too. But they asked me to take care of you." He holds Peter out towards her.

Emily trembles at the thought of getting closer to the scary man, but she wants to save Peter. With her jaw clenched, she sprints to Peter. She tries to bolt back to the doorway, but her wrist is locked in the man's large hand.

"Let go."

"Now, now, I'm really not that scary once you get to know me. And I have a son that's a couple years older than you. I think you and he are going to be great friends."

"I don't want any more friends." Emily's white lace-frilled socks slip on the carpet as she tries to peel herself from his grip.

Using one hand, the man lifts her off the ground and brings her face up to his. She screams in pain. Her dangled feet kick the man but make no impression. He keeps her in the air. "I know it's scary right now. But soon, you'll be having so much fun at my house that you'll forget all about this place."

"No, I won't." Defiance replaces her fear. But only a little.

The man puts her down, and against her protests, drags her down the stairs. She cranes her neck, trying to find her mom and dad, but they aren't in the living or dining rooms. All she sees are two dark red stains on the beige living room carpet that weren't there earlier.

Emily kicks and tries to pull away so she won't have to get into the large black car, whose front looks like it would open up and eat her. "Let go of me! HEL-"

The man shoves her into the backseat and the rest of her word is silenced.

Crying, she falls on the floor and the wound on her tongue starts to bleed again. She returns her mom's sweater to its healing place but it doesn't calm her fear.

The large driver's already in position, his companion seated in front of Emily. The faces a blur behind a wall of tears. Not moving from the floor, she rests her head against the seat and hopes everything is a bad dream. *Wake up*, she begs the universe.

"Sit." The scary man pats the seat beside him.

The only thing stopping Emily's hands from shaking is her grip on Peter and her mom's sweater.

The scary man pushes himself forward, and hunches over her, one arm resting on the seat back as the other tugs at the seatbelt. She sinks into the back of the seat trying to put as much space between them as possible. He smells weird, not like daddy's Old Spice.

The world around her is a blur, but metal clicks, and with a huff, the man moves away from her. The hairs on her arms stand tall. She stares at Peter and is afraid to look anywhere else.

If he can make her mom scream like she did, what might he do to her?

CHAPTER THREE

NOW

THREE RINGS ARE ALL it takes for Victoria's worst nightmare to abate.

"Thank God. I wasn't sure you'd call." Nicholas' soothing voice kisses her ears. She rubs her neck. Was it out of excitement or grief? Probably both.

"With a text like that? Of course I'd call. I was afraid..." Their complicated, and what those who don't know the truth about Victoria's origin, would call incestuous relationship, was the reason she stayed in The Family. The only reason she had not yet destroyed it. At least that's what she tells herself. In truth, the Townsends are her family. More or less. They protect her, employ her and give her a power she may not have known if life had turned out differently. She hates to admit it, but she likes who she is, and it's all because of them.

That doesn't mean her desire to escape the criminal life, and find her true self has been silenced. It calls to her daily; however, she's become adept at ignoring it. Mostly. Knowing Nicholas is alive, it screams louder than it has in years.

Nicholas fills the silence on his end of the line. "I'm sorry about that. I figured if I said Father was dead, you'd ignore me. This way-"

"I'd call."

"Ya." He clears his throat. "Listen, the funeral is in four days. I have Don arriving at your location tomorrow to take over leading your team. With a day to fill him in, that will get you here for the viewing."

"I don't know if I'll come."

Over the last five years, the ties that bind Victoria to the Townsends, to Nathan, have loosened. The semblance of freedom she's had tastes sweet.

Her decision to run a small team of two other people of her choosing, minimizes the chance that their loyalty to her would be swayed. Having heard nothing from Father, Nicholas or The Family regarding a few unsavoury incidents at the launch of her protection racket, she has no reason to believe they've been reporting back to those she has left behind.

Her time away has also given her the space to contemplate what Nathan's death would mean to her. Today, a wave of relief washed over her at hearing Nicholas' voice. It wasn't only because she still loved him, but because the beatings and manipulation at Nathan's hands would stop. Despite being adults, Nathan never failed to punish his children when they made a mistake.

Battling relief, was a sadness eating at her. She was unsure if it was Stockholm Syndrome, but Victoria felt like some days Nathan could be mistaken for a loving father. In his unique way. It was those days she'd miss.

Nicholas intrudes on her thoughts. "Yes, you will come home. If not for him, then for me."

The weight of Victoria's heart is almost unbearable. It had been two years since she last saw Nicholas in Paris for a crossover assignment. Their working lives required only one night of collaborative work since her departure from Nova Scotia. Prior to that, it had been three years with little to no contact. Victoria would be lying to herself if she said she didn't miss the only person in The Family she trusts. "I don't know. I mean, sure, it's Nathan's funeral, but would anyone really miss me? Besides, I don't know if I can deal with...*her*."

"Mother has been happier since you've been gone; but I'd take you over her in a fight any day. Anyway, I miss you. And when else am I going to get you back home?" Nicholas' sly smile travels the airwaves and Victoria's cheeks warm.

She cracks her knuckles against her leg, switches the hand holding the phone and repeats the action with her other hand. Then she bites the inside of her cheek. The pain reminds her of how strong she's become. Twenty-one years in the making, She's the strongest she's ever been. But

see in a few days. If only for twenty minutes. Victoria pushes her longing deep into her gut, to a place where secrets lie unattended. "I wish." She grips his t-shirt and pulls him in for a long, slow kiss. The warmth of his lips tempting her for more.

Brad's grip loosens from the door, but she pushes him away before his hands find their way around her waist. "I'm leaving tomorrow, so this is goodbye." Words colder than her touch.

"Ah, I see. One last night with your 'client' before you both head back to your families. I get it."

Victoria has no desire to protest his misunderstanding. She has no ties to the man in front of her and couldn't care less what he thought of her after she was gone. She simply smiles and closes the door to room 1204.

Just as she'd closed the door five years ago, if only part way, to her life at the Townsend compound. A life of emotional terror to which she was being called back to. A life from which she hopes Nathan's death will free her.

CHAPTER FOUR

THEN: NOVEMBER 2003

EMILY WISHES SHE COULD be like the grey November sky and release the tears welling up in her eyes. She hugs Peter close to her chest. His soft, worn body shakes in fear with her. She wants to scream for help at the cars crowding the Halifax streets. Knees clench together and bounce up and down. She has to pee, but is afraid to say anything. Part of her wants to ruin the bad man's nice leather seats but she knows upsetting the man beside her will be a bad idea. The other half doesn't want to ruin her dress.

Emily tries to distract herself by looking for clues to where they are going. She will need to tell her daddy when she talks to him again. Then he can tell the police.

The black exterior of the car continues on the inside. There's not a scratch or dent anywhere. The cream leather extends along the doors and features a silver door handle, four buttons, and one knob. The soft string music enters the car from two golden circles. Emily's too small to see the front of the car, but she presumes it's just as nice up there, with their own wide leather seats.

The armrest that separates the bad man and Emily has two compartments. As much as she is curious to look inside them, she doesn't.

The man pulls the dark curtains along his window and presses a button beside him. The ceiling sparkles with thousands of stars. A small gasp escapes Emily's mouth.

"Pretty, isn't it?" his voice has softened.

She keeps her eyes on the stars and nods.

"Your name's Emily, isn't it?"

She nods again.

"That's a beautiful name. My name is Nathan." He holds out his hand. "It's nice to meet you."

Emily peels her eyes away from the stars. Daddy always told her to be polite, so she unwraps her right hand off Peter and shakes Nathan's. She focuses on the hands and avoids his eyes. She doesn't expect his hand to be so soft. After two shakes, he lets go and her eyes return to the twinkling stars above.

"I'm going to be completely honest with you, Emily, which is something I rarely am with anyone. That means you are a very special person. Besides, I think you and I are going to be good friends."

Everything in Emily wants to scream, "I told you I don't want more friends." Instead, she clenches her teeth and stays silent. This way, maybe he'll tell her where her parents are.

"But you need to promise me you'll behave and do exactly what I say. Can you do that?"

She slowly nods, unsure what this stranger might ask her to do.

"As long as someone is looking me in the eye, I can always tell when they are lying. So, look at me and say I promise."

Emily has to lick the top of her mouth to erase the dryness from it before she can speak. Her eyes fall to her white socks, the bottoms brown with dirt from being dragged along her driveway. Mom won't be happy about that. She gathers up all of her courage and looks the man in the eye. Her stomach swirls. His eyes have turned kind. She doesn't understand. He's an evil man. How can he have friendly eyes? She whispers, "I promise."

"Good. When we arrive at home, my wife, Brigitta, will not be happy to see you. In fact, it's probably best you stay close to me for a little while. Brigitta can get ferocious and you don't want to be in her path when that happens. But I'll protect you." Nathan pats Emily's quivering knee. "The thing is, we have...well, had, a daughter your age. Her name was Victoria. She died a couple of weeks ago." Puddles form at the bottom of Nathan's brown eyes. He looks away from Emily, breathes deep and when he looks back, the puddles are gone.

"Why did she die?"

"Someone who didn't like me very much tried to hurt me, but Victoria ended up getting hurt instead."

Her heart hurts. Poor Victoria.

"Brigitta will not like having another little girl around. Not right away. But she'll come around."

Emily bites her lip harder than intended and it bleeds. Nathan passes her a pale blue handkerchief from his suit jacket pocket. Cedar and vanilla rest under her nose as she applies pressure to her wound.

He continues, "Victoria needed an operation, and the doctor didn't save her, like he should have. Do you know any really good doctors?"

The handkerchief muffles her voice. "mm..my...my dad."

"Correct. Nathan swallows hard. "It's hard for me to talk about, but what you need to know is that your dad was supposed to save her, but he didn't. It was hard for Brigitta and I to have a little girl, something Brigitta always wanted. We lost three babies before Victoria was born and now, she's gone, too."

Emily's kind heart can't help but show itself. "I'm sorry."

"Thank you. I haven't slept for days trying to come up with a plan. Some way to make it up to Brigitta. Do you know how I'm going to make our family whole again?"

Her head shakes, and she has to fight the urge to look at her feet. The man said to look him in the eyes when they're speaking and she didn't want to anger him. He probably won't help her find her parents if she does.

"I've known your parents for a long time. Although I hadn't met you, I knew they had a daughter Victoria's age. When I saw your photo, I could see your big smile and green eyes speaking to me. It was as if my little girl was staring up at me. It's a sign from God that the doctor who took my little girl away will also be the one to give her back."

"But she's dead, so you can't have her back."

"That's why you are coming to live with me."

"No, I live with Mom and Dad."

"Not anymore, you don't."

Emily discards the handkerchief beside her and buries her face into Peter's already damp head. He's no comfort at this moment. Her whole-body shakes. Her dress and seat become warm and wet. She can't stop the tears.

Nathan rubs her hand. "There's no need to cry. You're safe with me."

"I...I... I'm scared, and I made a mess."

"I see. No need to be scared. What can you do to fix the mess?"

She shrugs her shoulders. She longs to hug her mom and dad and can't think of anything else.

"Why don't you ask the nice man driving, Louis, to stop at the next department store he sees and we can get you cleaned up?" Nathan unlocks her seat belt and nods forward.

Emily places Peter on the wide arm rest as though he's seated in his own chair. Her legs stick to the leather as she scuttles her wet butt forward until her feet touch the carpeted floor. Drops trickle down her Jello-like legs. She digs her nails into the headrest of the seat in front of her to keep her balance as the car continues down the streets of Halifax.

Nathan nods again.

"Excuse me, can you please stop at a store?"

"Will do, young lady." Louis' voice paints a picture as though this is a normal day for him.

Emily's eyebrow curls when he winks at her in the mirror. Why are they being so nice? They took me away from my parents, my home, but they're acting like nothing's wrong.

She remains standing as she doesn't want to sit in the mess she made, but Nathan points at her seat. A wordless order. She re-enters the cooled puddle.

"That wasn't so bad, now, was it?"

Emily shakes her head and pulls Peter back to her chest. The car pulls into a parking lot and stops in front of the doors. Louis opens Nathan's door and the evening breeze pricks Emily's bare arms. The man who was in front of Emily opens her door and holds out his dry and scratchy hand to help her out.

Nathan takes Peter from Emily and passes him to Louis. "They will watch him while we're inside." He turns to Emily. "We don't want to lose him now, do we?"

"No." She checks on Peter's safety as he's perched on the dashboard. Louis retrieves a towel from the trunk and cleans Emily's mess. She lifts herself onto her tiptoes to see if her parents are hiding in there. Maybe everything is a mean joke to punish her for something she did. Not that she knows what that would be as she follows all of their rules. Mostly.

The trunk is bodiless.

Protected from the rain by the concrete building's overhang, Emily's head only swivels forward once the store's automatic doors open.

Nathan squats in front of her. His mean face is back. "You don't say a word to anyone, you understand?" He smooths out the shoulders of her dress and runs his hands down her arms until he retakes her hand.

She nods.

"Remember what I said about using words?"

"I understand." Emily says.

Nathan stands tall and a girl folding T-shirts at a table inside the entry welcomes him. "Is there anything I can help you with?"

"We've had a slight accident and we need a nice new dress. Something pink perhaps?" Nathan replies.

"I think we can find one of those" She bends to meet Emily's height. "And what is your name, young lady?" Her smile is inviting.

Emily wants to scream for help, but Nathan squeezes her hand and she clenches her teeth to prevent herself from speaking.

"This is Victoria." Nathan says.

CHAPTER FIVE

NOW & THEN: 2019

VICTORIA'S KNUCKLES TURN WHITE from her grip on the hard leather steering wheel. She stares at the keypad that opens the thick, black wrought-iron gate. Six buttons will whisk her back into the cruel world she's been tethered to, but from which she's had some much-needed freedom.

She turns off the windshield wipers and the torrent of rain swells the memories of the day she moved one step closer to that independence.

Nathan strides around his office, a sturdy six-foot, two-inch frame in his typical black double-breasted suit. Not a strand of his greying slicked-back hair is out of place. One hand flexes in his pants pocket, while the other holds a cigar waiting to be lit. "You think you can leave The Family? Leave us?"

Outside the double-hung windows, a flock of chickadees chirp and dance in circles across a tapestry of pinks and purples. Exercising an independence Victoria longs for. "You and I both know I'm not welcome here. Not really. I never have been."

"This is about Brigitta?"

"Not just her." It's also about him, but she'd never tell him that.

"What about Nicholas?" His all-knowing eyes locking onto hers. "He'll be devastated if you go."

She is prepared for him to play the Nicholas card and doesn't let it affect her. As much as it pains her to leave him, her survival means letting their past together go. "He'll be fine. He'll double down on his efforts to make you proud of him. Perhaps, you might actually tell him he's doing a great job."

Nathan huffs and twirls the coarse cigar between his fingers. "He's doing fine. But not great. Not like you. I should whip you for asking, but I'll give you points for having the guts to do so. You know too much, and you know there's no 'leaving' The Family." Nathan leans back against his large, antique oak desk. Immaculate placement of papers, pens, and an ashtray goes undisturbed. "So, what is it that you really want?"

Nathan is very intuitive at reading people and situations. The trick is making him believe he's smarter than the other person in the conversation. That he discovered the solution independently, not because of being guided towards a desired answer. It has taken Victoria years to master this, and she's kept the secret to herself. Not even Nicholas knows the tricks of this trade.

Victoria strolls around the room. She runs her finger along a few of the treasured volumes of books. She picks up a small brass sculpture of the Bluenose and fills with hope that she will be able to sail away from the man before her. The ship returned to its home, Victoria picks up a picture of Nathan, Brigitta, Nicholas and herself taken outside their favourite ice cream shop. Her fingers wrap around the gold gilded frame. Ice cream lipstick covers the faces of a nine-year-old Emily - as she still thought of herself back then, and a twelve-year-old Nicholas. Brigitta's beautiful smile doesn't hide her usual annoyance at the replacement daughter. Nathan's face, still free of wrinkles, stares down at the children. A rare glimpse of fatherly affection from a normally stern face.

Nathan's family and The Family mean the world to him. If she wants to win, she's going to have to make him think that her plan is beneficial to both.

Victoria has spent nights working out exactly how her leaving would be financially and strategically beneficial. If he doesn't benefit, there's no point in asking. She knows that he'd be happiest if the results enable him to manipulate others into doing what he wants.

Under no circumstances will she reveal her true intentions. If he gets any sense of what her idea means to her, he'll make it difficult to get, less enjoyable, or deny her.

If she were to leave without permission, she'd be dead. Nathan doesn't want that. If she stays, he won't be able to stop another daughter from dying, as this time she'd succeed with her suicide. He doesn't want that either.

The family photo is returned to its rightful place on a shelf by the window seat. She locks eyes with him. One glance away and he'll smell her fear. He'll refuse the request, leaving no chance for a second ask. "What if we started a new venture as part of the family business?"

Nathan's ears perk up to the potential of expanding his business, but he waits for all the facts before he speaks.

"Contract me out as a bodyguard for hire to high-profile individuals. People whose political, business, or legal lives are being threatened and who need protection. I know they could get this service from established outfits, but what makes us unique is we'll give them their first service at half the market rate."

Questions stack in Nathan's eyes and he bites on his cigar to restrain himself from asking them. Part of teaching his children to be thriving criminals included letting the other person do most of the talking. Often, they reveal what they're really seeking.

It also creates the opportunity to get a better understanding of an opponent.

"They foot the bill for my accommodation, transportation and living expenses. My services, which we would highlight, would include the removal of any known threats, would also be at a discount during their first experience with us. We won't disclose that I'll be gathering as much intelligence on them as possible, and they'll be compelled to work with us in more lucrative ways in the future."

A sly grin creeps across Nathan's face. He lights his cigar, takes a few puffs, and rolls his wrist for her to continue.

"Our challenge is to publicize our cost without giving our enemies an advantage. That part requires some finesse and a willingness to look weaker than we are. I know, I know. Weakness equals death, but hear me out. If our enemies think we are so desperate for business that we are practically giving it away, they'll focus on making a play for our other business ventures in the hopes our empire will collapse. They'll let us have this one piece. Meanwhile, we'll both defend our existing infrastructure and poach their clients from right under their noses. Yes, our underground reputation could take a hit, but it'll be worth it, especially with The Family on board." She maintains eye contact and lets Nathan ask the one question she's yet to answer.

"Why you? I could easily send Don or any of our very skilled assassins. You were all trained the same. Anyone in my employ could turn this idea into success."

"Three reasons. Statistically, men are more likely to hold positions of power. As much as I hate to admit it, men currently rule the world. Therefore, most of our clients in this venture would be male. I have a certain.. .appeal, that Don, or any other man who works for you, may not, in most circumstances."

Nathan can't hide the veins in his neck throbbing at the thought of men being sexually attracted to Victoria. She wasn't the only woman working for him, but her girl-next-door looks made her one of the most attractive.

"Second, I'm a better marksman. I'm faster. I'm less conspicuous. I can get people to talk. Plus, you trust me. Frankly, I'm the best person to start this venture. I'll pick a small team, one, maybe two people. Include others later when the demand increases, but for now, you cannot deny we need to start out strong and that means me."

Victoria stands beside Nathan and weaves her arm around his. She holds it as well as his stare, "Third, letting me outside the walls of this place long enough to breathe might just give me the desire to stay. Forever. Presently, I'm trapped, and we are aware of the consequences for animals in prolonged captivity."

Nathan glances at her scar, and his eyes glisten. She doesn't need to say the words for him to understand. He squeezes her hand and kisses the top of her head. "I've dreaded the day you'd come and ask me for an assignment outside of my immediate reach. It was bound to happen. Even with everything I've given you, I knew the property's stone walls could not hold you back forever. Part of me hoped whatever fuels you to be successful here, would keep you by my side. Running everything with me. Yes, Nicholas is a perfectly acceptable second in command. But you and I, we have something. Well, you know."

For her plan to work, Victoria monitors her breathing to ensure the anticipation of Nathan's agreement does not derail everything. She calls forth the rare happy memories she has with the man. A mask to cover her loathing of him for killing her parents. "Then you agree with my plan?"

"I agree it's a decent plan. More work needs to be done to make it brilliant. Only then will I decide who facilitates it."

As a blanket of darkness consumes the remains of the sunset, Victoria leans her head against his chest. Since she's mastered her tricks, Nathan's never been able to deny her what she wants. She smiles on the inside. She's won again. One day, she'll win the entire game when she burns the Townsend compound to the ground.

Chapter Six

Then: November 2003

Emily's new dress is light pink and has white, flowered lace over top and three bright pink flowers along her waist, with a ribbon tied around the back. She can't see the bow it forms behind her, but it digs into her as she sits back in the car. The orange, red, and yellow leaves wave at her amongst the dark green of balsam firs on the side of the careening highway. Her nerves jiggle beneath her new frilly socks and sparkling silver shoes.

Peter doesn't like her new outfit. He prefers her in her own clothes.

Emily's unsure if she likes it. It's pretty, but she feels weird. Like there are ants crawling on her arms and back and she can't shake them off. She supposes if she wants to see Mommy and Daddy again, she should play along. They're just clothes, after all.

What she doesn't understand is why Nathan told that girl in the store her name was Victoria? He knows it's Emily.

The car stops, and Emily cranes her neck to look out her window.

"Press that button and the window will go down." Nathan instructs.

A tall black fence that never ends stops the car, but not for long. With a whirring sound, the mouth of the fence opens.

"Welcome to your new home." Once again, he unbuckles her seatbelt. "Have a look."

"This isn't my home," Emily whispers.

"What was that?"

"Nothing." She stands, wraps her mother's Mickey Mouse sweater around her waist, and leans over the car door to keep herself steady in the moving vehicle. Her body presses against Peter to keep him in the car, with his chin resting on the door so he can see too. Tall, sturdy trees with lights reflected off their trunks line the driveway. She can't see the end of the dense forest surrounding the property. Pine, dirt and the remnants of fall float in the air. There are no other houses around.

A fountain sits in the middle of the driveway, so they have to drive around it. The trip ends at stone steps that lead up to a massive, bright yellow two-story house. Emily's house was really nice, but this one is beautiful. It looks like one of the Mexican hotels her parents took her to. It's like nothing she's ever seen in Nova Scotia.

She pushes back tears as she wraps one hand around the door handle. The other grips Peter. What if she ran?

But where would she go? Would she be fast enough?

Her hand tight around the handle, she falls out of the car when Nathan opens the door. He catches her and flips her upright in the driveway before she collides with the pavement. As if he knows her thoughts, he keeps hold of her free hand and they walk up the steps.

Two stone lions lie on pillars at the top of the stairs. They look like they're napping and are unconcerned that a stranger has entered their property. Someone shaped the fence's black material into flowers between the glass of the two large doors. They open into the prettiest house Emily's ever seen.

The heels of Emily's new shoes announce her presence on the stone floors. She cranes her neck and a large golden chandelier with fake candles and little black hats hangs from a ceiling that only a giant could touch. A cream-coloured stone and carpeted staircase leads to the second floor. Nathan escorts her through an archway that is twice as tall as him and that four people could stand in. Wooden tables, chests and ugly artwork decorates a long hallway. Why do people like hanging pictures of unsmiling people from so long ago? When she grows up, she'll have cheerful people on her walls.

They stop in a doorway. Nathan takes a deep breath, looks at Emily and whispers. "It's best if you say nothing. If you're to live here, we need Brigitta to like you. Only I can make that happen. Okay?"

"But I don't want to live here." She yanks her hand from his and runs towards the front door. Her shoes slap against the marble floor.

Nathan has her arm in his grasp before she gets six of her small steps away. "Where else do you think you can go?"

"Home," she pouts with a stomp.

"That home doesn't exist anymore. There's only this one. Or, you can live out in the forest, all by yourself, with all the wild and scary animals."

The trees outside the floor to ceiling windows dance in the wind like tall ghosts.

"Which would you prefer?" Nathan asks.

"I'd prefer to go home." She stomps her feet again.

He squeezes both of her arms. She tries to wriggle free. "Ouch, you're hurting me."

"I'll stop if you behave, but if you don't, Brigitta will hurt you worse."

"Nathan? Is that you?" A sharp voice filters out of the doorway they had been in moments ago. "What's going on out there?"

His eyes plead with Emily, like her daddy's do when he wants her to go along with something instead of telling Mommy the truth. Emily's shoulders slump and she drags her feet as Nathan walks her into a living room the size of a community pool.

Red and cream carpets hang on the walls. A large black piano sits in the corner, its lid open. There are two sets of living room furniture which mirror each other; except one looks at the piano and the other at a giant stone fireplace. Emily could stand inside the fireplace and there would still be space all around her.

The pretty things disappear with the shrill of Brigitta's voice. "Who's this?" Her long red nails point at the girl. The woman stumbles forward, causing the green olive from her drink to fall onto the blue carpet, and a splash of clear liquid joins it. Her eyes have a familiarity Emily cannot place.

Nathan moves her in front of his body, like a shield. She hugs Peter to protect him. Nathan's hands rest on her shoulders. "This is Emily. She's going to live with us. Make up for what was lost." He reaches for Brigitta's hand "Be our Victoria."

His soft yet stern voice confuses Emily. Is he asking or telling the strange and angry woman what is happening?

"Don't you dare say her name." The woman's face turns the same colour as her nails and her eyes bulge out of her head. Her drink glass shatters against the wall. "It's your fault she's gone...you were supposed to make Rodney pay for what he did, not bring her...to our home. No. She is not Victoria. Our daughter is not replaceable." Brigitta lunges for Emily's arm but she crouches down, releasing herself from Nathan's grasp. And runs.

She doesn't care that her shoes are a beacon for where she is, she just wants out. Raised voices get lost in the large house as she turns down unrecognizable hallways and runs through endless rooms. She pulls on every door handle to the outside world, but they refuse to release her.

She's out of breath but doesn't want to stop. She circles around, looking for an exit, as she needs to get out of here and find Mommy and Daddy. How do these scary people know her parents? What bad thing did Daddy do that she's stuck here?

A cool breeze kisses her right arm. Then she sees it. An open door. Green grass lies beyond. She just needs to make it through one more room. She runs as fast as she can.

"Hello?" a soft voice she can't see calls out.

Emily comes to a halt and ducks behind the kitchen island. Have they seen her or only heard her shoes?

Her heartbeat quickens. She's so close to the door. She places Peter on the floor and silently tells him to hold on while she tightens the knot of the grey sweater around her waist. Picking him up again, her footsteps go unheard as she shuffles like a duck to the end of the island and closer to her escape. Her fingers grip the cold corner of the kitchen island. She pushes herself towards the door.

"Who are you?"

Frozen like a sprinter mid race, only her eyes turn towards the voice.

A blond boy not much older than Emily leans against the island, his shoulders almost the height of the counter-top. He shovels cereal into his mouth and milk drips down his chin and back into the bowl. The crunch of the food echoes off the cabinetry. His blue eyes are kind.

The boy wipes his shirt sleeve along his mouth and the dishes clank against the sink. Then he holds out his hand, "I'm Nicholas."

Gripping Peter, Emily stares at his hand. He steps forward, arm still out-stretched. An echo of her dad's voice rings in her ears, "Emily, be polite."

She peels one hand off Peter and puts it inside Nicholas'. Warmth rushes over her and her fear dissipates a little.

"What's your name?" he asks.

"Em.. Emily." Her hand still in his, he guides her to the other side of the kitchen. Away from the door she longed to be on the other side of.

"Are you hungry? We're not supposed to have cereal for dinner, but ever since-"

"I want to go home."

"Where's home?"

"It's...in Halifax, across the river is an old tower."

"That's pretty far. Were you planning on walking?" he jokes.

"If I have to." She doesn't understand how Nicholas could be so calm with a strange girl in his house.

"All by yourself? You're funny."

"I'm not funny. I want to go home."

Nicholas' smile disappears. "Okay. Okay. I'll help you find your parents. Do you remember where in the house you left them?"

Tears cover Emily's cheeks and her shoulders slump forward. "They're not here. Three scary men took me. That's why I have to go home."

Nicholas' face goes pale. His eyes shift around the room. "Follow me." He pulls Emily out the kitchen door. The crisp night air cools her burning skin. Nicholas guides her around the side of the building. He winces and she notices his feet are bare as they walk along a gravel pathway. She's so close to freedom she can smell sewage in Halifax's harbour.

"Going somewhere?" A voice bellows from behind the children.

Nicholas squeezes Emily's hand and they sluggishly turn back towards the house. With the golden lights shining down off the building and up from out of the stone patio, Nathan looks ten feet tall on top of the steps. She can't see his eyes, but she can feel them target her nonetheless. Louis and the other big man from earlier step out from beside the building.

Nathan glares at Nicholas. "I'll deal with you later." With one hand squeezed on each of the children's shoulders, he directs them back into the house.

Emily will have to plan her escape for another time.

Brigitta, with her arms crossed, and her toe tapping against the floor, huffs at the miscreants. Her anger and displeasure cannot hide her beauty. Her eyes tighten their grip on Emily. "You are to keep your mouth shut, do exactly as I say and if you take one step out of line, I'll feed you to the bears. Understood?"

Emily's head refuses to nod and her lips won't move.

Brigitta yanks the girl away from Nicholas and grips her chin. Her long nails dig into skin. "When I ask you a question, you answer it."

Emily's bottom lip quivers and her head tries to agree, but inside Brigitta's grip, it barely moves.

Brigitta's eyes are on fire as she glares at Emily. "Good. And stop your crying, child. This house has no place for tears." Her grip lingers after she lets go of the girl's chin.

Nicholas retakes Emily's hand and guides her up the carpeted marble staircase. She grips Peter and the edge of her mother's sweater against her stomach. At least she has something of her own in this scary place.

She doesn't know why she looks back, but when she does, she sees Brigitta has disappeared and Nathan is staring at her. Hands in his pockets, he smiles and rocks back and forth on his heels.

Emily's dad's voice is back in her head, "It'll be alright. You're strong. You'll find a way back to us."

Chapter Seven

Now

THE BUZZ OF THE front gate brings her back to the present. Someone in the security booth must have noticed her sitting there and opened the gate before she could enter the code. Victoria stretches her tense fingers, while her palms touch the steering wheel, allowing the blood to return. Brigitta will feed off her unease and she will not give her the satisfaction.

The familiar, haunting yellow mansion comes into view. Vehicles litter the driveway. The fear Nathan instilled in those who worked for, or with, him continues after death. They know Nicholas will hand out retribution to those with excuses for not attending the events around his father's funeral. If not a bullet, then gruelling work until the person loses their usefulness. Those working the protection racket are the only exceptions.

Four people in black suits line the front steps. None react to the buckets of rain the sky throws at them. A man Victoria doesn't recognize opens her door. She leaves the keys in the ignition for him. She holds up her face to the fresh rain and saunters to the house. The less time she has to spend inside these cold-blooded walls, the better.

Water clings to Victoria's skin as it travels down her black leather jacket and pierces her black tights. Hair sticks to her face and eyelashes. Her reflection in the glass of the front door causes her to laugh: Brigitta will not like this. She revels in the thought as her military-style black boots cross the threshold.

A wave of longing to escape this criminal world envelopes her. What's stopped her? She's never been able to come up with a plan where Nicholas can get out, too. Not that he wants to leave, which is part of the problem.

Every time she brings up the subject of leaving the life behind, running away together, he scoffs at the idea. Despite knowing people who could get them new identities, Nicholas believes the need to always look over their shoulders would take the fun out of their new life. Besides, he's poised to become the Director of The Family. All that money and power is a definite temptation to stay.

Voices trickle under the archway beside the staircase. They grab hold of Victoria like a lasso and pull her forward. Nathan's employees, associates, and friends - if you'd call them that - whisper and glare as she passes. Judgment about her appearance, and perhaps existence, oozes from their eyes.

Head held high, Victoria smiles and takes pleasure in their discomfort. Her typical black attire mirrors the attendees. Her casual style is not reflective of the suits and dresses. As though she carries the Black Death, those near her take three steps back and create a path down the center of the ballroom.

The polished hardwood floor mirrors the banister on a stairwell in the corner leading to a second-floor balcony. Sentries guard the balcony and doors to prevent guests from exploring the house, stealing artifacts, or accost the grieving family.

Positioned in the curve of an expansive bay window is Nathan's shiny black coffin, lined with a silver trim and pallbearer rails. The lid is open, but the body is unseen from Victoria's vantage point. Spiders crawl up her spine. His death wasn't real until this moment. Her mind, body, and soul fight the contradiction of emotions travelling through her core. Emotions she had shut off for so long.

Not only did the man kill her parents, he'd stolen her childhood, turning her into an obedient criminal with a deadly mind and even deadlier hands.

Yet Nathan also gave her everything she ever asked for. Well, to a point, and after years of figuring out 'how' to ask. Not being his biological daughter never stopped him from loving her like she was, his affection shown in untraditional ways, always to the benefit of himself, but never made

Victoria feel unwanted. In fact, when he was home, he'd spend more time with her than Nicholas. This caused strife between the Townsends. There was no escaping the discord which filled this house.

When she was younger, the males would shield her from Brigitta's wrath until she was big enough to fight back. Even then, she understood Nathan continued to protect her behind closed doors. Now, one of her protectors is gone and yet a sense of satisfaction blankets her.

Victoria buries the thoughts in the back of her mind. She just needs to survive this week and maybe she can get the support she needs from Nicholas, and thereby Brigitta, to leave forever. In reality, she knows her fake mother would prefer to have her killed, but she'll make Brigitta see why that would not be to The Family's benefit. The protection racket is making a lot of money and the organization doesn't need more change than it's already going through. She can maintain her position on the outskirts, if she must. For now.

As Victoria reaches the end of the parted sea of bodies, the matriarch of the house becomes visible. The sheer black veil covering Brigitta's long blond hair and Botox-riddled face cannot hide her disgust as she digests Victoria's wet and ragged attire. Her large diamond wedding ring sparkles in the light of the crystal chandeliers, as her hands ball into fists. She takes a step towards her surrogate daughter, but a hand grips her shoulder and holds her back. The knives Brigitta's eyes throw pierce Victoria's many layers of armour. After all these years, she can still get under her skin.

Victoria retracts her own daggers. Her gaze travels along the hand keeping Brigitta from her, across the broad shoulders and follows a line of scarred skin that peeks out from the collar of a white dress shirt and continues faintly up the side of the boyish, yet worn, face of the only person she wants to see on this short trip home.

Nicholas. Protector number two once again steps between her and Brigitta.

Living within a criminal organization entails hiding feelings while still experiencing them passionately. Even after years apart, his eyes shout a thousand unspoken words: gratefulness she came back, worry and delight over her audacity to show up looking like a drowned rat, affection, happiness, sorrow, and anger that she left him.

With Brigitta somewhat distracted by another guest, Nicholas steps forward and wraps his arms around Victoria. Comfort and safety hug her. His warm, marine and bergamot cologne elicits a lifetime of memories. He kisses her cheek and holds her body out in front of him. "You look like shit."

"I could look worse."

"Could you?" Nicholas winks, and Victoria revels in the fact the wet front of his suit will irk Brigitta for a while. He guides Victoria to the other end of the coffin. "I'm glad you're here. Even if you didn't think to go upstairs and change first."

"The look on her face was worth it." Victoria knows Brigitta's eyes will remain on her as she cordially accepts condolences from guests. Her fake smile hiding a mixture of hatred and fear that her rival for Nathan's affection will ruin the day.

Victoria winks and smirks at her, while pondering what she might do to make the fears come true. Perhaps an obnoxious speech? Not really her style. Knocking over the casket? Now that would cause a scene; however, that would be too low - even for her. Satisfied the torture of Brigitta being kept in suspense will be enough, Victoria turns her focus to Nathan.

Even in death, Nathan's face keeps the appearance of someone who grew up on the streets and fought his way to power. Someone meticulously pressed his black and white pinstriped suit and adorned it with his favourite cufflinks. The sight of which causes her stomach to ride a roller coaster of love and hate.

Growing up with the Townsends was hard. Punishment for disobedience was cruel, and watched over by the man lying before her. She wanted to be the one to kill him, but something or someone beat her to it.

She rubs her hands on her pants to wipe away the unwanted grief bubbling inside of her. She tries to flick away the craving she developed for the smiles Nathan displayed in private, when his eyes turned kind and she momentarily felt safe. Loved.

Her eyes sting and she cuts off the emotional torment. There is no time for feelings and there was no way she will show Brigitta that Nathan's death is affecting her.

Although not religious, she still says a brief prayer, that after years of battling external and internal enemies, Nathan has found peace.

Irritated by the itchiness of her hair being plastered carelessly on her face, she pushes it into a tattered mess behind her ears. She survey's the room again and finds Paul Inglis' tall lanky frame not far from Brigitta, as usual. The head of the Inglis outfit, and an ally to The Family, but a group yet to be approved to join. She recalls Nathan's disdain for the man, telling her the Inglis' would never be approved while he still breathed the ocean air.

Victoria's never liked the man and hopes he won't be gracing the halls of the compound much.

Next, her eyes fall on Irving McKinnon along the far wall. He's pays little attention to the person talking beside him. Like Brigitta, his eyes are on Victoria.

His white hair, sprinkled with grey, accents his soft blue eyes. His seventy years of life hidden behind a well-tailored suit and rigorous adherence to exercise and a healthy diet. He is one of the few people Victoria knows who takes their health as seriously as their business without being forced to. He will not let a heart attack take away his power.

If Victoria didn't know any better, Irving appeared like a gentle old man. However, she did know better. There was a reason his nickname was The Snake. He'd crush the life out of a person or business before they knew what happened.

His wealth, power and connections to the legitimate and illegal business world evolved into the creation of The Family, and his apparent invincibility. Nathan, and now Nicholas, may be the Director of The Family, but Irving is the God.

She knows she should talk to him, but dares not approach him as disheveled as she is. For Nicholas' benefit, she understands the level of decorum needed to interact with Irving. She swallows hard and diverts from his gaze and back to the living man beside her. "Should we give Brigitta's glaring eyes a break and get out of this sardine can of entitlement and lies?"

Nicholas hesitates and fumbles with his pocket flaps. "How would it look if the new Director left his grieving mother's side and ignored those we work most closely with? They are already vipers trying to seize more power." Nicholas' hands continue to fumble with his meticulous suit. "It would be nice if you stood with us."

"Ha. Brigitta would love that." Victoria catches her eye as the woman kisses the cheeks of one of their suppliers, while shaking his hand. The smile on Brigitta's face shields the stranglehold she desires to wrap around Victoria's neck. "You know what? Sure. I'll even be nice enough to change first."

Hands out of his pockets, Nicholas cups her head and kisses her smooth forehead. "I appreciate that. And maybe shower as well. The flies will start circling soon."

"You don't like the perfume of a nine-hour flight, shitty fast food and wet dog? How rude." She squeezes Nicholas' wrists and once again parts the sea of people while whispers die in her wake.

Chapter Eight

Then: November – December 2003

On her first night at the Townsend compound, Emily is locked in a large bedroom, with pale pink walls and a white four-poster bed. Normally, she would be excited to have a princess bed, but she hates it and everything about the room.

"Let me out!" Her fists pound, while her feet alternate kicking the wooden door. It stands tall. A few scuffs from her shoes, but otherwise left undamaged.

No one responds to her repeated cries.

Her throat sore, she looks around the room for another means of escape. She opens a bedroom window. She squeezes Peter Rabbit at the thought of jumping, as there is nothing she can use to climb down.

The bathroom window cannot be opened. A jetted tub sits in the corner. She would normally like to play in it, but she doesn't.

With no way out, she returns to the bedroom and slumps into the cushioned window seat. The evening air through the screen cooling her warm skin.

Across the room, by the bed, is a closet that could hold all the clothes she would ever want. It even has its own doorway.

"It's okay Peter. I'll get us out of here. We'll find Mommy and Daddy." She squeezes him tight. The blanket of fear cannot compete with exhaustion, and Emily falls asleep to crickets and frogs singing their lullaby in the woods.

A soft shake of her shoulder pulls her out of a dream where she and her dad are painting rocks to sell at her school's holiday craft fair. She looks forward to the annual traditional of the splatter of paint on the craft table expanding, while she and Dad laugh, sing Christmas Carols, and make miniature scenic pictures.

"Wake up." The dark eyes of the bad man stare down at her.

As she remembers where she is, and what happened, the anticipation that in a couple of weeks she and her dad would be on the beach choosing the best rocks fades into an ounce of hope. Still there, but shadowed by fear. Her stomach gurgles.

"It's time for breakfast." He grabs her hand and doesn't let go when she tries to take it back. "You don't have to eat everything, but you must eat something."

"I want to go home."

"We are not having this conversation again. You are home and that is the end of that." He tugs on her arm to get her moving.

Peter falls to the floor. Her fingers stretched wide as she reaches out for him.

"Leave him. There are no toys allowed in the dining room." The somewhat gentle voice from the car is gone.

Emily mouths "sorry" to her friend as she follows meekly behind the large man.

The daylight does not make the mansion feel any more inviting than the dark of the night before did. In fact, there is something scarier about the place, but Emily can't figure out what it is. Maybe it's not knowing where her parents are or if she'll ever see them again. Or maybe it's the warm hand that her small one sits inside.

Before Emily knows it, they are standing in a grand dining room. The aroma of the bacon and eggs from the dishes in the center of a long oval wood table fuel her to keep moving. She needs to eat if she wants the energy to escape.

The table is positioned in the center of the room, on top of a red and blue carpet. A matching cabinet sits along the wall opposite a large stone fireplace. A wall of windows, and a glass door, look out into the backyard.

Nathan leads Emily to a chair in front of the fireplace. He lets go of her hand, and she considers making a run for it. Before she can, she's pushed into the chair he had pulled out for her. He takes his place to her right, at the head of the table, in front of the windows.

Nicholas bounces into the room. "Good morning, Father. Emily." He smiles at her.

She wonders what he can be so happy about. Is having a girl trapped in their house normal? The hairs on her arms tingle.

"Nicholas, what have I said about containing your energy?"

"Sorry." He pulls his shoulders back, hides the smile, and calmly sits opposite his new sister.

Nathan drops a ladle full of eggs on Emily's plate and a couple slices of bacon. She pushes it around with her fork, and resigns herself to eating.

He pats her hand. "I knew you were hungry. Now, Brigitta is going to take a while to get used to you being here. It's best if you stay out of her way until then."

"I don't-"

"DO NOT INTERRUPT ME WHEN I'M SPEAKING." Anger flashes in Nathan's eyes and Emily clenches her hands together and squeezes, so the pain stops her from speaking. Fearful tears well up.

She glances at Nicholas, who stares at her silent and still.

Nathan regains his composure by taking a moment to butter some toast. "Monday to Friday, you will attend Nicholas' tutoring sessions and spend your evenings catching up to his level. You may be three years behind him in school, but you'll do just fine if you put in the work. You will have one hour each night and weekends for play. The rest of the time, you will do as Nicholas does. I want a report of your week every Friday at dinner. There will be times when you will have to interact with Brigitta, and during those times, you should be on your best behaviour. I have people stationed all over this property, and if you ever try to leave, they will catch you and punish you. So, wipe any thought of a life outside of this family from your mind right now. Nicholas will not help you try to escape. He knows the consequences of disobedience. Get up, boy, and turn around."

As ordered, Nicholas' back faces Emily. Nathan pulls up his blue t-shirt to reveal four red scars that cross his entire back. "Do you want this to happen to you?"

She shakes her head.

"Then follow the rules, do what you're told and you won't get hurt." The harsh voice evaporates into calm. "For today, Nicholas has the day off from his studies. He'll show you around and tell you the rules."

All of her muscles hurt as she tries to contain her screams for freedom. She doesn't want to be hurt like Nicholas, but she doesn't want to be here. Unsure of what to do, she mirrors the boy. She watches the food leave her plate and enter her mouth. Bite after bite until her plate is empty.

Six weeks later, Emily still cries herself to sleep every night. No matter how many times Nathan tells her to forget about her parents, she fights to keep their images in her mind. Replays memories to keep them alive until she can see them again.

Even poor Peter hasn't cheered her up enough to take him on any imaginary adventures. When she's not forced to go to lessons or play outside, she spends most of her time sitting in the cushioned window seat overlooking the backyard. Why can't my hair be long like Rapunzel's and a nice prince come save me?, she wonders.

Sometimes she and Nicholas play board-games. Mostly, he tries to convince her life won't be so bad with his family. Emily's not sure why he seems eager to replace his sister. Sure, he's nice enough, and she has fun with him, but it's not the same. She wants to go back to her house.

Nathan comes to tuck her into bed each night, just like Daddy used to.

She doesn't care if she needs to go to bed before everyone else. It gives her time to be alone. Every night, hoping for a different answer, she takes a deep breath and asks, "are you going to let me go home?"

He smooths out the comforter, pinches his lips, and shakes his head.

She hugs Peter to her chest.

"Emily..."

It's the first time he's called her that since coming here. She can't help but look at him.

"I've given you time to get out all of your anger and grief. I've tried to be nice, even though you are disturbing everyone around you. Now, I see I need to treat you like an adult. So, no more sugar coating anything. Your parents are gone. Just like I said they were when we first met. You can't go back to your mom and dad, because they are no longer there. Everyone thinks you're dead."

Peter falls beside her as Emily covers both of her ears with the hope the words can be unheard. She sinks further into the covers.

Nathan unfolds a newspaper, dated December 23, 2003, and reads, "Spencer family found dead. DNA tests have confirmed that the three bodies found by hikers last week in the Boggy Lake Wilderness Area are those of Dr. Rodney and Arlene Spencer, along with their daughter Emily."

Emily's chest hurts, like an anvil from Looney Tunes sits on top of it. She feels like she's floating and everything goes black.

"Emily? Can you hear me?" A soft hand rubs her cheek.

Her eyes flicker as Nathan comes into view. She doesn't know if she's more afraid of him or the tingling radiating through her skin. He pulls her to a seated position and holds her in his arms. She bursts like a damn at the thought of never seeing her daddy again. Never snuggling up on the couch and eating popcorn until her stomach hurts. She soaks Nathan's pale blue shirt with tears.

"It's alright now. You fainted. I'll get you a warm cloth for your head."

He does as he says, and the warmth brings her a little comfort.

He sits on the edge of her bed. She wonders if that's worry on his face, but with a deep breath, it disappears. "I will not apologize for being blunt with you. It's time you stopped acting like a petty child, suck back your tears, and embrace reality. There's no family to go back to. This is the only place that will give you a good life. You have until Christmas Day to decide if you're going to give me one-hundred percent of you, or if I need to force you. And trust me, you will have a lot fewer privileges - including losing this very nice bedroom, if I have to force you to be one of us." Nathan leans over to kiss her forehead and she slinks under the covers.

Emily feels him rise from the bed. Before he leaves, she pulls the covers to just under her chin. "How can the police think I'm dead if I'm right here?"

"I can make anything happen, and anyone believe anything."

CHAPTER NINE

NOW

Victoria feels like she's wearing burlap instead of a tight black lace dress. She loved dresses as a child. Now, they are only a tool to get what she requires. Not only will her outfit continue to piss Brigitta off, it will attract the eyes of the people she's unfamiliar with.

Through the crowd, stationed at the entry, a young man of about twenty, catches her attention. A small smile escapes his lips, and he runs his fingers over his stubby hair. He and a soldier she recognizes swap their positions, which tells her the kid works for Nathan. Well, Nicholas now.

She monitors him and identifies he's not very skilled. He can't keep his eyes off her when he should be watching the crowd. There are a few other soldiers, in their matching black suits and ties, that she doesn't recognize in the ballroom. Most give her a quick glance and return to their duties as she makes her way to Irving, who stands by the bar.

He passes her a pre-filled glass of red wine. "Victoria, nice to see you again. You're looking well. At least, better than you were thirty minutes ago."

She holds a witty comeback between her teeth and instead says, "Thank you. I know you are...were, like a father to Nathan. Condolences for your loss."

A cough stifles in his throat, "you as well."

They each sip their drinks and Irving continues, "The different leaders in The Family have reassured me they will support Nathan's heir to continue as Director. I can't guarantee that support will last, but it will get you and your brother through the transition. Give you time to secure your position."

"It's good to know I'll only have one battle on my hands during my brief stay here." Victoria catches a glimmer in Irving's eye, and a small smirk at the side of his mouth.

"You don't plan on staying home long?"

"No. I'll return to my post after Nicholas' installation as Director. I have work to do."

"You have been doing a hell of a job with the protection racket. I didn't have the same confidence in its success as Nathan did. He really advocated for you on that venture."

Her heartstrings tighten knowing Nathan did what he could to give her what she wanted without completely losing her. To avoid a discussion about Nathan, and navigating the minefield of emotions that could come up, she changes the subject. "I was always told not to ask you this, but, as you saw, I'm up for taking a few risks today. What made you decide to start a criminal empire, when you have your hands full with an assortment of highly profitable legitimate businesses?"

"What did Nathan tell you?"

"He told me the answer wasn't important. What was important, was what we did with the gift we've been given."

"He's right." Irving finishes his drink and waves off a refill the bartender dutifully offers. "Short answer, greed, and I needed a source of cash to pay off government and regulatory officials. I'd need to explain the outgoing funds if it came from a legitimate business."

"You'd think between the forestry, construction, oil and shipbuilding, you'd be able to hide something somewhere?"

"Not when people are always trying to topple the giants. It's hard to believe, but it was easier to join the criminal underworld to capitalize on a consumption filled economy than to participate in capitalism itself. The hard part, is not getting caught."

"Hence, each of the 'six families' having legitimate and illegal business-es."

"You're well versed in how this business operates. What is it you are really hoping to get out of this conversation?"

Victoria smiles. "I figured it would be rude not to say hi. Now, I'm trying to waste as much time as possible before standing at the front of the room to shake the hands of people who care very little for me."

"I think you'd be surprised how much support you have here." He flicks his watch. "I must leave. Please tell Nicholas I won't be able to attend the funeral. A few last-minute meetings about an acquisition I'm making came up." With a handshake, he departs and Victoria takes up her position in the receiving line.

Three hours of condolences have rubbed her hands raw as the last pair of guests bid the Townsends farewell. An evening birdsong filters through open windows, the remnants of the bustle of the day.

Now, only Nicholas' tall lean frame walls Brigitta and Victoria from each other. "Before the two of you tear each other apart, let's remember the situation we find ourselves in. Just because those closest to us were loyal to Father, doesn't mean they will be loyal to me, or either of you. If they see, or sense, we are not a strong team, they will, betray us." Nicholas steps forward, turns and his gaze shifts between the two women. "Can we all agree to hold it together for the sake of The Family?"

Brigitta twirls the sapphire band on her right wrist, one of the many trinkets Nathan bought to placate her rage. "I agree to not make a scene; however, I will not hold back my opinion if I feel it must be heard."

"Naturally," slips out before Victoria can catch it. "I mean, I agree to only defend myself if the situation arises. I will not instigate a fight, insult, or risk the reputation of this family." That is until she deems it necessary.

"As that's likely the best I'll get, I'll take it. It's been a long day, and Devin has made Father's favourite, lasagna and all the fixings. Shall we?" He holds an arm out to guide the women to the equally grand dining room.

Brigitta squeezes Nathan's hand one last time as she passes his coffin, and with her head high, leads the way.

Side by side, Nicholas and Victoria trail behind. The tension of being closer than they have been in two years causes them to sweat. Victoria can feel his eyes looking upon her, but she keeps hers forward. Their fingers graze each other.

Brigitta coughs. The eyes in the back of her head see all.

Conversation filters into the hallway and halts when the matriarch steps into the wide dining room doorway, commanding all attention. As though she was the Queen of England, Nicholas and Victoria flank her sides but stay two steps behind her. Until Nathan is buried tomorrow, and out of respect for the widow, The Family bestows the power upon Brigitta. Once Nathan is laid to rest, Nicholas will step up.

The aroma of baked cheese, ground meat, and a secret spice blend Devin reveals to no one, taunts the eight men and one woman who break from their huddled group and step behind the ornate wooden chairs surrounding the long dining table. When Victoria was a teenager, Nathan had the inner circle of his soldiers eat with the family. He thought it made them feel like they were Townsends and garnered deeper loyalty. Business meetings remained in the boardroom, yet it was inevitable some business would come up during the meal, but never anything personal.

The last rays of sunshine spotlights Nathan's empty chair. A sliver of guilt stabs Victoria's heart. Or is it grief? Whatever it is, Victoria ignores it to focus on the four people in the room she doesn't recognize. One woman and three men have earned a spot at the Townsend's table since her departure, along with four other loyal workers whom Victoria grew up around.

Brigitta positions herself behind the chair at the foot of the table, closest to the hallway. Nicholas and Victoria stride to the other end. Tomorrow Nicholas will ascend to Nathan's throne. For now, they take the positions they've maintained for ten and seven years, respectively, on either side. She realizes there are not more bodies than seats, and wonders if Nathan had kept hers empty while she was away.

Bowed heads and a moment of silence remember their fallen leader. With a soft cough, Brigitta waves her hand and everyone takes their seats.

The crowd waits until Louis serves Brigitta and then they scramble like wild animals to fill their plates from sliver platters adorning the middle of the table. A Michelin star restaurant rates lower than Devin's cooking and everyone wants to sleep on an overstuffed stomach.

Victoria recognizes that grief and alcohol quench Brigitta's appetite, her food pushed around her plate like a petulant child. No one can blame her for that today.

With everyone else distracted by their plates, Victoria nibbles on her hearty meat-packed pasta as she assesses the strangers in the room. Her hand grips her knife more like a weapon than a utensil.

Across from Louis sits the young man who had been staring at her earlier. A little rough around the edges, he chews with his mouth open. It takes a few moments, but he catches Brigitta's glare and closes his mouth, then smiles and winks at Victoria.

With a strategic twirl of a strand of hair, she looks away. It took little to find the person who'll tell her what's been happening in The Family behind Nathan and Nicholas' back. The black lace dress did what she wanted it to.

With everyone hunched over the table, Victoria doesn't have to crane much to take in the woman three seats down from her. Red hair pulled into a tight bun, stern face, good posture and trimmed nails with a bit of dirt underneath. These clues tell Victoria she works with her hands. Not just another errand runner. Although, the fact she's seated at the table is more evidence of that.

Nathan's personal bodyguard usually took the seat beside Victoria. Given Nathan's death, she suspects the current occupant has only sat there for a couple of days. It was highly unlikely the previous resident remained breathing for much longer than Nathan did, having let him die.

It occurs to her that she doesn't know Nathan's cause of death, but knows better than to ask at the table. She pins the question in her mind for later.

She looks to her left, and watches the light blue eyes of the large bald man beside her survey the room, as he shovels salad into his mouth. Tattoos cover his hands and neck, and she wonders if his suit hides a canvas of art.

Next, Victoria's gaze falls on the last stranger, who occupies the seat next to Nicholas. His position at the table tells her he's been third in line for the crown, so to speak. Her skin tingles. In the years that she's been gone, this dark, wavy-haired, bearded stranger has somehow climbed the ranks, without Victoria knowing so much as his name. Electricity runs through her veins. Something's not right.

She continues to analyze the man, his oil-black eyes meet hers. He raises his glass of red wine and nods with half a smile. She doesn't return it and he refocuses on his plate. His black suit jacket strains against a muscular frame. Louis and the stranger next to Victoria are almost double his girth.

He's more akin to Nicholas' slender build; but, not as tall. Fine wrinkles grow out from his eyes and there's a subtle scar along his left cheek. He won't be hard to look at for the week she's here. Which is good. She's going to have to keep a close eye on him, along with the others, until she's satisfied that they're not here to harm Nicholas.

They can go after Brigitta and the rest of the crew as much as they like. She'll kill anyone who targets Nicholas.

Chapter Ten

Then: December 2003

With Nathan gone, Emily throws off the covers and retrieves the newspaper from the window seat, where he had discarded it. She has a hard time reading some words in the article, but she recognizes 'missing for weeks', 'bodies, and 'dead'.

She hasn't heard her dad's voice for a while, but it speaks loudly from the face on the front page. "It's time to be strong. Mommy and I will always be in your heart. Never forget us and we will meet again. Pretend this is your family until you can get free."

She grips the sides of the creased newspaper as she kisses her parents, wearing the party hats and big smiles, from her fifth birthday party. Tears fall on her reflection and the five-year-old self blurs. Afraid they will spread to the other faces; she hides the newspaper behind the books at the bottom of a three-shelf bookcase. She pulls out her mom's faded sweater for comfort but finding none, she climbs back into bed with Peter Rabbit where he catches her nightly tears.

Nicholas' ears have become attuned to Emily's cries from the next room. Even though his bed is against the wall of her bathroom, the sound travels through the ceiling vents with ease. He can hear every fight with the staff and every attempt by Nathan to gain her trust.

Unsure why the real Victoria is being replaced, Nicholas disguises his displeasure with the intruder and obeys orders to be friends. He lets her win the games they play so he can retrieve information she's too happy to share about her family and where she came from. He's learned that Emily's dad was a surgeon, and he is positive he's heard the name Rodney before, but he can't place it. All he knows is, the sooner he can get her back to the city, the better. Then father can pay attention to him again.

It isn't until Nicholas overhears this most recent exchange that his displeasure turns to pity. Although adults consider him a child at nine and three-quarters, his heart aches for the small girl when she finds out her parents are dead. He may not have liked his sister much, but he'd give anything to have his family back together. To have Victoria run and jump on his bed in the morning to wake him up.

On his way to his piano lessons, he stops outside Emily's door. Maybe the person on the other side deserves his friendship for real? It's not her fault father's revenge took away her parents. Head down, he leaves her to her tears and trudges down the stairs. Even though he'll get a beating, he vows one day he'll show Emily the secret hole under the fence that she can escape through.

Chapter Eleven

Now

CARRYING HER GRIEF AND a body full of alcohol, Brigitta stumbles out of the dining room after the meal. Louis tries to assist her, but she pushes him away, almost falling over in the process. "I'm fine. I can get upstairs on my own." She's never been one to accept help from anyone besides Nathan. Even that was a struggle. Louis trails behind her like a lost, but obedient pet.

Nicholas waits until the slam of Brigitta's bedroom door signals she won't disturb the conversation. All eyes are on him as he takes a commanding step behind Nathan's chair and grips the curved wooden back. "Today's been a long day. Normally, I'd dismiss you all to whatever frivolity you want to get up to, but tomorrow will be no better. In fact, because the cemetery will expose the attendees, we need heightened diligence. For those who haven't figured it out, this is Victoria. Her reputation speaks for itself, so the only thing I will say is that she out ranks all of you. She deserves the same respect you give me and there are to be no questions if she asks you to do anything. Understood?"

Everyone nods and she stares down at those with lingering eyes. They flinch first.

"Janet, you and Louis scan the vehicles now and again in the morning." Nicholas looks at the man seated beside him. "Aidan, you run through the rest of the security plan and assignments with the crew while I update Vic. If anyone needs us, we'll be in Father's office."

Aidan stands and rubs his hands together. "Right, well, you've all heard it before, but-" Victoria misses the end of the sentence as Nicholas hustles her out of the dining room but presumes it will concern the instructions for the soldiers.

She's taken aback when Nicholas opens the door to Nathan's office and stacks of papers cover most of the floor, shelves and desk. She remembers him as maintaining scrupulous order in both business and personal matters. None of which is evident now. The books on the shelves lining the walls have a smell of stale cigar embedded in them.

"What happened here?"

"You know how Father battled insomnia, paranoia, and kept a lot of information to himself after the assassination attempts on him?"

She nods.

"Well, your leaving the compound heightened his delusions. Especially, when he started to forget things, not that he would admit his memory was going. He took not using computers to the extreme. He had them all removed from the house. If we didn't require cell phones for work, I'm sure he would have eliminated their use as well. He did what he could on paper. Then he kept that paper to make sure he could prove he was right should anyone question him."

"Nothing like handing the police a goldmine if they ever raided the place."

"I know. I tried to talk to him about it, but you know Father."

Did she ever. Nathan's way always remained the sole option, despite insurmountable evidence against it. Victoria shuffles papers away from the green upholstered bench in front of the mullioned window. She was hoping Nathan's recent unannounced visit to England a couple of months ago, with his allegations of a perpetrator messing with his memory, was a tactic he was using to make her come back. Looking around her, she senses she was wrong. She wonders if she had taken him more seriously, and returned, could she have stopped his death?

With no point travelling down a road she can't change; she cracks the nerves out of her fingers. "I'm sorry I left. You know that, right? I couldn't stay here any longer."

Nicholas sits beside her, his back to the window. With his formidable persona left in the hallway, he grips the velvety bench and stares at his shoes. "I just wish you would have told me before Father announced your new assignment. We told each other everything. Or at least I thought we did."

Her skin burns when she takes his hand in hers. Their eyes meet. "I was afraid that you would overreact and ruin my plan. I know it would have come from a place of love and protection, but this place has suffocated me since I first stepped into it. If I had to stay here any longer, I would have killed myself."

The last sentence lingers in the air as Nicholas sniffles back tears. The forbidden emotions within the Townsend compound did not apply to their relationship. It was the one place they felt safe enough to laugh, cry, scream and share everything they felt. After her first attempt to end her life, he spent months sitting up all night listening through the vent on the wall between their bedrooms. If anything were to happen, he'd hear it and stop it. When his exhaustion affected his training to the point his father noticed, he slept in shifts. In between, he'd crack open her bedroom door and ensure she was safe. He'd prove his usefulness to his father, and himself, by ensuring this Victoria remained alive.

He lived like this until the day she left the compound to work the protection racket. After that, he required pills to help him sleep. Otherwise, the fear of knowing Victoria's life was out of his hands kept his mind twirling all night.

Victoria has a hard time believing Nicholas is as unaffected by Nathan's death as he appears to be letting on. "How are you doing? Like, really doing with his death?"

"I'm fine."

"Really? Were you expecting it?"

"What? No, of course not." He kicks a piece of paper. "I mean, not really. He was going crazy, and I wondered if there was something more medical to it. He'd never let me join his appointments with the doctor, so I hoped he would tell mother and I if there was something we needed to worry about."

"Well, I appreciate you looking after everything while the world was falling apart around you. I just worry that you looked up to him, not only as a father, but as a mentor. Now, he's gone. You're carrying a lot."

"You know, I've carried a lot my whole life. Now, isn't any different."

"But now, Irving's eyes are on you more than ever before. One step out of line-"

"You think I don't know that?" Nicholas tosses the papers in his hand aside and they flutter to the floor. "I have Irving and the five families watching to make sure I can lead The Family. Everyone thought they had years before they saw this day, but now it's here. I doubt any of them think I'm ready. Even though I know I am."

"You are ready." Victoria says.

"Don't patronize me."

"I'm not. I'm being supportive."

"Like you were when you left?"

"And we're back to this."

"Yes, we are. I had to work twice as hard to prove myself after you were gone. At least when you were here, the shadow I lived behind wasn't as big. Most of what Father talked about was how his precious daughter was making the new business venture successful. How lucrative the information you were gathering would be to bring shady people deeper into our dark world. There was no, 'great job Nicholas' on handling that takeover, or the absorption of the cigarette cartel 's distribution path and removing our competition. No pat on the back, or congratulatory discussions at dinner. I may have had the title of Second-in-Command, but I didn't feel like it. Rather, he made me feel smaller than when you were here. Like, all I was ever good for was to be his lackey."

Victoria wraps her arms around the broken man. He holds her tightly, and the heat from the anger and hurt coursing through his veins radiates through his suit and her dress.

She doesn't move. She lets him have this moment, without judgment or being watched.

Moments later, he loosens his grip on her, sniffles, and rises. "I don't want to talk about this again."

"Okay." Giving Nicholas his space, she turns to tackle the clutter.

"A lot more has happened since you've been gone, and Father's insistence on minimal contact means I haven't been able to keep you apprised of the biggest concern."

"How he died?"

"No." Nicholas runs his fingers through his hair and over his face. "Father was adamant there's a rat on the compound."

Chapter Twelve

Then: December 2003

Both of Emily's hands grip the glass doorknob to her room. The waved edges dig into her skin. Her knees knock together as she opens the door. Before stepping into the hallway, she holds her breath and listens. Silence. In her stocking feet, she inches down the hallway on high alert. She pauses on each step of the winding staircase.

A ten-foot Christmas tree stands along the curve in the staircase's wall. The multi-coloured lights illuminate the ornaments. Emily knows there are no presents underneath. They belong under the other large tree in the living room.

Stepping off the stairs, the front door is almost within her reach. It calls for her to open it. Two guards outside pace back and forth like the pendulum in the grandfather clock her dad kept in the living room. She's so engrossed with the expressionless men that she doesn't notice the person behind her.

"Listen to me when I'm speaking to you." Brigitta's shrill voice pierces through her and she turns on her heels.

"I'm sorry, I was-"

"I don't care what you were doing. I thought Nathan told you to stay out of my way?" The woman towers over her and seems to wait for something, but Emily is unsure how to respond. "Well, get out of here. And don't go into the parlour today, otherwise I'll take great pleasure in giving you a *Merry*

Christmas." Her voice is anything but merry, and a shiver scurries down Emily's spine.

Unsure where or what a parlour is, Emily runs as fast as she can down the closest hallway, her stocking feet sliding on the pristine floors. She can't recall where the kitchen is, and after getting lost a few times, finally finds it. A tall, round man that Emily hasn't met wears a white jacket and stands at the stove. The left side of the jacket has the name Devin stitched in black.

He flips his frying pan, tossing a pancake into the air and catching it. "Good morning, young lady. Would you like some breakfast?"

Emily's stomach longs for the fluffy, buttery circles of delight. She nods.

"Head through that door and I'll bring you a plate. If I don't eat them all first." He winks and she can't help but smile back.

Her step lightens at the thought of future pools of maple syrup, but she stops in her tracks at the sight of the next room's occupants.

Aware of the new arrival, Nathan folds his newspaper and places it on the table. Nicholas smiles and sits up straighter. Disappointed she isn't alone, she half smiles back.

"Well, have a seat." Nathan points to the empty chair on his left.

Emily does what she's told, keeping her gaze on her folded hands in her lap.

"Father got me a new bike for Christmas and there's one for you, too. Do you want to go for a ride after breakfast?" The joy in Nicholas' voice bounces across the wide table.

Nathan speaks before Emily can. "That's a good idea. One benefit of a green Christmas. Only after you both finish your regular duties, helping Devin clean up the dishes. Just because it's a holiday, it doesn't mean the life lessons stop."

As if he heard his name, Devin arrives with two plates stacked tall with pancakes and one with a single poached egg and two slices of plain whole wheat toast. Without a word, he whirls around the table making deliveries and is back in the kitchen before Emily can say thank you.

Nicholas and Emily drench their pancakes. She can't help but smile when Nicholas stuffs himself with a folded pancake and pretends it's his mouth. Nathan glares but lets the shenanigans continue.

Once all the plates are empty, and despite her desire to get as far away from Nathan as possible, Emily remembers her manners. "May I please be excused from the table?" she asks.

"Well now, Nicholas, you could learn a few things from her. Before anyone goes anywhere, we all need to have a little talk." Nathan leans back in his chair, rests his elbows on the curved arms, folds his hands together, and locks eyes with Emily. "You've heard, and learned, most of the rules of this family. The one I haven't shared is that you will address me as Father; not Nathan, not Mr. Townsend, but Father. Just as Nicholas does."

The lake of maple syrup in Emily's stomach churns. The last thing she wants is to call him Father. But her daddy is gone. What else can she do but play along? At least, until she can figure out a way to escape. She begrudgingly nods.

"There are only five people who know Victoria is..." Nathan rubs the back of his neck. "Emily no longer exists. Just like the newspaper article said. You will answer to Victoria. You will introduce yourself as Victoria. You are Victoria."

Emily digs her stubby nails into her legs. The pain keeps her from screaming 'my name is Emily' at the top of her lungs. She'll do what her dad's voice told her to last night. Whatever it takes to survive. Right now, that means silence.

"Now, both of you help Devin with the dishes."

Nicholas grabs his and Nathan's plates, cutlery, and cups. "Yes, Father."

Emily pushes her chair back and grabs her own.

"Victoria?" Nathan asks.

Her chest tightens at being called by a name that isn't hers. She looks to Nicholas, who mouths what she's supposed to say.

"Yes..." the word sticks to the tip of her tongue. After a few starts and stops, she spits out, "Father." The word tastes like dirt.

"Good. I have some work to do in the city, so after your bike ride, keep yourselves occupied without causing trouble and stay out of Brigitta's way."

"Yes, Father." They say in unison and leave him to finish reading the newspaper.

Emily grips the handlebars of her new purple bike as she rides up and down the long driveway. She's happy there's no snow. It would feel more like a real Christmas. Which it can't be without her parents.

She wonders if Santa left her presents at her house. She didn't see the tree in the living room here before Nicholas ushered her outside. Was there a stocking for her?

She wishes that she was cuddled up on the couch, her dad cracking different nuts out of their shells as the three of them watched Christmas movies. Her mom getting up during commercials to baste the turkey.

Tears run down her cheeks. All she wants for Christmas is a hug from her parents.

Tires screech, and out of breath, Nicholas comes to a stop beside her by the front gate. "Let's try them on the grass."

She wipes away her tears, "um...I'll stay on the driveway."

"Come on. It'll be fun."

"I don't want to, okay? Just because I have to live here, doesn't mean I have to do whatever you want."

Nicholas looks around and she realizes she shouldn't have talked about being forced to be with the Townsends. Thankfully, the guards at the front door couldn't hear them.

"I only learned how to ride a bike in the summer, so I can't do that."

"Oh, right. I guess you are pretty young." He smiles, "race you to the house." He pushes off.

She wonders if she could fit through the bars of the fence. It would be tight, but maybe, just maybe.

"Come on," Nicholas hollers.

She decides it will be better to escape when Nicholas isn't with her. Then maybe he won't get in trouble. She straddles her bike and walks it so that it faces the house. Her feet fumble with the peddles. She gets control and chases after him. He waits until she's close to him to restart the race.

In two different windows of the mansion, Brigitta and Nathan watch over the oblivious children.

In the upstairs den, grief overwhelms Brigitta, and she grips the window frame to keep her standing. All she wants for Christmas is to hold her little girl again.

Nathan cuts the end off a cigar and, even unlit, a spicy earthiness tickles his tongue. All he wants for Christmas is to keep the girl below in line, train her to be an asset to The Family, and make sure she never finds out what really happened in the house on Rockcliffe Street.

CHAPTER THIRTEEN

NOW

VICTORIA'S RIBS GRIP HER heart like long bony fingers as she registers what Nicholas has revealed. She had hoped Nathan's similar revelation to her a few weeks prior was his paranoia talking. Maybe it still was. She knew Nicholas wasn't aware of Nathan's trip to see her, or that she was aware of his concerns, so she acts as though this is news to her. "A rat? Are you serious?" She doesn't let him respond before she dances around the stacks of papers, and books, to find a small piece of uncluttered floor. "I would have thought that after the last person to betray us, Nathan was too smart and cautious to let anyone suspicious near him. But the state of this office makes me wonder if you're right."

Should she reveal to Nicholas that Nathan thought someone was trying to kill him? Considering Nathan thought that Nicholas was the threat, she decides to keep her knowledge to herself.

She pulls her hair back into a ball and releases it. "This mess isn't like Nathan. It's like he's lost in the chaos. Add to it the unfamiliar faces at dinner, half of me believes he was paranoid and the other half believes he was on to something. Where did that kid, Janet, Aidan and the behemoth of a man who was sitting beside me come from?" She can't take it anymore and organizes the papers into a more structured mess, knowing she'll need a shower afterwards to wash off the dust and odour of cigar smoke.

Nicholas rolls his eyes with a smile. "The kid's name is Finn. He was one of the street gang that moved drugs and cigarettes. He took a few chances and made us a lot of money. Father rewarded him for it."

"Took a few chances with or without permission?"

Papers crinkle as Nicholas shifts them from the antique Georgian chintz couch to the floor, sits and crosses his legs. "Without."

"Wow. The kid's got balls, I'll give him that. But it sounds like he's a little too ambitious to follow the rules. Which could mean he'll continue to stray outside the lines. I have some tricks up my sleeve that will figure him out quick enough."

"Vic, don't." Hurt blankets his affection for her.

"Don't what?" She playfully hides her smile behind a fan of papers.

"He's just a kid."

"Is he over 20?"

"21."

"Then no harm done. I'll have some fun and we'll get the information we need."

"You're ruthless."

"So are you. Remember Nadia?"

Nicholas laughs. "Would you stop cleaning and sit down?"

"You know if I stop, I'll go crazy. Now, tell me about Janet."

"Janet, formerly known as Sofia, came to us through one of the other Families, the Harris's. Long story short, an enemy syndicate in South America was after them and they knew their family members were at risk of being used as bargaining chips or revenge. With her life in danger, her family asked for our help. Give her a new life."

"And a new name, which seems to be a popular tactic around here." Victoria allows the comment to linger in the air for a moment before she continues. "Why not have her work with her own family?"

"Too obvious. Besides, the Harris' are our most trusted partners within The Family."

"And what better way for them to take control of us and the organization than by sending us someone who has little to no loyalty to us?"

"She's loyal. Trust me." Nicholas rubs the long scar that rides up the side of his neck.

"I see. And you're chiding me about having sex with Finn to get information?" Victoria keeps hidden the fact that the thought of Nicholas with Janet sends her stomach into cartwheels.

"She's not our enemy. Besides, I ended it when the "L" word was on the tip of her tongue." He chuckles and helps to stack papers. He did not align the edges of his stacks as perfectly as Victoria did. Corners stuck out and towers leaned slightly.

"You think every woman you're with falls in love with you." Victoria shakes her head to get the idea of Nicholas being in love with anyone out of her head. "Besides sex, is Janet competent in any other area here?"

"Yes, very. We started her in the armoury with in-house inventory management, then she worked her way up to organizing those shipments. Her impeccable creation of the fraudulent shipping manifests we need to allow transportation of all goods to occur in broad daylight, mean we've had fewer issues with the Halifax Port Authority. That led Father to invite her to the table two years ago. She's quick on the draw when needed, takes no one's bullshit and gets the job done when no one else will. Reminds me of someone else I know."

"Serious question. Do you trust her? Really trust her? Or should I be concerned about her likeness to me in other aspects, too?"

"She's given me no reason not to trust her. And you know I'm very careful not to spill The Family's secrets between the sheets."

"Hmm. I'll also look after her."

"Do you plan on sleeping with everyone you don't know?" he smirks.

"If I have to, but you know I don't like to travel lands you've already conquered. Moving on. Who was that gigantic man in Carlos' chair?"

"You know Erik. He's been working for us since we were teenagers on patrol and reconnaissance."

"Wait, that's Erik? When did he become the size of a gorilla?"

"A few years ago, Father told him to bulk up if he ever wanted to be a top bodyguard and he took it seriously."

"I'll say. How's he performing in the position since Carlos died in that horrific fall off the container ship?"

"George took over first, but with Father's death, we had to, you know, feed the fishes as they say."

"Could you be more cliché?" Victoria didn't want to sound like a broken record, but she had to ask. "Was George involved in...?"

"Father's death?"

"I'm confident George wasn't a problem. He reported back to me the worse father got. Besides, George was with him almost twenty-four-seven. He had few opportunities to speak with anyone beyond our walls, so I have no concerns he was working with anyone to take father out."

"I suppose." Victoria was grateful the lives she took were because of self-defence or evidence of their guilt. "This Aidan guy. How's he third in command if I've never met him?"

"You left, remember?"

"How often must I apologize? But, let's get back on topic." The last thing Victoria wanted was a heart to heart. "Who is this guy and how the hell did he climb up the ranks so quickly?"

"Honestly, he saved Father's life three years ago and has remained here ever since. I ran Aidan's background check and had him watched for months before he moved onto the compound and found nothing alarming. The army gave him a second chance after being convicted for possession with the intent to sell. That didn't work out. Eight years ago, a court martial found him guilty of selling OxyContin to his fellow soldiers. He spent three years at the Canadian Forces Prison in Edmonton. Did you know they call it Club Ed?" Nicholas chuckles.

"This is no time for jokes. A convicted drug dealer sits beside you at the table. Hardly the company Nathan would keep so high in the ranks."

"Father works with a range of criminals and Aidan's always abided by our side of the law. A career criminal who had never found a home until now. Father gave him a chance and approved his promotion. Besides, he's also a skilled marksman with amazing tactical awareness. Something we need as our world becomes more dangerous."

"I saw you two years ago in Paris and you didn't think to tell me any of this? What else aren't you telling me?" Done with the papers in front of her, Victoria moves to the desk. Half finished cigars litter the top, and she has to remove the buried garbage can from under a pile of couch pillows to toss them out.

"We had one night in Paris after three years apart. I didn't want to spend it discussing business. Look, he's a good guy. He's gotten me out of a couple jams and didn't report it to Father."

"Of course he has. Or maybe instead of being a good guy, he's a guy with an excellent cover."

"Do you not trust that I did my job?"

"Sorry. A lot has changed around here, and when you mention a potential rat, I'm going to suspect everyone until we find them." Nathan was right, Nicholas had dropped the ball somewhere. But how far had it fallen? And if Nicholas wasn't involved, was he in danger?

Chapter Fourteen

Then: February 2004

While Emily slept, a Nor'easter careened over Nova Scotia. The brownish-green grass from the day before was buried in heaps white. Tree limbs drooped with the weight of their uninvited companion. It will be weeks before the blades penetrate their cover like zombies reaching hands out of a grave.

The vents in her room sing a warm, welcoming song for the day. Emily wishes they wouldn't. Not today. There will be nothing happy about today.

She knows her seventh birthday won't include a party. No songs. No candles for her to make a wish upon. No 'surprise!' from her parents telling her this is all a big joke and she can come home now.

Emily buries her head under the covers and cries. This is the worst birthday ever. Way worse than the time a kid in kindergarten dumped worms on her head.

There's a gentle knock on her door.

She ignores it.

Whoever it is knocks louder.

She hopes they go away.

The creak of the hinge tells her they haven't. Instead, footsteps get closer. Soft breathing is above her. She holds back her tears and pretends to be sleeping.

A light thump on the nightstand beside her, the shuffling of feet, more creaking and silence.

Emily waits and inches the blanket down. Alone, she raises herself to sitting. The sun peaks out from the clouds and spotlights a thin package, wrapped in paper with colourful balloons on it.

She bites her lip and looks around as though the walls have eyes.

The curiosity too much, she digs into the paper. She opens the book to a random page and inhales the new book smell she loves. Roald Dahl's *Matilda*, calls for her to join its imaginary world. She can't help but smile when she turns to the front of the book. Maybe this birthday won't be all bad.

A small note falls out.

"I'm sorry today will be sad for you and that we can't celebrate.

My sister loved this book - I hope you will too.

Maybe you'll develop powers like Matilda, and the adults will have to listen to you instead. That would be cool!

Looks like we get a snow day from lessons. Come dig out a fort with me!

Nicholas

P.S. Don't tell anyone I got you a gift."

Emily's heart warms knowing that she has one person thinking about her birthday. As much as she wants to hide in bed and read, she rubs her puffy eyes and puts the book under her pillow for later. She hides the note in the box with the reminders of her parents. Reminders that people care for her.

Emily can hear Nathan on the phone in his office and tip toes past. Sad 1980s pop music erupts from the parlour she's never allowed in.

She finds Nicholas staring out the dining-room windows. Crisp white blankets the entire property and forest. The only wrinkles created by the wind.

He turns to her, "you came down. I wasn't sure..." he hugs her and whispers, "happy birthday."

She tries to smile but can't.

His warm hand pulls her into the kitchen where his toe taps as she shovels some cereal down. She's not hungry, but he won't let her leave until she's done. "You're gonna need your strength if we are going to make the best fort ever."

Emily dances from foot to foot on the cold stone floor of the mudroom at the back of the house. Her socks do little to maintain warmth while she shuffles into some lavender snow pants. Nicholas helps tighten the suspenders, and she realizes Victoria must have been taller than her.

The puffiness of the pants makes it hard to put on the matching winter boots. She's glad they slide on and her cold toes find some comfort off the ground.

Now more than double her width, Emily waddles like a penguin out of the house. She feels silly, especially when she sees Nicholas has a better handle on his outfit and walks normally.

A chill kisses her nose and cheeks. Nothing too harsh, just enough to remind her to keep her mittens and toque on.

Motors rumble as the soldiers battle the leftovers of the storm with snowblowers. Pathways with snow mounds on each side are being created towards their quarters, down the driveway, and around the house. Emily's reminded of a moat around a castle, but without the trickling water.

"Over here" Nicholas calls. The bobble on the top of his toque is a beacon for his location. "Okay, let's dig." He hands her some small gardening shovels, which Emily figures he's set aside for this very purpose.

On their hands and knees, they dig. And dig.

"Are you sure this is safe?" she asks as it snows inside their tunnel.

"Ya. I make these all the time. Just keep digging."

After an hour of pushing the heavy snow into the pathway, Emily is not sure where in the yard they are and is exhausted. She longs to curl up in bed with her new book. She sits against the wall of snow and looks up at the ice ceiling above her. "I'm tired."

"Don't give up. Just a little further."

"My hands are wet and cold."

"I promise you some hot chocolate when we are done. Please, help a little longer."

"Ugh, fine. But you better put in a lot of marshmallows."

"Deal."

After the uneven circle of the 'living area' is dug out, the children lay with heavy breath on the hard damp floor, the sputtering and chugging of engines gets closer. Emily covers her ears as the sound echoes down the tunnel.

Flakes fall from above and the walls around her shake.

Nicholas looks to be saying something with a smile, but she can't hear him.

Then, with a thunderous crack, he's gone.

As is half of the cave. There's a wall of snow between where she is and where he was.

Wide-eyed, Emily drops her arms from her ears. Looking towards where she thinks the exit should be, it's gone too. She tries to get to her knees. The cave floor is as smooth as an ice rink and she falls over. The ground rumbles. She screams.

No one hears her.

Rolling onto her stomach, she pushes herself onto all fours. Fuelled by panic, she digs where she last saw her friend.

She doesn't know how long she's been digging. All she can think about is going faster. What if he can't breathe?

Her small hands barely make a dent in the snow. Heaving, she wonders why everyone who likes her leaves?

She keeps digging. Finally, she hits something hard. A boot. She found a boot!

Double-speed, her hands work faster than they have ever worked before. A leg. The pants glisten. She shakes it. It doesn't shake back.

A red mitten, but no hand.

Something clangs near her. There it is again. She looks, but there's no way out. No one's there.

She doesn't stop digging and follows the leg. His face is close. She knows it.

Tears turn into icicles on her eyelashes. She tries to blink them away, but they refuse to leave.

She finds the bottom of Nicholas' jacket. So close.

Something grabs her foot. "Ahh!"

"It's okay. It's okay." Louis wraps her into his large body. He drags her away from Nicholas.

"No, he-"

"We'll get him. He'll be okay." He passes her to Carlos, who guides her over and around mounds of snow in the broken open tunnel.

Nathan, in nothing more than a suit jacket, and Brigitta shivering in an elegant housecoat, crane their necks to see who is behind Carlos' large body, but Emily knows she's not who they are looking for.

"Where's Nicholas?" Brigitta exclaims, "Where's my baby boy?"

"Ma'am, Louis is digging him out. I'm sure he'll-"

"Don't you assure me of anything. You go back in there and get my boy."

"Yes, Ma'am."

Emily doesn't want her saviour to go. Even if he was one of the people who took her away from her parents. Today, he found her.

With the snowblowers immobile, sound travels easily and Emily is confident Louis said, "We need to get the snow out of his airway." She's not sure what it means, but they must have found him.

Tears stream down Brigitta's face and she clutches her robe. Emily feels sad for the mean woman. A daughter gone and now maybe a son. Before she can stop herself, she wraps her arms around the woman's legs. Daddy always said a hug can make anyone feel better.

"Get away from me, you wretched child." She tosses Emily backwards, pushing her along the bank of her fictional moat.

She slides down the side and lands hard on her butt. She wants to cry out but doesn't. She knows it will do no good.

Nathan repositions her to the side of him that is opposite Brigitta. His eyes are sad again. She watches his eyebrows lift, and she follows his gaze.

Brigitta's wail and Nicholas' limp body drains the hope from Emily.

The other men follow Louis as he carries the boy inside with Brigitta screaming and giving orders hurrying alongside.

Emily's padded legs can't keep up. Nathan scoops her up into his arms and rushes after the group.

Without stopping to remove her snowsuit, everyone rushes down to the basement.

She watches as Louis takes command of the situation inside a weird bedroom she's never seen before. Nicholas hadn't included it on the tour. Machines come to life and startle her as she pictures her grandpa in the hospital.

"Is he going to be okay?"

Nathan tosses her boots aside. "I'm sure he will be."

"We were only playing…I didn't know…" The weight of her extra layers lift but she can't feel it. She's scared Nicholas' eyes won't open, just like her grandpa's never did.

Once again, in Nathan's arms, she's above the crowd as those around her work at lightning speed.

They strip Nicholas naked. Cords are attached to his chest like he's an alien and beeps fill the room. He's wrapped in a shiny silver blanket. Louis asks Brigitta to lie beside her son to help warm him up. Her arms, a second barrier to further cold.

Nathan puts Emily down. She tries to look around the bodies of the adults, but all she sees are legs and parts of the bed.

She retreats to the back corner. Following the wall to the floor, she knows Nathan won't like it, but she can't stop crying. Silently, she prays, "God, please help my friend. He's been really nice to me. Laughs with me. Tries to make me feel like I belong. He doesn't deserve to die. I promise, I'll follow the rules the best I can. I'll be Victoria for them if you wake him up."

CHAPTER FIFTEEN

NOW

WORKING TOGETHER, THE MOUNTAINS of paper are now stacked against the walls of Nathan's office. The occupants move without the worry of a landslide.

Victoria uses the remains of a yellow pad of lined paper to sweep some cigar ashes into the garbage can and avoids looking at the family photo now prominently displayed on his desk, rather than the bookcase. "If you're confident that none of the newer soldiers are the rat, then who do you think is?"

Nicholas rubs the bridge of his nose. "I'm not sure there even is one. Father was out of his mind before he died."

"I can tell." She thought back to Nathan's last visit. He had left England two days after he arrived to deal with an urgent work matter. It meant they couldn't test his theory that someone was pulling the strings of his memory loss. If someone was drugging him with something that would present as dementia or paranoia, the remains of his last potential dose were still in his system when he left for the airport. If he had been able to stay longer, and the symptoms disappeared they would have had proof. The disarray around her was more evidence the man may have been unnecessarily paranoid and had legitimately deteriorated.

"Ew gross." She dives beneath the desk and comes up with her thumb and pointer finger gripping the thin, pink tail of a small, grey mouse. It wriggles and tries to scurry across the surrounding air.

Nicholas opens the window, and she tosses it outside. "Leave the window open. This room needs to be aired out." Victoria goes to return to the mess. Nicholas blocks her by resting his hand on her arm. Mischievousness twinkles in his eyes. Her thighs warm as temptation tickles her. Nicholas leans in. She turns away, and he lets his hand fall.

"We promised we wouldn't. Not after…" Her eyes itch as a tear threatens to escape. She pushes it back to prevent the pain of the past from being released.

Her words cut Nicholas down and he collapses on the bench. "And how many times did we break that promise?"

"We can't. Especially now. You're about to be the most powerful man in Nova Scotia's underworld. You can't have any distractions. Or weaknesses." She steps behind Nathan's large desk to help keep distance between them. As much as she's missed him, she doesn't want a distraction either. She needs to neutralize any internal threat and then get the two of them out of this game.

Nicholas runs his finger along his eyebrow. A nervous tell. "Don't leave. In a week, when this is all over, don't leave. Don can take over your work in England and Europe. He's done a remarkable job cleaning up your incident."

"Do we have to talk about this again? Wasn't a two-hour debriefing on the plane home enough? I made a mistake and once we figure out who Mr. Singer was working for, I'll correct it."

"All I'm saying is, it doesn't have to be you who works all over Canada or overseas. Hell, even Janet could do it if you think a woman is more apt to gather information. Besides, I won't be as strict with you as Father. If you need to get away now and then, I could send you somewhere here on the eastern side of this continent." Nicholas returns to the clutter.

If she can't get them both out of here alive, working closer would enable her to monitor Nicholas, in a manner of speaking. At least she'd be able to come back a lot faster if disaster struck. "I make no promises. If Brigitta remains on her best behaviour, I may stay longer. But don't get your hopes up, as I doubt it will be forever."

"I'll take whatever I can get."

Victoria continues to stack papers into meaningless piles. "Now, can we please focus on this rat?"

"Lets talk about it another time? We need to focus on getting through tomorrow alive. To help ensure that, you, me and Mother will take separate vehicles to and from the cemetery."

"What are we, the Royal Family?"

"Pretty much."

"The three of us will also stand apart. Mother on one side of the burial plot, me at the foot and you on the other side. Louis will guard Mother, Erik, myself, and that leaves Aidan for you."

"At least I'll have something nice to look at." Victoria was confident she could smell a rat, so having him close would be beneficial. As Nicholas laid out Aidan's plans for decoy cars and Finn's role of taking pictures of the crowd to see who's talking to whom, she had to admit that it made sense. Still plenty could go wrong, and her gut was telling her it would.

Nicholas tosses some papers haphazardly on the desk. "I'm going to give myself paper cuts if we keep at this. Besides, we should get some rest."

"Before we do, are you going to tell me how Nathan died, or is that supposed to remain a mystery like the mountains of paperwork in this office?"

"Ah, right?" Nicholas taps his finger on the top of a pile. "Coroner said it was a heart attack. Probably brought on by stress, heavy drinking and smoking."

"Nothing unusual in his blood?" Besides the cigars and bourbon, Nathan kept himself in good shape and ate a balanced diet. Victoria doubted a heart attack took him down.

"The coroner said no, but I'm waiting to hear from our guy to confirm. He can do a more thorough review than what public dollars would pay for. Especially, when law enforcement only cares that Father is dead. Not the how behind it. I'm just waiting for his report."

"When will we hear?"

"His wife just died after a hard battle with cancer. I didn't want to be a complete asshole and ask him to delay his wife's services to attend to our needs, so it'll be a few days. End of the week tops."

"Not ideal, but I understand. Who found him?"

"I did."

Finding his body must have been excruciating. Victoria's mouth opens to speak, but Nicholas holds up his hand, lowers his head, and leaves.

About to follow his boss, Erik stops in the doorway. "You alright?"

"Don't you have somewhere else to be?"

He nods and turns towards the stairs. A guard should never be too far from his subject.

"Actually wait. I want to talk to you. Come in and close the door."

Erik does as instructed and stands, hand over wrist, in front of the door.

Victoria takes a position in front of him, and although much smaller, she's just as intimidating. She noticed nothing outwardly suspicious about the man, but a good rat wouldn't be.

"I'm going to skip the pleasantries and the how have you been. We've gotten along in the past. I don't see why we can't right now. Although, I shouldn't have to say it, I will. This conversation is to stay between us. Nicholas is not to be informed. If he asks, tell him I wanted to know how he was doing after Father's death. Do you understand?"

Erik nods.

"Good." She gives him some space but maintains eye contact. "As I'd hate to kill you. Well, I might not hate it, but I'd be disappointed to have to do it. Tell me about when Nicholas found Father."

Erik swallows, "Mr. Townsend, Nathan, didn't show up at breakfast. It had become common for him to only eat with Nicholas and Brigitta occasionally, so no one thought anything of it. Afterwards, we came here to get our orders for the day. That's when we found him lying on the floor. His hand stretched out as though he was reaching for the door."

Satisfaction and sadness battle inside Victoria's mind. Her parent's deaths were painful, so why shouldn't Nathan's be? On the other hand, the image of the powerful man she once knew, frail and struggling on the floor, hurt. A little.

"You stay close to Nicholas, so I know you hear confidential information. This is where I need you to be completely honest with me. No holding back on account of your loyalty to Nicholas. What do you know about how Father died?"

Erik squints for a moment and must have realized Victoria was serious as he looks up and to the left in thought. "As far as I know, it was a heart attack."

"You have no suspicions there was foul play?"

A minuscule twitch releases from the corner of his eye. "I don't-"

"Let me stop you right there. You know something. Even if you think it's nothing, I need to know about it."

He straightens his shoulders. "Nathan kept telling Nicholas there was a rat on the compound. Nicholas didn't believe him, but looked into it and found nothing. The fact Nathan is dead makes me think he wasn't wrong."

"Who would be your short list of people around here that would want Nathan dead?"

"I don't know. No one has been especially obvious or fighting with Nathan. Except for Nicholas and Brigitta, but that's normal."

"What were these fights about?"

"Nicholas called Nathan out on the poor business decisions he seems to have made over the last six months. I don't know the details of the decisions Nathan made. All I know is The Family has lost some money and business prospects and is not happy. Nicholas took over handling some of the business without Nathan's authorization and they came to blows."

"When was this?"

"A few months back. They've been fighting constantly since, but somehow kept everything running smoothly enough that Irving wasn't called in by The Family to fix the problems."

The hairs on her arms stand on end. Erik's story lines up with Nathan's fear that Nicholas was coming after him. "This next question I need you to answer immediately. Whether based on gut or knowledge, there can be no hesitation. If there is, I'll consider you as being complicit." She steps toe to toe with the man, who looks down to meet her eyes. "Was Nicholas angry enough to do something about it?"

"No. Never."

"Who else have you spoken to about the fighting?"

"No one."

She eyes him quizzically, "Who are you closest too on the compound - besides Nicholas?"

"I keep to myself, really. I'm nice to everyone, but the life expectancy for the soldiers in this line of work isn't long. There's no point in getting close to anyone."

He wasn't wrong; she thought. "What about Brigitta? What were she and Father fighting about?"

"That he spent all of his time in here and barely paid attention to her. And he only acknowledged Nicholas when it involved the business. Even then, it wasn't praise." He scratches the back of his hand.

"What is it?"

"I was up late one night, couldn't sleep, and was reading in the library upstairs. I know the books aren't for the soldiers but-"

"I don't care about the books. Frankly, read as many as you want. What happened?"

"Brigitta and Nathan were in their bedroom. She was pleading with him to hand over the reins to Nicholas. She felt her son was ready and wanted to spend more time with her husband. Nathan refused and told her that a new leader would only take over once he was dead."

"What did Nicholas say when you told him?"

Erik hesitates, "I didn't."

"Why not?"

"That's how The Family works. One must die for the other to succeed. It didn't seem like anything unusual had happened. Just another fight."

Victoria wonders if she should come out and ask Erik if he's the rat. Will he tip anyone else off that she's on the hunt? Or is he innocent and will he keep their conversation private? Unsure, but with no time to waste with weeding out the threat, she grips his wrist, twists his arm back, and he collapses to his knees. She pushes him onto his chest and pulls the arm to the moment before the shoulder blade would pop out of its socket. "You said with Nathan's death you think there might be a rat living amongst us - is that you?"

"No." He huffs. "I swear. I just do my job, keep my head down and hope I live another day. I have no grand ambitions."

She releases some of the pressure on his shoulder and then pulls it back again. "We'll see about that. Know that I am watching you." She lets go of his arm. "You can go."

Erik pushes himself to his feet in one swift movement. He turns before leaving the office. "If you need a hunting partner. Let me know."

Victoria nods for him to leave and watches as he climbs the stairs two at a time. She wonders if he wants to help because he's loyal or wants to be informed of what she learns. Trust around here is pretty thin, and she's not ready to take chances with anyone.

Unable to help herself, she finishes straightening the papers Nicholas tossed on the floor. A mash up of accounting records, property listings, pages torn from books, and supply orders. All with illegible handwriting covering them. Nathan must have gone mad. The question was, was it genetics or at the behest of someone else?

A breeze through the open window picks up a piece of paper, and it makes a run for it under the furniture. Without looking at it, she adds it to one of the paper mountains encircling Nathan's desk.

Now, to find the files on the new 'recruits'. After seeing the office, and the number of new people in the Townsend's inner circle, Victoria is angry at herself for not believing Nathan when he came to her with his concerns. Rather, she placated him. She vows to find the rat and make them pay. Not necessarily as revenge for Nathan, but to ensure her mistake was rectified.

Chapter Sixteen

Then: July 2004

A subtle knock-on Emily's door signals it's time. She throws the blanket off her fully dressed body, stuffs pillows where she had been and returns the blanket to its position. No one disturbs her at night, but she and Nicholas don't want to take any chances.

Emily slinks out of her room. Peter Rabbit, her mom's sweater with the small bloodstain, and the newspaper article about her parents' death, are tucked into a small polar bear-shaped backpack. Only these possessions and the weight of her future rests on her shoulders.

"Ready?" Nicholas adjusts his ball cap.

"Ready." She grips the straps of her bag.

After the tunnel collapsed, she thought he would be angry at her for what happened and keep his distance. When he finally opened his eyes, it was like nothing had changed. He was still her friend and wanted to help her find her family.

The journey from the stairs to the kitchen door goes unhindered. A waft of humidity smacks them in the face as they step into the cloudy summer night. Emily's stomach is in knots made of nerves and excitement.

Hand in hand, the children weave and dodge the few soldiers on duty at two in the morning. Crouched low, they move to the south side of the wrought-iron fence where Nicholas first showed her the small crevice under it. It was barely noticeable, but big enough for her to shimmy through.

Nicholas had succeeded on two occasions, but with nowhere to go, he simply returned.

"Give me your backpack. I'll toss it over once you're on the other side."

With a deep breath, the scent of the freshly mowed grass encourages Emily to lie on her stomach and stretch her arms under the fence. This is it. She's going to make it. She grips the cool grass and pulls her body through. She lies there for a moment, unable to believe she's out. Rolling onto her back, she sees Nicholas smiling on the other side of the bars.

Dirt brushed off her pants and hands, she holds out her palms to catch the backpack.

Positioned like a basketball player at the free throw line, the smile fades from Nicholas' face.

A yelp escapes Emily when a hand squeezes her shoulder. She looks up. The darkness hides the person's face, but the voice pours terror into her veins.

"Going somewhere?" Nathan asks.

Teeth chatter in response. He thrusts her towards the open main gate to her left. Nicholas matches her steps on the other side, their eyes glued to each other. Two men meet them at the main entrance, and once all occupants are secured behind the locked fence, they follow behind their leader.

The warm glow of the lights on the trees lining the driveway highlights the blanket of fog hovering above the earth. Emily wishes the mist would carry her away.

Fearful of what punishment awaits her, Emily stumbles over her own feet when she attempts to climb the stairs to the house, but Nathan's tight grip guides her forward. She's too scared to ask where they are going. Nicholas' free hand slides into one of hers and she feels a little safer. Not much. But a little.

The red barn-like building where the crew sleeps has a single yellow light on over the front door. Moths circle it as though the bulb emits their only lifeline.

Past the sleeping quarters, they enter the stables where horses announce their displeasure at being woken from their slumber as fluorescent bulbs flicker to life. The scents of manure and mouldering hay and straw is sickening.

"Nicholas, get what we need." Nathan orders.

"Yes, Father." He squeezes her hand, lets it go, and runs into a room at the end of the building. He returns with a long black stick that looks like a tiny oar.

One man moves a wooden horse, with a brown saddle on top, into the middle of the barn. Nicholas places Emily's backpack on the ground, then takes off his t-shirt only so far that it dangles around his neck. He bends over the saddle slightly; his hands grip the tough leather trim.

Nathan didn't enjoy punishing his children, he believed actions have consequences and his children needed to learn that before they embarked on the dark and dangerous road of the family business.

Although neither Emily nor Nicholas would ever believe it, each lash delivered shreds his already tormented soul a little more. His whole life, he, and others, learned lessons through hardened punishment. Whether it be on the streets before he met Irving McKinnon, or once he was in his employ.

He found Irving's, and his, soldiers responded to the fear of punishment more often than leniency. In Nathan's business, lines were not to be crossed. Only once was he foolish enough to forgo retribution and it almost cost him his life.

Sure, Emily and Nicholas were children, but they also needed to learn quickly that favouritism has no place on the Townsend compound.

Emily's fragile skin blisters from the punishment and a few drops of blood bond her wounds to her shirt.

Nathan turns her to him, rubs her arms and pulls her into his chest, careful to not press the fresh wounds. "I don't enjoy hurting either of you, but there are rules. One of which is you can't leave these grounds without my permission. I'm not sure where you thought you'd be able to go. There are kilometers of forest and road before you would find anyone." The sad eyes from the day Nathan took Emily return. "There are also a lot of bad people out there. People who won't be as nice to you as I've been. I hope you can see that I can give you a good life. One day, hopefully soon, we will come to love each other, like a family."

Still as a statue, Emily doesn't know what to do. She wants to cry, scream, run. Anything to get Nathan's hands off her. She's smart enough to know that won't help her situation. She's trapped. Stuck in the life of a dead girl and she wishes they could change places. At least she'd be in heaven with her actual parents. In a place that knows no sorrow or pain. Only happiness. A feeling Emily is confident she'll never have again. Instead, her hopes are being eaten away by a rage that will only be satisfied when Nathan is dead.

He gently releases Emily's arms and Nicholas' hand returns to hers. With the adults following behind them, watching every move, the children make a silent vow.

Nicholas to always protect Emily.

Emily to become strong and smart enough to kill Nathan.

CHAPTER SEVENTEEN

NOW

GIVEN THE HEIGHTENED THREAT at the funeral, Victoria wears a sleek black suit and is not squeezed into an uncomfortable sheath dress like Brigitta. Ironically, it was Brigitta's idea that Victoria wears the suit. Perhaps jealously reigns over yesterday's skin-tight ensemble. Or maybe she wants the reassurance that when Victoria is less restricted, she can better protect her and Nicholas. Regardless, Victoria appreciates the comfort while relaxing in a Rolls Royce heading to the McKinnon cemetery, a private plot of land owned by Nathan's boss.

As repayment for The Family keeping law enforcement from tying Irving's involvement to anything illegal, elite members are buried beside generations of McKinnons in graves marked only with a number at the bottom, often hidden by blades of grass. Without a name, anyone interested in locating a specific body would either have to have inside information, or dig up multiple graves. A legal nightmare for the righteous and a tedious torture for grave robbers.

Victoria focuses one eye on Aidan while keeping watch on the surroundings outside of the car. Nicholas has threatened dire consequences if anything happens to her, so Aidan stays vigilant, his head on a swivel.

She's impressed by his diligence, having plotted the route of the convoy. He identified there was only one left turn and one intersection to travel straight through, compared to six right turns had they taken a different path. As such, he insisted on Nicholas, Brigitta, and Victoria sitting on the right side of the cars to avoid a direct hit in a vehicle ambush. Despite his attention to detail, he doesn't earn her trust.

She spent the night reviewing Nicholas' background work on him, which she found in the back of a filing cabinet in Nathan's paper-strewn office. Everything looks to be in order, but her gut tells her something's not right. Some detail has been missed. Given what happened in England when she ignored her gut, she'll not be so easily swayed by Nicholas' reassurances.

A few strands of Aidan's dark voluminous brushed-back hair hang over his forehead. Victoria's desire for order screams for him to push it back into place. He doesn't seem to mind. His form-fitted suit jacket is unbuttoned, as is his seat belt.

Victoria has no time to waste figuring out if he's the rat. Even though it's unlikely he'd admit to anything today, especially with the driver present, she can at least get a sense of his character.

With her head against the headrest, fresh, expensive leather overtakes the subtle hint of men's cologne from beside and in front of her. She catches his eye as he glances from left to right. They lock eyes briefly, and he sits back in his seat without Victoria having to instruct him to do so, keeping his gaze fixed on her. His fingers tap on the armrest of his door.

Whether out of politeness or strategy, Aidan waits for Victoria to speak first. "As you know, Father hated chit chat, bullshit, lies and traitors. Something he passed onto me. Now's your chance to be honest and share anything important about yourself I should know."

Without breaking eye contact, Aidan pushes the wayward hair back into place. Finally, thinks Victoria.

"Ma'am, everything you need to know about me is in the dossier I'm sure you've read."

"First, don't call me Ma'am. I'm twenty-seven, not fifty. It's Victoria. No need to be formal with me. Second, you and I may have different definitions of 'need to know'. Your file reads a little too conveniently like the perfect back story of a future mobster. What is suspicious is that you joined an organization at thirty-one. Most career criminals are in the business before they turn twenty-five, hell twenty even. Why such a late bloomer?"

"I preferred to work independently."

"What changed?"

"Businesses like your father's stopped hiring outsiders and my income was significantly reduced. I was struggling. Serendipitously, I found myself at Moonshine Cafe that day, witnessing a passenger brandishing a gun from a car. In Lunenburg County, Nathan was a well-known figure, even if he remained somewhat of a myth elsewhere in the province. I knew the bullets were for him. Thankfully, the shooter waited for the sidewalk to clear. I got your father under the table before the first bullet struck the shop window. I rushed him out the back door as the offenders fled. Nathan was grateful. Hired me to find the culprit. I had the guy within the week, and here I am."

"You're not telling me anything I don't already know. It's still too opportune that you were there. It's not like people go to Chester in droves mid-week. Not on a day when you can't see beyond the fog. Perfect day for an ambush? Yes. Perfect day to plant a rat? Also, yes." Victoria juts out her chin and her lush lips disappear into a thin line as she assesses the man beside her. "How *did* you find the shooter without cameras and in bad weather?"

"Witness statements and town gossip, mostly. It didn't take long for news to travel about the silver Toyota Camry sporting a bright-red cartoon lobster bumper sticker."

"There's nothing unusual about that."

"It was wearing a yellow fisher hat with a pipe sticking out of its mouth."

"Ah, that is strange. You know that gossip has its limitations?"

"I have connections in the RCMP who ran some checks for me."

"They monitor those. They must be linked to a specific file and have a valid purpose."

"Technically, the shooting at the cafe was a file. My contacts were smart enough to fear repercussion from Nathan if they didn't help. They took the information I gathered, ran it, and gave me the results. They delayed their counterparts, who wish to take your family down, for a few hours, which gave me the lead time needed to deal with the situation before the cops showed up."

"You used Father's name, rather than your own resources, to get on his good side. I don't know whether to throttle you or commend you."

"Technically, I was working for him."

"Do your technicalities help you sleep at night, given everything you've done and do?"

Aidan shifted in his seat and licked his lips.

"At least you're not a complete psychopath." Glancing out the window, she realizes she only has a few more minutes left to get the answers she's looking for.

"Your quick rise in the ranks makes a nice little bow on a perfect story. Too perfect."

Aidan holds Victoria's stare. "Would you trust me if my story were different?"

"No."

"Then I guess it doesn't matter what I say, now does it?"

Victoria grips her door handle to prevent her from slapping the man. "What are your intentions towards my family?"

"You make it sound like I'm dating...nevermind. I was practically out of work, and your father offered me an opportunity. I didn't see any reason to turn him down."

"You just jumped in with blind loyalty, then?"

"Something like that. We both know Nathan rewarded those who supported him. Unlike certain families who devalue you until they think you've proven yourself."

"Are you a rat?"

"No." He replies without taking a beat, a flinch or flicker of doubt.

"It can be a lucrative position, spying for the enemy. Your short time with us means you don't have a deep-seated loyalty. With your tactical skill set, and the fact you had Father, and now have Nicholas fooled into trusting you, it wouldn't be hard to pull off."

Aidan focuses on Victoria, rests his arm along the backseat, and leans in. "This family gave me a life when I was about to lose it. I had nothing left. Next to Louis, I'm the most loyal person on this team. I'd bet my life on it."

Victoria searches his eyes for a shadow of a lie. She comes up empty-handed, but maybe he's a fantastic actor. "Let's hope you don't lose that bet. I'll kill you myself if I find out you're going after my family."

He reaches for her shoulder to reassure her, then pulls back before contact. "I understand why you don't trust me. I wouldn't either, in your position. Although, with you being gone for so long, one could question where your loyalty stands."

Victoria is about to slap the insubordinate bastard, but he catches her wrist before her palm can collide with his face. "Don't you dare question me," she says through gritted teeth.

Aidan releases her. "That crossed the line. I'm sorry. You may proceed." He turns his cheek to take the blow.

"Oh, why thank you for giving me permission." Victoria decides the moment has passed. It's less fun when he's expecting it. "I see you don't fear pissing me off. Not something I'd recommend from now on, by the way." As they talk, she's warming to the idea of having a verbal, if not physical, sparring partner that isn't Nicholas. "Give me one good reason why I shouldn't kick your ass the moment we get out of this car."

"Nicholas."

"Excuse me?"

"If you want to embarrass Nicholas in front of your outfit, not to mention your enemies, who are bound to be paying their respects today, then go ahead, kick my ass. That's up to you. However, if you want him, and The Family, to have the respect of those present, I'd recommend keeping your hands to yourself. Not to mention, Brigitta would see the act as disrespectful to your father. Although, I don't think you worry too much about that."

Victoria clenches her jaw as her blood boils, and her desire to strangle him grows. She must be losing her ability to mask her feelings if he has assessed the circumstances so well. Her mind rolls in circles as she questions if she's just over-analyzing the situation. She's sure, with his rank, that he's aware of what land mines not to step on between herself and Brigitta. Victoria decides that it's better not to provide assurance or disagreement to his statement. If she has lost her touch, it's more important she gets back in control and finds the rat.

The car turns into the cemetery and Aidan takes up his head-swiveling reconnaissance. Faceless statues of winged angels mark the entrance. There is a long line of cars parked along the back road. A large crowd gathers around the fenced family gravesite.

"Stay here while I make sure everything is safe." Aidan reaches for the door handle and emerges into the blaring sunlight.

Victoria doesn't wait to be told what to do. The fresh spring breeze refreshes her and she saunters to her guard. "There's a secret hiding in you, and I will find it."

Chapter Eighteen

Then: September 2007

A THUNDERCLAP SHOCKS EMILY from lying on her stomach to sitting. Nicholas doesn't seem bothered and picks up a railway card from the face-down stack at the edge of the Ticket to Ride game board.

"Did you hear that?" Emily asks.

"Huh? Oh, it's nothing." Nicholas says.

Emily leaves the game and examines the star-studded September night sky through the double-paned windows in Nicholas' bedroom. Not a cloud in sight. Smoke drifts up from the middle of the forest. Otherwise, there is no sign of life outside.

She's frozen in place as she recalls the screams and sudden silence that overtook her world almost four years ago. A similar silence fills the air now.

She scrunches her eyes shut to brush away the thoughts from her mind. Maybe it wasn't what she believed? Maybe it was fireworks? Perhaps some-one hit something with a shovel by the barracks or horse stalls and the wind carried the sound to the house?

Nicholas puts down three of his red train pieces between Santa Fe and Oklahoma City and looks up. "You don't have to worry. Sounds like Father took care of the rat."

"There are rats?"

"No, silly, not like the ugly rodent. But a person. Someone was selling Father's secrets to his enemies."

Her blank expression urges Nicholas to continue.

"Father's work is very secretive. Only certain people are allowed to know how the business works. If anyone shares the information with someone they shouldn't be, they are called a rat. Then, Father exterminates them."

"I know I'm only ten, but what does the sound have to do with rats?" Emily wasn't sure she wanted to know, but what Nicholas was saying wasn't making sense.

He joins her at the window. "You know how Father is very strict about keeping information about what happens around here to ourselves?"

She nods.

"Well, someone was just killed for revealing Father's secrets to people he doesn't like."

Emily's eyes widen. Nicholas used the word kill with ease. As though the definition didn't carry the weight of a life. Or was finite.

Nicholas continues. "We call them enemies."

She silently tries the word enemies on for size. "How do you know what happened?"

"This morning, I was listening at Father's office door when he was talking to Louis and Carlos. They said they found the person who provided our enemies' crew the coordinates so they could hijack Father's latest gun shipment. They agreed to handle the rat problem after dinner, when everyone had returned for the evening."

"Guns?"

Nicholas ducks his head out of his bedroom door to make sure no one is doing what he did this morning. Confident of some privacy, he continues. "You can't tell anyone I told you, okay? You're just a kid and shouldn't know this stuff."

"You're a kid too."

Nicholas thrusts out his chest. "Well, I'm older. Besides, I'm going to run the family business someday. Father says so. So, I'm going to have to learn how everything works. Might as well start now. I listen in on some conversations here and there. No big deal."

"He'd hurt you if he found out."

"But Father won't find out, right?"

Emily shakes her head, purses her lips, locks them and throws away the invisible key.

"Good. Now, if you get scared, you tell me and I'll stop."

"I'm not a scaredy-cat."

"You jumped when the gun went off."

"Well... Well, I didn't know what it was. What if someone was coming to hurt us?"

"That won't happen. Not here, anyway. Father has people to protect us."

"Like he protected Victoria?" The moment the words left her mouth, Emily wanted to shovel them back in.

Nicholas swallows hard. "Part of Father's business is transporting weapons, drugs, and protecting locals. I know he cleans people's money for them. There could be more, but I'm sure there are parts of the business I don't know yet."

"How do you clean money, like putting it in a washing machine?"

Nicholas laughs. "No, silly. Remember how the other day he took us to look at that big yellow house in Mahone Bay? The one with the For Sale sign?"

Emily nods. It was a beautiful house with a short porch out front and looked out onto the water. The salty mist from the harbour had tip-toed on her skin. She liked it a lot better than this place. It seemed more inviting. More friendly. More like a home rather than a prison. She thought they might move there, until Father patted her on the head, as though it was a stupid question.

"No, we aren't moving." He said. "I'm buying it for a friend." And that is where he left it.

Nicholas continues, "Well, Father uses what's called dirty money. Money that was earned by doing something bad, and buys property, or vehicles, horses, or anything big and expensive. At some point he'll sell whatever he bought, and that's what's called cleaning money."

"How do you know that?"

"Before you arrived, I asked Tutor Glenn what Father does with everything he buys. He didn't tell me right away, but the next day I had a lesson on, what's it called? Right, money laundering. I put the pieces together."

"Why would Glenn teach you that?"

"He probably told Father I was asking questions and was instructed to. You'll see that a lot of what the tutors teach us relates to the business. And there's nothing in our lesson plans that isn't approved by Father."

"Right." Emily wasn't sure how learning about the Prime Ministers of Canada or religious studies would help with a business, but she cut off the thought and refocused. Nathan was like those bad guys with guns in the old movies she had watched with Daddy. But probably worse. She knew there was a reason she didn't like Nathan. Although, saying 'Father' when she was in his, or his soldier's, presence had become more natural than she liked. At night, she pulled out the newspaper article to remind herself who her real dad was. But with life becoming normal here, and no way for her to get out, she feared one day she wouldn't remember him at all.

A thought crept forward in her mind and sent shivers down her back. "Do you know why Nathan killed my parents?"

Nicholas tilts his head as though assessing whether she can handle what he's about to tell her. "All I know is, Father was furious when your dad didn't save Victoria's life. And Father can be very mean when he's upset. He barely slept or put on clean clothes for two weeks. He walked around here like a zombie, muttering about teaching your dad about how it feels to lose his daughter. But your dad would need to be alive for that to happen, so I guess your dad made mine change his mind. Maybe he exchanged his life for yours?"

Emily thought she wanted to talk about this, but it hurts too much. Tears paint her cheeks and chin.

Giving up on the board game, she follows Nicholas down to the kitchen.

Shadows dance in the moonlight on the quartz counter-top until Nicholas turns on the pot-lights. He climbs on the counter with ease, passes her a couple of ceramic bowls, and hops down without a sound. No wonder he goes unnoticed when he eavesdrops. After four scoops of smooth chocolate ice cream are divided into the bowls, they sit at the table in the alcove in silence as the rich chocolate coats their taste buds.

Emily scrapes the sides of her bowl, hoping for one more drop. Giving up on her efforts, but not removing her eyes from her dish, she asks. "What was Victoria like?"

Nicholas clears his throat. "Um, well. I don't know."

Emily pushes herself around the bench and places her hand on his. She's not sure how to comfort someone, but this helps her sometimes.

"She liked to sing and dance. Not that she was very good at it."

"Was she funny?"

"No. Or I don't think so." He squeezes her hand. "Can I tell you another secret?"

"Yes."

"I didn't really like my sister. She was always mean to me."

"Why was she mean to you?"

"I don't know. She told on me whenever she caught me doing something I shouldn't be. Then, when I was getting yelled at or whipped, she'd make funny faces at me behind Father's back."

"That's not very nice."

"No, it's not. You're much nicer."

Emily can't help but smile. She clings to her friendship with Nicholas as though her life depends on it. Which she suspects it does. She couldn't survive this family without him.

"Can I ask you another question?"

"Sure."

"Why does your mom hate me so much? I mean, I know she misses Victoria, but what happened isn't my fault."

"I don't know. She doesn't like it when I talk about you. She got furious when I asked her to be nicer to you. Even slapped my cheek so hard her ring cut it open, and she never hurts me."

"Oh. I'm sorry you were hurt because of me."

He wraps his arm around her, and she snuggles into his side. "It's not your fault."

"Yes, it is. If I wasn't here, she wouldn't hate me, and then she wouldn't hurt you."

"Even if you weren't here, she'd still be mad. And she probably won't hurt me again. She wouldn't stop crying and kept apologizing afterwards."

"I hope she doesn't. It's not fair."

With the air of someone older and wiser than his years, Nicholas advises, "not much around here is fair."

The cool night air tickles Emily's socked feet, and she searches for its source. Nathan emerges from an outside door with Carlos. Noticing the children, he whispers something to the large man, who nods to the children and leaves the house.

Nathan sits on the opposite side of the booth from the children. Calm and collected, he rests his folded hands on the table. "Do either of you have questions about what happened tonight?"

They both shake their heads.

"I'm giving you the opportunity to ask questions, otherwise we will never talk about this again."

Emily doesn't know if it is the sugar from the ice cream, her childhood curiosity, or the realization she probably won't get out of this family anytime soon that propels her to ask, "Did you kill someone?"

Nathan pulls a cigar from his inside jacket pocket, twirls it between two fingers, and lowers his eyes to meet Emily's. "I did not pull the trigger, but someone died tonight."

His honesty glues her tongue to the top of her mouth.

"But they deserved it right, Father?" Nicholas asks.

"Yes. They always deserve it. And they only die when they become a threat to The Family. To your mother, to you," he turns back to Emily, "and you. Everything I built is for the both of you. We must punish anyone who tries to take that away."

"Why do they have to die? Whenever I got in trouble, I was just sent to my room for a while. Or I wasn't allowed to do something I really wanted to do."

"Sometimes, when someone makes a slight mistake, the punishment is less severe. But, when it's as bad as what Oscar did, I needed to not only punish him, but show everyone else that works with me, or against me, what I'm capable of. Scare them a little so that they don't hurt me, or you, again."

"Does someone want to hurt me?" Emily asks.

Nathan taps his pointer fingers. "No. No. But they will. One day."

Emily's eyebrows squish together.

Nathan continues, "I don't say that to scare you. Well, actually I do. Life with us will not be like the life you remember. It will be a good life, but there are some things that we have to do differently. And one of those things is to look out for one another. Protect one another. There will always be someone looking to take what we have."

"And this person tried to take something of yours?" Emily didn't want to let on that Nicholas had told her about the gun shipment. She was learning the game.

"Exactly."

"What happens to them now that they're dead?"

"I have a team that takes care of that. You don't need to know the details. Just be aware that you are protected, but you always have to be careful who you trust and what you tell people. Not everyone wants to be your friend. Be sure to tell me if anyone you meet scares you. Your gut is your greatest asset."

"My gut?"

"That feeling you get that something bad is going to, or is happening, when it may seem like the situation is normal. That's your gut. We rely a lot on that around here."

Chapter Nineteen

Now

Lush fir and maple trees that have laid claim to the land for hundreds of years overlook a half-acre of immaculately mowed grass. The leaves wave goodbye in the wind to the souls below, while squirrels squeak as they jump between branches.

Victoria hasn't seen many of The Family for years, but besides a few additional grey, or in some case less hair, and some added weight around the middle, the members are the same. The mass of bodies in black meld together in the rare sun and stand motionless, eyes glazed and unfocused on the casket. The Reverend's monotone voice reads words Victoria tunes out.

Erik stands large beside Nicholas and casts a shadow over the people behind them. Like Victoria, he's paying little attention to the actual service.

Finn and Janet, accompanied by two of the Harris' crew, stand on a small hill behind the crowd. Finn takes the occasional photograph, but despite his eyes being hidden behind the lens, Victoria feels them land on her often. The other three have a hand inside their jackets, ready to react if needed.

Beside her, Aidan stands at attention. His shifting from foot to foot was only noticeable to Victoria.

Across from her, Brigitta accepts a handkerchief from Paul, seated beside her, and dabs away her tears.

She sees that Nicholas is having a harder time masking his disgust at Paul's presence. He glares at the man and is rubbing his hands raw.

She tries to stay focused on the crowd, as Nathan's allegations that some-one was trying to kill him replay in her mind. With sentries around her, and a lengthy program ahead of her, her mind wanders to the last time she saw him alive. Maybe she'll find a clue to who the rat is.

The dreary sky matches the mood inside Victoria's ornate hotel room. Nathan refuses to leave the comfort of the surrounding walls. A room ser-vice cart cluttered with half-eaten food sits to the side of the couch. In between questions, she picks at the cold French fries.

"If someone is after you, then we must have missed something. Someone. Of all the suspects we've talked about, who do you trust the least?" she asks.

"Paul."

"Yet, you're adamant it isn't him. Tell me why again."

"He has too much to lose. Even if he got some of the other families on his side, without Irving's backing, he'd be dead." Seated beside her, Nathan rests his elbows on his knees and massages his temples. Dark bags from lack of sleep accent his brown eyes.

"What if he took out Irving? Or garnered his support somehow?"

"Never! Irving wouldn't do that to me. We've built this empire together. Of all the people to replace me with, not that I'm replaceable, it wouldn't be him."

"I'm just trying to look at this from all angles. Paul's been cavorting with Brigitta for years. Maybe he wants to take over your entire life." The irony of a replacement Nathan is not lost on her.

"My wife is as close as he gets to being me. As you know, she's spying on him more than he is on us. The information he tells her would surprise you and it all comes back to me."

Victoria wants to point out how perhaps Brigitta isn't the dutiful wife he thought she was. Seven years of playing games with Paul may have warped her reality. But, they've already talked about her rival many times, so she leaves her questions unasked. Instead, she focuses on Paul. "He's worked for you for nine years in his role as the Director of the Halifax Port workers. Maybe he's not satisfied with the sizeable sums we pay him to ignore containers appearing or disappearing. Perhaps he wants more power and knows you keep impeding his progress? Going after you seems like the logical next step."

"Not if he wants The Family to trust him. If he kills me, what stops him from killing them?"

He had a point. At the same time, power hungry people do stupid things. That was part of the reason her protection detail was so successful. People made mistakes and needed her to keep them alive long enough to fix them.

Nathan continues, "There's a reason I've prevented the Inglis clan from joining The Family. Paul's a wild card. You can never trust a wild card."

She smiled knowing that she was a wild card, and Nathan really shouldn't trust her.

CHAPTER TWENTY

NOW

AN ELBOW JAB INTO Victoria's side brings her back to the present. Aidan coughs, and she realizes it is her turn to speak. Nicholas had spoken at the church, in front of the faith, and local communities. Her message was reserved for the private burial with family and criminals.

She steps forward, but doesn't stray from her side of the coffin. A piece of paper crinkles as she removes it from her inside jacket pocket and unfolds it. The sound magnified by the silence. She scans the notes she tossed on the page late last night, after she was done with Aidan's paperwork. Most of it is illegible. Disregarding her previous thoughts, she hands the paper to Aidan. She doesn't know, or care, what he does with it.

"I'm not sure there is anything I can say about the magnitude of the man that lies before us, that you don't already know. He wouldn't want me to show you his more sentimental side. Like the fact that every Christmas until Queen Elizabeth II died, he turned on her Christmas message hoping to hear the memories of his own mother's voice within the queen's. Or that he never forgot a birthday. Even if he was away, a mysterious package would always wait for Nicholas or me at the foot of our bed when we awoke. What he would want me to say, is that he was devoted to his wife and children."

The echo of Paul clearing his throat travels through the uncomfortable shuffling of the crowd.

Victoria's eyes lock with his. "Father would do anything to protect us. We will do the same to protect his legacy. If anyone tries to come after our family. Tries to take what is ours, yours will be the next grave to be filled with dirt." She steps back.

The Reverend retakes his position. "Right, well. Amen?"

The crowd responds in kind.

The bland voice says a last prayer.

Afterward, those who wish to place roses on top of Nathan's casket, while the family waits for a moment to themselves, do so before returning to their vehicles.

Aided by Paul, Brigitta rises from her seat. She picks up a silky red rose from a nearby table, kisses it with lips of the same colour, places it gently on top of Nathan's casket, and returns to her position. Paul remains in his position to her right, and Louis stands behind her surveilling the area.

As the casket descends, Victoria resists the temptation to jump on top of it, open the lid, and release her pent-up frustrations on the man who destroyed her life. She steps behind Nicholas to toss her own flower, Aidan glued to her side, as if the four feet she needs to travel were the most dangerous she will ever walk.

As Nicholas walks towards the vehicles, he tries to take his mother with him, but she refuses. Rather than joining those in the crowd returning to their vehicles, she wants a semi-private moment with her husband after everyone else has left.

Victoria reaches for a rose; a thorn pricks her finger. A drop of blood stains the stem. A part of her forever with Nathan.

Her feet stick to the fake grass turf that drapes the edges of the hole in the ground. Her eyes burn and she squeezes them shut to soothe them. This moment is harder than she expected. Five years ago, she got as far away from the Townsends as their reach would allow her. Today, she cannot break free from the man who ensnared her in an unrequested existence. She smells the rose and drops it on top of the others. Aidan places his hand on her back to guide her away, but she brushes him off. She'll move when she's ready. When she's done silently cursing Nathan for her lost childhood. For this life.

A deafening boom and an unseen wave of force knocks Victoria off her feet. Dirt erupts from the grave. Dust, dirt and shrapnel, hinder her view of the scene. Her ears ring. Wafts of sandalwood cologne signals Aidan is on top of her. The ground under her vibrates from the stampede of the crowd. Some take cover in vehicles; others hunt for the culprit.

Only when Aidan is satisfied no further devices will go off, does he move issuing orders while pulling Victoria back to her feet. "Stay close to me!"

She tries to spit the dirt out of her mouth, but gritty remnants remain.

Crouched over and running to the car, Victoria cranes her neck and tries to find Nicholas. The dust and the swarm of bodies are thick. She can't find him.

"Keep low," Aidan hisses shielding her with his body as they scuttle forward.

The whistle of bullets flies around her and he shoves her into the back of a car. Shots ping off the vehicle's bullet-proof siding as tires screech and speed their occupants to safety.

It's not until they are out of the cemetery, with Aidan seated beside her, that Victoria feels a warm puddle suck her pants against her leg. "I'm hit."

Decency has no place in a disaster. She eases her pants down to her knees. A bullet-sized hole marks her left thigh. Blood gushes down her leg and onto the leather seat.

Leaping into action, Aidan rips off his plain black tie and creates a tourniquet around her leg.

She closes her eyes and is grateful for the pain the pressure causes, knowing it means she should at least make it to the safe house before she bleeds out.

Bloody fingers grab her wrists, checking for a pulse. "I'm still alive, thank you very much." She pulls away from Aidan. "I thought your job was to make sure I didn't get shot? Or blown up, for that matter."

"My job is to keep you alive. No one said anything about ensuring there were no holes in you." Aidan responds. He looks out the back window and his finger dances as he counts cars. "We have all our vehicles. Now we wait to see if everyone is accounted for."

Her wound still oozing, he guides her leg over the armrest between them, her foot now in his lap, and ties the arms of his jacket around her.

"Whose job was it to secure the grave site?"

Aidan's shoulders slump "Mine."

"What the hell was that then, you incompetent bastard?" Gritting her teeth against the pain, she flings her leg off the armrest. She wants to break his nose, but needs his attention on her, and not himself, so instead she punches his shoulder. "I swear to God, if Nicholas has so much as a scratch on him, you will find yourself inside an unmarked grave in the forest. Now, I know enough about incendiary devices to realize a full-blown bomb did not explode back there. Otherwise, I'd be dead. So, you better start telling me how an ambush happened right under your nose."

Was that fear she saw creep across the chiseled face? Was the rat caught?

"I did everything by the book, right down to climbing into that hole this morning before picking you up for the cemetery."

"Who stayed to watch the grave while we were at the church?"

Aidan creates a shield with his hands, "Now, don't kill me-"

"Oh, that's not a good way to start a sentence." The pain in her leg forgotten, she reaches into her jacket pocket and pulls out the red-handled switchblade Nathan gave her for her fourteenth birthday. She snaps it open with a flip of her wrist and raises it to his jugular. "A little more blood in this car won't make a difference. Now talk before I lose my patience. Or all of my blood."

"Paul's men were on site, making sure it was safe for him. We've been working together on a few jobs lately, and I knew he was going to sit beside Brigitta, so I didn't think they would risk him getting hurt."

"Didn't think, or intentionally created a cover story to blame someone else? I knew I couldn't trust you and my gut is always right." A thin trail of blood trickles down Aidan's neck and along her knife blade.

"I swear I'm not part of the attack against your family." Aidan's jaw clenches and he lowers his hands, gripping his seat instead of using his military training to disarm his injured companion.

"How do you expect me to believe you? I don't see any bullet holes in you. It doesn't look like the explosion affected you at all. Convenient?"

"I wasn't lying when I said this family has given me a purpose in life. I'm not dumb enough to risk losing that."

"But dumb enough to allow someone to launch an attack at the funeral. Guaranteed that all the bullets flying around weren't Townsend bullets. You'll be lucky if we let you keep your head after this."

A wave of pain and Victoria's world spins. She pinches her eyes shut to make it stop, grateful she ate nothing for breakfast as her stomach churns.

Her knife falls into Aidan's lap as she topples sideways towards him. The armrest digs into her side and a grey fog overtakes her. The car comes to a sudden halt and a waft of heat washes over her cooling skin. Erik's enormous arms wrap around her.

Nicholas' voice is faint. "What the hell happened to her?" A body slams against the car and Aidan's apologies echo in the air.

Chapter Twenty-One

Then: August 2012

Abject complacency rules Emily's life now. She eats when she's told to eat, mindlessly uses up her allotted hour a day of free time and follows behind Nicholas to an in-house classroom where three tutors try to instill the Nova Scotia curriculum, on top of those Nathan deems necessary for the business. "It's never too young for you to learn the basics. I won't be around forever," he states when the children complain about the volumes of homework assigned to them.

With most of her time spent on homework and reading, Emily caught up to Nicholas' grade within two years of her arrival. Now they are both finishing grade eleven. Emily's dad always said knowledge was power, and she plans to get as much of it as possible in the hopes she'll find a way out.

Part of that knowledge includes observing everything that happens around her. She longs to join the strict physical training routine, undergone by the soldiers so that, like them, she can turn her body into a weapon. For now, she's restricted to basic self-defence lessons.

Every Sunday, in the seventh pew from the front at St. Augustine's Catholic Church, Emily prays Nathan's departure from this world happens sooner rather than later. She isn't sure God is listening. It's not like He condoned people seeking the death of another. Let alone the fact He hasn't helped her discover the answers to why her life turned out this way.

The only enjoyment Emily gets from church are the angelic voices of the choir. But even that has waned. It's hard to find pleasure in a place when it's exploited by evil.

Over the years, her courage to speak her mind has increased. She treads carefully and has learned what, and when, she can ask questions. Like today, while Nathan sits at his desk, and she is on the floor in front of the couch, her legs stretched under the coffee table, and her math homework staring up at her finished. "Why do we even go to church?"

"It's important." Nathan's eyes don't move from his paperwork.

"I gathered that, as we do nothing without it having a purpose. But, the things that go on around here don't exactly follow the rules of the Bible."

Nathan stops reviewing the paperwork for the latest gun shipment arriving next week. "If you know it has a purpose, why are you asking? Why not just do as you're told? Like everyone else around here."

Nervous that she's pushed too far, she bites the inside of her mouth, but doesn't back down. "When have I ever been like anyone else?"

"That's what will make you a great asset to our family. To The Family. Someday. So long as you learn when to tow the line, and when it's safe to explore the grey area outside of it."

Hearing no anger in his voice, Emily perceives she has permission to continue with her questioning. "I've seen the whispered conversations between you and other members of your organization at church picnics and bazaars. Is the church just another place to conduct business?"

Nathan nods. "It's also about community. Putting a face to the name of all the rumours and working to dispel them from people's minds."

"Wouldn't you want people to be afraid of you, even a little?"

"The fear is still there. People will often overlook what goes on in the dark if they can't see it or if what they can see is generosity. That's partly why we help with the Food Bank, fund children's activities, and sponsor events all over the province. Not to mention the millions donated to local charities every year."

Emily can't understand how people can be so blind. Then again, they couldn't even see she wasn't Nathan's daughter. Maybe people believed what they wanted. "No one questions where the money is coming from?"

"Some might, but they never turn it down."

Of course they don't, she thinks to herself. "Do you even believe in God?"

Nathan looks up at the ceiling. "Some days. Those are rare."

"Then it's okay if I don't believe?"

"How you feel about God, or whatever may or may not be out there, is up to you. As long as you keep playing your part on Sunday. Faithful living may be on the decline, but many people around here still take it seriously. The longer we can be seen as faithful Catholics, the more often we'll be forgiven by others for our acts."

"Are you saying that if you stopped going to church, people wouldn't tolerate you or your business anymore?"

"It's more complicated than that, but it's easier if we stay the course."

"Right." Emily shuffles her practice test into a pile and inserts it into the textbook, fiddling with the corners of the papers.

"What else are you wanting to know?" he nods towards her physical tell and she smooths out the paper.

"What is your plan for me?" The question lingers in the air without a twitch from Nathan. Emily's nerves can't handle the silence. "You must know what you want from me in all of this. The Family and the Townsends, where is my place in it?" The question she asks to herself is, what obstacles does she have to climb to find her freedom?

"Must I? Well, that is for me to know and you to find out."

Chapter Twenty-Two

Now

Cold flat metal shocks Victoria's body and clears the hazy curtain hanging over her eyes. The fluorescent lights hanging from The Barn's ceiling blind her and she has to look away. It's been many years since she's visited the Townsend's functional safe-house, of sorts. With a tile floor that's easy to clean, the darker side of their business is also taken care of here. Whether that be torture or clean up.

The registered owner of the land, an unrelated name, ensures no direct Townsend ties.

Once a vibrant red, the building's outer shell of chipped paint and deteriorating wood creates the perfect mask for the metal structure built within its walls. The rickety old barn is unlikely to catch a passerby's attention, except to ponder its stability.

With the unknown threat moments ago, Victoria knew that even if she wasn't shot, someone would bring her here, rather than the compound. At least, until they got the all clear. Pain shoots up her spine, "Argh!"

Nicholas stands beside her. "Here, bite down on this," he says, putting his black Prada belt between her teeth.

Erik replaces his sunglasses with eyeglasses and pulls out a scalpel. Today, he's not just a bodyguard but the doctor.

There's no time to administer anesthesia, and Victoria would reject it if it was offered. She needs to keep her faculties. Squeezing Nicholas' hand, she meets his scared eyes and bites down on the leather as the scalpel pierces her skin. She's had to perform a bullet extraction on herself twice, but that experience doesn't lessen the pain now.

Thankfully, the bullet hasn't splintered, and with the help of Finn holding her leg steady, Erik's meticulous work retrieves it within minutes. After a splash of antiseptic, some stitches, and multiple mouthfuls of whiskey, she pushes herself back on her feet. Ready for revenge.

"Where the hell is Aidan? He and I need to have a little chat." Victoria stumbles still woozy from shock. The man she's looking for has disappeared.

"Calm down, Vic, plenty of time for that. We need to get you dressed first." Nicholas holds her steady.

Erik rips open the plastic cover off of a clean pair of pants he's pulled from a storage locker. With Finn maneuvering her legs, and Nicholas keeping her shoulders straight, they struggle but finally get the pants on her.

"I asked where is Aidan?"

"I sent him home." Nicholas says.

"I'm sorry? You allowed him to return to the house?"

"It wasn't his fault."

The veins in Victoria's neck pulse. Why does Nicholas seem so unmoved by the incident? She has to be missing something. She scans her surroundings. Only Erik, Nicholas and Finn remain.

Nicholas' eyes show no concern or anger but a silent pleading for her to calm down. Unattended, she hobbles around the perimeter of the barn, piecing it all together.

When she's ready, she steps in front of Nicholas, leaning against the cleaned operating table. "Please explain to me why you almost had me killed today."

CHAPTER TWENTY-THREE

THEN: AUGUST 2012

WITH A RARE WEEKDAY afternoon to themselves, Nicholas and Emily leave their towels by a large grey boulder the size of a compact car, halfway into the forest. It's seated beside a waist deep river that winds its way through the trees. They call it Rocky, for no reason other than it made the younger Emily happy. They had considered painting it a rainbow of colours, but did not want the transportation of supplies to attract unwanted attention to their secret place.

The cool water was a welcome bath for their sweaty bodies. The swimming pool would be warmer, but within sight of many eyes. Here, they can be themselves and here, Nicholas calls her Emily.

"Hey, Em. Betcha, I can catch one of these fish with my bare hands."

"Haha, no way you can do that."

"Wanna bet?" Birds chirp their encouragement while perched above in the rustling trees.

"Okay. What will I win?"

"What do you want?"

"I get to drive your car."

"Haha. Father barely lets me drive it. And what happens if the police catch you?"

"Like the police are going to do anything." She wasn't wrong. The police were either on Nathan's payroll, feared the man enough to leave him alone, or were so discouraged they hadn't been able to make anything stick in a court of law that they didn't bother to try.

"Fine. And if I win…" Nicholas scratches his chin as if he's deep in thought. "I get to kiss you."

Emily can feel the blood rush to her face. Despite standing in the chilled river, her cheeks burn. She rinses the telltale sweat from her face. Curious what it would be like to be kissed, she can't stop the shy "Okay" from slipping between her lips.

Nicholas grins and gets to work on finding a fish. "Here's one. Now, I just need to get ahead of it." He leans down and slips. The shallow water splashes and washes over him, then continues its slow trickle through the winding forest.

"I win! Get those car keys ready."

"Best two out of three?"

"Fine, but add doing my stable chores to my winnings."

Nicholas climbs up on a rock protruding from the water and surveys the stream. Back in the water, he crosses to the other side and stops just short of the edge. He squats with his feet gripping the mud on the river floor and waits.

"I'm cold. Can you hurry up and lose?" Emily dances in the river as the August sun refuses to warm her.

He smiles and his hands dive into the water. He pulls out a long, wriggling eel. "Yes." He thrusts the eel towards Emily. It escapes its capture before Nicholas can torture her with it. "Told you I could do it. Now, do I get my prize?"

Emily's heart pounds as though it wants to leap out of her chest. She can't look Nicholas in the eyes. "What if I'd rather kiss the eel?" She jokes.

"Oh, ouch." He brushes back his wet hair. "I mean, if you really don't want to, I won't force you. But, a bet's a bet." He winks.

Emily turns away, her wet hands slide off the smooth, thin plant roots, keeping her in the river. The voices in her head battle with each other. She likes Nicholas, but does she like him like that? There are no other boys around here, so how else would she get her first kiss? Is he thinking the same thing, and just using her? She struggles to get out of the river. The tug on her other arm pulls her out of the whirling words in her head.

"You're going the wrong way." Nicholas says.

"What? Oh. Oops."

"Are my good looks dismantling your inner compass?" He remarks.

"Ya, sure. That's exactly it." She playfully pushes him aside and gets herself back on track towards Rocky.

Once there, she wraps herself in her large blue and white stripped towel. A shield to hide confused feelings. Nicholas dries himself off as much as possible, climbs up and lies down beside her.

Surprised by her courage, Emily says, "If you still want to kiss me, you can."

Nicholas smiles and sits up. She mirrors him. Unsure what to do, she keeps her eyes open.

"Are you going to stare at me the whole time?"

"I dunno. It's not like I've done this before."

"Close your eyes."

She does what he tells her. Without warning, their lips meet. Emily's engulfed in warmth and her head swoons. Nicholas' supple lips taste like clean river water.

"STOP THAT."

The booming voice ricochets off the trees around them and they part as though a flame has come between them. Their stomachs drop at the sight of Brigitta, her eyes as wide as her gaping mouth. Her hands outstretched like claws. "Get over here this instant."

With heads lowered, they hasten down the rock.

"You two are disgusting." She wraps her hands around their wrists like handcuffs and she drags them through the forest, their towels discarded behind them. "Nicholas, when your father hears about this, he might just send you to Mr. McKinnon's boys' school like he's always talking about."

"You can't do that." Emily protests.

"Not another word from you, you little hussy."

"It's not her fault." Nicholas pleads.

"You shut up too."

Everything in Emily wants to use her defence training to free herself, but she doesn't want the extra lashings, on top of whatever they'd get for kissing. Nathan has coached her to let whatever Brigitta does to her slide off her back.

The soldiers in the yard stare as the three fly past. Brigitta's reflection in the glass of the open back door contorts into the devil.

Brigitta lets go of Nicholas' arm long enough to open Nathan's office door. Then the handcuff returns. "Do you know what I just found these two doing in the forest?"

Nathan places a hand over the receiver of his phone. "Closed doors require a knock first," Nathan speaks into his phone, "I'll have to call you back," and hangs up. With the call ended, he turns his focus back on the intruders. "You were saying."

"They were kissing. Kissing."

A master at hiding his emotions, Nathan doesn't so much as twitch at the announcement. Emily's been trying to emulate his skills. Even now, there's no reaction to Brigitta rubbing her wrist raw.

Nathan looks between Nicholas and Emily. "Is that so?"

"I've said it before, and I'll say it again. She is not trustworthy." Brigitta seethes.

"It wasn't her-"

"Nicholas shut up. Everything is her fault." Brigitta retorts.

Attentive to his wife, Nathan stands and moves around the desk toward them. He caresses Brigitta's jaw line. "Now, darling. Why don't you unhand the children and I'll sort this out?"

With force, she lets go, causing them both to flounder sideways. "There better be consequences for this." With a door slam, she's gone.

Nathan points to the brown leather couch aligned with his desk. "Sit." They obey. "Speak."

Drawing from experience, Emily understands brief responses are preferred. She looks to Nicholas, who perfects his posture and tries to make himself as big as possible. Their cheeks flush at the retelling, nothing left out.

Nathan paces the office for a few minutes with his chin resting in his hand. He lights a cigar. The smoke billows towards the ceiling and Emily's nose twitches from the harsh, earthy aroma.

Nathan resumes his place behind the desk. "I suppose this was bound to happen. But you're brother and sister, for Christ's sake. What if someone else saw you? The damage you could cause this family…" he takes a long draw on the cigar. "Now that you've satisfied your curiosity, it will never happen again. If I catch so much as a whiff of you two being together, Nicholas will finish his schooling elsewhere and you…" His eyes reveal a heartbreak she hasn't seen before. "Well, I don't know what I'll do with you yet, but it won't be good. Understand?"

They both nod ferociously.

"I'll discuss your punishments with Brigitta, as lashings don't seem to be a deterrent around here. I suspect, at minimum, you'll be giving the crew a break from cleaning their barracks. And I'd stay away from each other when Brigitta's around lest you increase her suspicion of you." With a wave of his hand, they are dismissed.

They don't wait for him to change his mind but rush out of the room and up the stairs. Nicholas huffs as he leans against the banister overlooking the main entryway. "If we have to clean the barracks for months, it was worth it." He tosses the hair out of his eyes and winks.

Emily playfully side checks him. "Like you have anything to compare it to."

"Either way. I'll do it again if I have the chance."

"No, you won't. If you get sent away, then it's just me and her. You can't let that happen. She'll kill me."

The truth evaporates the smile from Nicholas' face.

CHAPTER TWENTY-FOUR

NOW

VICTORIA'S BALLED-UP FISTS CAN barely contain her rage on the trip back to the house, as Nicholas recounts the plan he set in motion for the funeral. She doesn't know if she's angrier that he kept it from her or mad at herself for not picking up that he had a secret. Things have changed since she's been gone. She doesn't like it.

"If Paul was the target, why was I almost blown up?"

"You weren't almost blown up. It was supposed to be a distraction so that our shooters could take him out. You weren't even supposed to be in that spot when it went off." he says.

"Then why the hell didn't you tell me, or wait until I had walked away?"

"I saw Paul whisper to mother and stand up, so I figured he was leaving. It was then or never. I'm sorry."

Victoria ignores the apology and continues to wrap her head around what happened.

"And what if someone had replaced your device with an actual bomb? What would you have done then?"

"Stop being hysterical. That's not what happened."

"Hysterical? I'll show you hysterical." She catches Finn's eye across from her. With three deep breaths, she tries to calm herself. "After you detonated whatever was in that grave, who was to kill Paul?"

"I was." says Nicholas.

"So, he's dead?"

"No."

Victoria shakes her head in disbelief.

Before she can ask why not, Nicholas continues, "His guards were on top of him too quickly. It was like they were prepared. I made a mistake. I'm sorry."

Her anger prevents her from continuing the conversation.

Traffic along the route to the Townsend compound is calm, with the drive marked by occasional grunts from Victoria when the tires collided with potholes.

She doesn't have to ask if anyone privy to the plan questioned Nicholas' judgment. She knows they haven't. Otherwise, none of this would have happened. Nicholas was a great idea man, but his carry-through was weak.

With the potential leak in their organization, logically, Paul's crew may have been tipped off. The question remained, who was the turncoat? Could the leak be plugged before it was too late?

Victoria closes her eyes and tries to transform her anger into a calm sensibility. It doesn't work. She can't believe the mess they are in now. "I hope you have something impressive to say to our soldiers when word gets around that you failed. You look like an incompetent leader at the worst time. You need to act fast to maintain and build on the trust Nathan created in this crew. If you don't, you lose control quick."

Nicholas was silent.

"While we're at it, why was I kept in the dark? Now I look like an idiot. Thank you for that."

"It was for your own good."

Every muscle inside her twitches. She hates when people tell her something is for her own good. Her anger explodes as her fist meets Nicholas' leg.

"Ow. I guess I deserve that."

"Oh, you deserve a lot more than that, mister. You asked me to come back here for you. And you don't even bring me up to speed on what you have planned. Had I known, I would have made sure I was out of the way."

"And you probably would have made sure Mother had tripped into the grave or something."

He wasn't wrong. Victoria would have found a way to at least have Brigitta injured. "Would that be so bad? Oh, sorry, that was out loud."

"I couldn't risk your hatred resulting in a world where both father and mother were dead and our enemies were making a move. Yes, I'm prepared for a move to be made, but I'd rather not give them a shiny red arrow saying, 'Over here, this family's falling apart, time to move in'." Nicholas tightens and straightens his black tie to prepare for their arrival home. Even after the incident at the cemetery, and acting as a surgical assistant, he maintains order in his appearance in front of his troops. "There is one advantage to how things turned out."

"Oh, really? Please, enlighten me, as I don't see how me having a hole in my leg, and the pain that goes with it, is helpful."

"It looks like we are the ones under threat."

"What happens when The Family, or Irving for goodness sakes, asks what happened? I'm not sure they'll be happy that you put their lives at risk."

"The Family knew the plan. Irving, well, I wanted to prove myself without having to run to him like a child for approval."

"Great. Just great. I look like an idiot and Irving is going to be pissed that you didn't tell him you were going to desecrate his graveyard. I don't know what's going on inside your head, but a sure-fire way to shift the balance of power away from you is to piss Irving off."

"I know. But, I've got it handled."

"Like you handled-"

"Don't"

Victoria closes her eyes and tells herself that poking the wounds of his failure will get them now where. Hopefully, he can get himself out of the hole he's in. She diverts the conversation to the tactics of what comes next. "And what exactly do you plan on doing about this Paul problem? Brigitta having a side piece while Father was alive was one thing. He kept her in line, and she'd never have betrayed him. But now, I can see her getting a little self-righteous at wanting more power in her hands. As it is, she's practically the Queen Mother. A figurehead with some input behind the scenes. The fact I've moved up a spot has likely got her riled up. What if she makes a move from the inside?"

She knows she struck a nerve. But wants to see if he'll take the bait with a potential rat in the car.

"We can discuss that later," he says, "but I can guarantee you that there will be no confusion about who's in charge here."

"Fine, but tell me this. How do you plan to ensure everyone trusts me, given you apparently don't?"

"I trust you and they know it. I told them the truth about why you were being kept out of the loop. You'll be happy to know some of them would have supported you throwing Mother into the grave."

"Really? You'll have to let me know who they are so I can thank them for their support." Victoria takes in the soothing forest scenery around her; but it does little to calm her. "Was Brigitta aware of this plan? If so, maybe she leaked it to ensure that she and Paul weren't harmed. Or, if she wasn't aware, how do you know someone didn't leak it to her?" Victoria's eyes fell on Finn, who hasn't kept his eyes off of her since they got into the vehicle.

He winks and licks his lips at her. Which looks more like a dog with peanut butter stuck on its face than anything she would want to get near. She can't help but curl her lip in disgust.

Nicholas rubs his brow. "Mother didn't know, but she is a loyal member of this family, of The Family, so please stop questioning it. She's not a rat. Yes, she-" He cuts himself off before he says too much. "Look, she's not going anywhere, so you need to deal with your issues and move on." Eyes wide, Nicholas silently wills Victoria to at least pause the conversation until they are alone.

Over the years, Victoria knows he has tried to get the women on each other's sides, but the hatred is too deep-rooted. It doesn't mean he's given up, it's just no longer his priority. His priority is fixing this mess.

She tries to heed his silent warning; but the opportunity to seed some information and see if it will grow elsewhere is too tempting. If it does, she'll have narrowed down the number of people who could be the betrayer.

"What about Aidan? Did he know the plan? Could he have informed on what you were going to do? It's not like he rushed me out of the way of the explosion." She then remembers how Aidan had, in fact, tried to move her along. Oh well, seed planted.

"As he handled the overall plan, yes, he was aware. No, he didn't tell Paul or Brigitta."

"How can you be so sure? You sent him home so quickly, I never got to interrogate him."

Nicholas' face reddens, and not from the heat of the day. "I've had enough of this, and you need to drop it. Aidan isn't a rat."

Although in the mood to keep the fight going, Victoria backs off, but doesn't entirely give up. "I have this hole in my leg, and Aidan's job was to protect me, what is the likelihood I'll be able to hand out some punishment? Not sure we've had a beheading recently. Might be nice to sharpen the old sword."

"He saved your life."

"Correction, Erik saved my life. Thank you, Erik."

Erik nods in the review mirror. "You're welcome, my lady."

"Thoughts on punishment, oh fearless leader?" She jokes.

"Vic, if we beheaded everyone who made a slight mistake, we'd have no employees."

She raises her leg and pushes through the pain. "You call this a slight mistake? Oh, I look forward to kicking your ass once my leg heals. And you better hope it happens quickly. The longer I have to wait, the worse you're going to hurt."

Nicholas takes her hand. It's soft and warm. He kisses it, and a familiar urge rushes over her.

"I've missed you," he says.

For someone not wanting Victoria to speak about personal matters, she is shocked at how forward he is with the personal displays of affection. She pulls her hand away from Finn's inquisitive eyes and brushes off the gesture as unimportant. "If you won't punish Aidan, I sure as hell will."

Knowing she won't give up until she can take her anger out on someone, which Nicholas preferred wasn't him, he gives in. "Just make sure he can still function afterwards. Most of the time, he does great work."

"As evidenced by today." She glares, then rests her head back, and closes her eyes. She knows Nicholas is leaving out some important details but will give up prying until they are alone. Although, with Finn in on their conversation, and his apparent desire to impress her, perhaps he'll give up the information a lot easier than the secret keeper beside her.

The bustle of the Townsend homestead ceases when Nicholas and Victoria enter the over-sized living room. With each step, pain pulsates up and down her leg, and reverberates throughout her body.

Louis has brought Brigitta up to speed on the day's events and she reserves her scowl for Victoria as she digs her nails into the arms of her fabric chair, rather than releasing a torrent of anger about the desecrated grave.

Victoria locates Aidan standing by the tall panelled glass doors that lead out into the backyard. He holds her gaze, makes his way across the room and hands her a glass of whiskey.

She finishes it in one gulp. Never looking away. She hands back the glass, and with both of Aidan's hands full, punches him in the nose.

Blood gushes from the wound on the unsuspecting victim.

Nicholas steps before Victoria before she can land another punch and turns to Aidan. "Why don't you take Vic upstairs, get cleaned up, and make sure she rests?" He turns to his sister, "You, try not to kill him."

Victoria smiles but knows she doesn't have the energy to enact more punishment now. "Well, now. I don't think Aidan's the right person for the job, do you? Not after his errors today. No, I think I'll have Finn help me." Victoria slides her arm into Finn's; who stands a little taller and unsuccessfully hides a smile under a bitten lip.

Hurt washes across Nicholas' face, but Victoria ignores it. He put her through hell today. Now, it's his turn.

She limps out of the room, Finn in tow, and Nicholas' anger bounces off walls as he demands an explanation for the bullet hole in his sister's leg.

Victoria fights the urge to turn around and stand in solidarity with him.

Chapter Twenty-Five

Then: October 2014

Steam from Nicholas' shower stall billows under the white curtain into the locker room. "Enjoy that, did you?" He spits the words out as he pours the contents of his water bottle over his head.

"Kicking almost everyone's, especially your, ass? Why yes, I did." She turns the water on in one of the change room shower stalls, and wipes off the first layer of sweat with a towel, tosses it into a basket, and grabs a spring-fresh scented one for after her shower. She tosses a few others in front of the empty stalls in preparation for the other soldiers' arrival.

"I mean throwing yourself at those men. It's disgusting. You're seventeen, for Christ's sake!"

"I literally had to throw myself at them to take them down. Just like everyone else. Was there another move you expected me to make?"

Nicholas clenches his jaw. "Did you have to be half naked to do it?"

"Seriously. You and the rest of the guys don't even wear shirts, and you're angry about a little cleavage?" She fondles her covered breasts. "These aren't even that big." Sure, her first week in skin tight workout gear propelled her to the top ten in the round robin fights. Not that it swayed the more experienced and older men. They knocked her down like an inflatable clown. And just like that clown, week after week, she got back up. Her outfit was no longer an advantage.

Nicholas tries to hide his hypo-criticism while he paces the empty locker room. "Look, I'm just worried about you. These men don't see a lot of women and you, well, look at you."

"Why yes, I have a body. But I doubt any of them are dumb enough to touch it outside of training. Nathan would have them killed."

"That's beside the point. And the others will be here soon. You wouldn't want them to hear you calling Father by his name, would you? Follow the God damn rules!"

"Fine. *Father* would have them killed. And if that isn't your point, what is?"

"Just don't do it again, okay?"

"What are you going to do when I do?"

Nicholas' face goes beet red. He hangs his head, shakes it, and his shoulders out, resigning to what he has to do. He charges at Emily, pushes her against the wall of lockers, and pins her wrists at her sides. "Don't make me hurt you."

Emily searches his eyes to see if the evil that resides in Nathan lives within him. She can't tell, but takes the chance he won't hurt her. "Would you whip me like Father does, or do you have a different beating in mind?"

He turns his head towards the mirror. "Vic, please don't make me do this. Just say you won't wear shirts like that again."

"Oh my god, this is what a woman's workout top looks like. I didn't design it."

He rests his head against her forehead. "I'm sorry."

"For what?"

Head raised; he knees her in the stomach. She topples over breathlessly. Stuck to the floor in disbelief.

"Say you won't wear it," he demands.

"What are you doing?" she gasps.

He kicks her again, but with less force.

Emily pushes herself to her knees. He grabs her hair and pulls her head back, grabs her neck and whispers. "I won't stop until you say it."

Her desire to not let him win wars with her curiosity to find out why he is beating her. "Fine. I won't wear the stupid shirt again, okay?"

He releases her and she collapses. She rolls over and pushes herself up to sitting against the cool metal, while trying to catch her breath. Nicholas sits on the bench, his head in his hands.

A shadow slides along the wall behind the lockers. The red nails identify the intruder before her face appears. "Good job, my boy. Although I would have hit her a couple more times." Brigitta runs her fingers through his hair. "She needs to be reminded of who's in control here. That her body will not fool you." She glares at Emily. "And you will not beat Nicholas in another fight, understand?"

Emily rises to her feet and stands nose to nose with Brigitta. Before she can tell her, she declines her request to let Nicholas win, Rufus barges in, a hand over his eyes. "Is everyone decent in here?"

Brigitta and Emily stand their ground.

Deflated, Nicholas responds, "Yes."

Rufus takes in the standoff and decides it's better not to address it. "You two change into your sweats and meet me on the training field. You have five minutes."

"Five minutes until what?" Nicholas asks.

"Until your next training session." Without waiting for a reply, his large body exits.

Nicholas squeezes himself between the women. "Mom, you got what you wanted. Just go."

She departs but makes her displeasure known through her muttering and door slamming.

Emily can't look at Nicholas. For ten years, he's protected her. Now, at the whim of his mother, he felt compelled to use his hands against her. They've had wars of words that cut like knives, but never have they intentionally caused each other physical harm outside of training.

She turns off the shower, and despite the floor being wet, changes as commanded behind the curtain, the cuffs of her grey sweatpants stained with water.

Lockers clang and questions fill the room as people wonder what Rufus is up to while they change.

When Victoria is done, she pushes past Nicholas and finds Rufus on the training field.

Nicholas scurries close behind and takes his place around the circle.

Everyone wears the same grey sweatpants and sweater. Military boots tied tight. Pinks and red stain the sky as the sun sets over the horizon. The yellow hue of the yard lights illuminates the property. Everyone's face is stoic, but their darting eyes tell Emily they don't know why they are here either.

Nathan steps into the middle of the circle. "I thought we'd take our training to the next level. The forest used to be a barrier from our enemies; however, we cannot rely on it defending us. We must be prepared should our enemies take to the trees. So tonight, we will pair you off, take you to a remote location, and require you to make your way back to this house with nothing more than a few tools. Anyone who makes it through my defenses wins $25,000."

A murmur runs through the crowd. Nathan raises his hand and the chatter cuts off. "We will fill any weakness we discover, making it even harder for stragglers to penetrate the wall of guards I'm setting up. You have forty-eight hours to make it back here. If you are not back by then, don't return."

Rufus hands every other person a hiker's backpack. "You have a flashlight, some matches. Two jackets and one sleeping bag. The idea is not only to identify weaknesses in the fortification of this compound, but to test your survival skills."

He passes out shot glasses and fills them with a clear drink from a silver Thermos. "A toast before you depart." He raises the Thermos. "May your journey be fruitful and may Mr. Townsend forever reign these halls."

In unison, everyone but Rufus downs their drink. As much as Emily would like to get one over on Nicholas, her gut tells her there's more in their cups than what meets the eye, so she pulls his arm down before his glass reaches his lips. She looks to Nathan, at the center of the circle. Hands behind his back, he strides over to them.

"Why the hesitation?" he looks to Nicholas, whose eyes direct Nathan to Emily.

"There's something in this drink, isn't there?" She asks.

"Why would you suspect that?"

"How else do you expect us to not figure out where you've put us in the forest? A blindfold won't hide the clues of the terrain we would travel over. Dropping us from a helicopter would give us a full view of the forest and which way we'd want to be heading."

Nathan smiles and squeezes Emily's shoulders. "You're a smart girl." He turns to the crowd. "I suggest everyone sit down before they fall over." As ordered, they obey.

"How long will we be unconscious for?" Emily asks.

"Not more than a couple of hours."

As she looks up at him, she's reminded of the scary man perched at the top of her stairwell holding Peter Rabbit. His eyes meet hers. "Drink up."

Nathan's hands ease Emily to the ground and a hint of mint tickles her tastebuds. Within minutes, darkness envelopes her.

CHAPTER TWENTY-SIX

NOW

PALE FROM THE LOSS of blood, the mirror reflects a ghost rather than a seductress. The bullet hole and limp are not the sexiest thing in the world, but she'll use them to her advantage. Not that Victoria believes it'll be hard to get Finn talking.

She splashes some water onto her face, gives her hair a shake and straightens the flowing, light blue silk, thin strapped lingerie to show as much of her petite bosom as possible without giving everything away.

When she exits the bathroom, Finn's playing nervously with the dark green blackout curtains that hang in her bay window. The full moon illuminates the yard and she hopes her time with this young man will shine light on what's been happening around here.

"You okay over there?" She asks. The strong pain killers she took after her fist collided with Aidan's nose are working their magic and the pain of moving her leg subsides.

Startled, Finn falls onto the window seat awkwardly. A pillow tumbles to the floor, and he leans on his elbow against the glass, his head in his hand. "Ah, ya. I'm cool."

"Right...first things first, please don't speak like a wanna be gangster. Got it?"

Finn blushes like a child caught with a cookie before dinner, and nods.

"Good. Next," she overemphasizes her hobble as she makes her way to the window and sits beside him. An abundance of AXE body spray burns her eyes. She hadn't noticed it on the way to the room. Then again, she was focused on retribution for Nicholas' antics. "It makes me feel a lot better to know that you have Nicholas' back." With Finn's ego nicely stroked, her hand finds a comfortable place on his leg. A bulge in his trousers tells her she'll get anything she wants out of him.

"Tell me everything I need to know about Aidan. He's obviously not as smart as you if he fucked up today's plan."

Finn licks his lips and has a hard time keeping his eyes off Victoria's chest. "Um, well, when I arrived, Aidan was already in the third position. Way I hear it, Nathan took a liking to him after Aidan saved his life. But I've also heard that Aidan knew to be there that day. As for today, what better way for him to get you out of your position as second in command and step into it himself? He's been coveting moving up further."

"And you know this how?"

"I heard him and Janet talking just before Mr. Townsend died." Finn leans back on his palms and tosses his next words nonchalantly to her. "You know Nicholas and Janet have hooked up a few times?"

"Is it the 1990s? Just say they've had sex. Now, what were Aidan and Janet saying?"

Finn's cheeks blush at her bluntness. "Janet insisted she had control over Nicholas and would soon be pulling the strings from the background. Their plan, if you came back, was for Aidan to distract or remove you. Your reputation for being a skilled and ruthless defender of The Family goes beyond the Townsend compound. They know their plan won't succeed if you stay."

"I suppose I should be glad to hear people haven't forgotten about me. Or what I can do." She wonders why they would think killing her off within two days was the best way forward? It just seems reckless to cause this much disruption with the risk of Nicholas doubling down on maintaining power and pushing everyone away. "What else did you hear?"

"Nothing. A guard came around the corner and scared them off." Finn's right eyelid twitches.

Locking eyes with him, she runs her finger along his leg and up his shirt. The eye twitch quickens. Victoria places his hand on her inner thigh and grabs the neck of his shirt, pulling him closer to her, their noses touching. "You wouldn't lie to me about any of this, would you?"

"N-n-never."

She feels his heartbeat pound through her hand on his chest. "Then why do you seem so nervous?"

"I..it's. God, you're beautiful and I'd be lying if I said I've ever been with someone like you before."

"Is that so? Well, we may get to that. Before anything else, who did you discuss Janet and Aidan with?"

"I tried to approach Mr. Townsend, Nathan, but he was focused on his office papers. He dismissed me without giving me a chance to speak. I didn't want to just blurt it out and cause chaos if someone else overheard. And Nicholas has had a lot to deal with since his death, so I was waiting for a better time."

Victoria considers dragging Finn to see Nicholas and share what her gut has been telling her, but she knows he'll brush it off as another rant during a long day of tirades. It would be better to talk to him when he's not annoyed by her accusations and she has more evidence from a trusted source.

She considers how internal threats loom over the Townsend's, and Finn has barely tried to reveal them. If he were truly loyal, he'd have made sure Nathan knew immediately. Keeping it a secret only makes sense if Finn is working with the other two. Or he might let the plan unfold so that his position remains uncompromised in case they succeed.

"Do you have more evidence of this plan?"

"Oh...I. It's not like they wrote it down."

"I may not be a lawyer, but it seems you have a lot of circumstantial evidence and no actual proof. How do I know you aren't the one trying to stir up trouble?"

The seat cushion shifts as Finn squirms in his seat. "Why would I do that?"

"I can think of a few reasons. One, you're trying to have sex with me and think that shows some sort of loyalty and I'll simply give in. P.S. that is not how to get into my bed. Two, you're ambitious and likely believe if I get Aidan and Janet out of the way, you'd move up the ranks. Three, you're exploiting our instability by working for another family or enemy."

"I suppose there's some truth to one and two. Yes, to sex, and, yes, I want to climb higher. But I wouldn't intentionally cause a rift for this family to get it. That's what I know, and you can do with it what you wish. I assumed you would be less emotionally attached and have a clearer perspective since you were away and didn't care about appearances at the wake."

"You think Nicholas isn't seeing clearly right now?"

"Well..." Finn chooses his words wisely, "He has a lot going on. With wanting to ensure you're taken care of, that Brigitta doesn't cause a disturbance, the extra funeral plans, and taking over a large organization, his eyes are all over the place, and are not focused on what's in front of him." Gaining confidence, shoulders back, head high, he continues, "We all know he trusts you, so not wanting to waste too much time with this information, I figured if I brought it to you, and you told him, he might pay attention."

Victoria's eyes travel Finn's body, "But you didn't bring it to me. I asked you."

"True. But I would have told you, anyway. I was waiting until after, you know."

"Seriously, if you can't say the word sex, I'm not sure we can have it."

"I can say sex. Sex sounds less...sexy. Vulgar even."

"You're Catholic, aren't you?"

He nods.

Wanting Finn to be a resource of information, Victoria decides torturing him to figure out if he's telling the truth or not can wait. Right now, she wants to forget today. "Bring the bench at the end of the bed over and rest my leg on it."

Finn drags the bench across the tight-knit carpet and lifts her ankles to rest on it.

"Now, get on your knees."

He kneels between her open legs. She holds his chin in her hand. His green eyes dart between her thighs and her eyes. "You know I'll bring you a lot of pain before I kill you if you ever hurt my family, right?"

He nods as best he can within her grip.

"Good." She releases him and leans back against the window. "But for now. You've got a job to do."

Chapter Twenty-Seven

Then: October 2014

EMILY'S LYING ON SOMETHING hard and cold. Pain shoots through her skull when she tries to move her head. She keeps as still as possible and her eyes remain closed. She feels around. Is that a wooden floor? And pine needles? The air is damp and musty. Fear prickles her nostrils, and despite the excruciating pain searing down the back of her head and neck, the smell of burning wood rouses her to her feet. She finds the closest wall and leans against it while she gets her bearings.

The fuzzy world around her comes into focus. The structure itself is a cheap makeshift hunting cabin the size of a small garage. A figure huddles close to the fire, rubbing their hands. The shadows from the flames keep the identity of the person hidden until they speak.

"Took you long enough to wake up." Nicholas turns his head towards her, the rest of his body clings to the fire. "Look in the side pouch of the backpack. There will be a vial of pink liquid. Drink it and the hangover you're feeling will be gone in a few minutes."

Without acknowledging his words, she follows his instructions. The vial has a label that states "drink me first". Its glass partner is empty inside the pocket. Did Nicholas even question what was in the vial or has his trust in Nathan become so explicit he wasn't worried that someone would try to kill him?

She smells the contents of the cylinder. A hint of sweetness. "How long ago did you drink yours?"

He tilts his watch toward the firelight, "about an hour."

Given he's still alive, she drinks the cool liquid. Either way, the hangover will end.

"Come warm up and then we'll get going."

She finds a place on the unrolled sleeping bag as far from Nicholas as possible, yet still close to the fire. Which doesn't leave much space between them. The shadows and flickers of orange dance on his face as he stares intently at the flames.

"I'm sorry about earlier," he says.

"Hmph." Still upset with him, Emily hugs her knees and the muscles in her stomach echo the pain he had caused.

"You know how Mother gets with each ounce of power you gain around here."

"Power? I have no power."

"You did this afternoon."

"Those men probably let me win. Nothing to do with skill. Or my boobs, by the way. They will put me back in my place next week. You didn't have to do it for them."

"For someone so smart, you are clueless sometimes. It's not the power over the soldiers Mother is worried about, not exactly. Sure, she doesn't like how some of the them are watching you more than her. No, it's the power you have over Father."

Emily's been honing her manipulation skills, especially when it comes to Nathan. She doesn't use it a lot. It would attract attention and Nathan would figure out what she's up to. Her goal isn't to supersede Nicholas, as Brigitta thinks it is. She just wants a say in decisions affecting her life. "So, I occasionally take advantage of his grief for your sister. But, it gets me physical things, and usually those that Brigitta is trying to deny me. If I had any genuine power, I'd get myself out of here."

"You'd still leave after all this time?" The hurt in his voice pierces her heart.

Emily wants to stay mad at him, but he's just as much a puppet in Brigitta and Nathan's game as anyone else in their circle. She inches herself toward him until their shoulders touch. "We've talked about this. A life of crime, jail, and likely death sooner than I want is not the life I want. If I get the chance to leave, I will." Her head tilts, "Like tonight."

"What about tonight?"

"For someone so smart, you are clueless sometimes." She jokes and drapes her hands over his shoulder, rests her chin on top, and whispers as though she needs to keep the trees outside from hearing, "We can leave."

The words linger in the air between her lips and Nicholas' ear.

Nicholas glances at her and refocuses on the fire. "Father didn't mean for *us* to follow his instructions of not returning at all if we're not back within forty-eight hours."

As with snow on a warm winter's day, Emily's hangover melts away. Charged by anticipation, she rises from the sleeping bag. "This forest is vast. Anyone could get lost in it. With our survival training, we could last for weeks out here. Find our way to Halifax and go anywhere."

"Father won't stop looking until he finds us. He'd have park rangers scouring the forest. Helicopters in the air 24/7. That means no fire. No warmth or a way to cook any animals we kill. Men would guard every bus terminal, the airport, train station, and port. We'd have to find a car to steal, and then another one, and another one to cover our tracks. Which given we have no money, our tracks would be pretty hard to cover since we'd need to steal more than cars. If we got away, it wouldn't be for long. And think about the punishment when we're found. Even Father's preference for you wouldn't save you from the horrendous beating and subsequent gruelling labour he'd have us perform."

"I'll admit we'd need to really think this out, but we could do it." She was desperate to hold on to hope.

"No, Em, we can't. And I don't want to. Yes, Mother and Father are shit. But the life we have here is better than the one we'd have out there."

Emily shudders.

"You know what I mean. No matter what we do to hide, the underground will find us. So, there's no point in trying."

"He killed my parents and you just want me to keep living like nothing's happened. Like Victoria didn't die and I'm supposed to be her. Like the real me, Emily, never existed. Every morning, I wake up and force myself to go on with his charade until I can find a way to either kill him or get out. I'm not giving up. Now, I'm going out into that forest to find a way out of this hellhole you call a life." A cool gust of wind slaps her in the face when she exits the cabin.

"Stop." Nicholas calls after her.

She turns back and Nicholas holds out the backpack. "Look in the bag."

She hesitates, knowing she'll need the supplies he's holding out to her. She crouches, unzips the top and parts the opening. Staring up at her is a map of the forest.

Nicholas stands beside her. "Open it."

Fully erect, she opens the map like an accordion. Her eyes bulge wide. A curving red line between two points stares back at her. One point is the location of the house. She suspects that the other point was the cabin they were left in.

"We can't get lost when we've been given the way home," Nicholas reinforces the fact that they are trapped.

"But...why would they give people maps?"

"Father doesn't care if anyone else gets lost. Us, he wants to find very little trouble. Turn it over."

Burn before you get home.

"No one else has a map," she realizes.

"Exactly. And they've put a tracker in the bag."

"What? Where?"

Nicholas empties the contents of the backpack. Instinct propels Emily to take the knife as soon as it hits the floor. She wraps the holster around her waist.

"Feel along the inside seam. It's small, but it's there."

Her hand caresses the canvas. It takes a few rounds of searching to find a lump. She uses the knife to open the fabric and out falls a small black square. No bigger than a quarter. She turns it between her knuckles.

"You see, you're stuck. Guaranteed, if that thing doesn't move in the next couple of hours, people will come looking for us. That wouldn't give anyone much of a head start. And if it doesn't move along the highlighted path, people will probably come looking for us. And if it loses its signal?"

"People come looking for us. Damn it."

"Father's a lot smarter than you give him credit for."

"Oh, I know he's smart. He faked my death, remember?" She wears down the leaves fallen around the cabin as her mind races over what to do next. Opportunity is within her grasp and yet she can't turn this situation to her advantage.

"Would you stop pacing? You're making me dizzy."

She turns to Nicholas on the step of the cabin. Her hands a tent in front of her lips.

"No." Nicholas says.

"It's the only way."

"I can't let that happen."

"Say I overpowered you and knocked you out."

"You know the trouble I'd been in if that happened. Father would never trust me again. Without that, I'm no better than a lowly soldier. I'll never be in charge."

"Then help me figure out a way for both of us to leave." The pacing continues.

Nicholas grabs her arm. "Stop being naive. We've been over this. There's no way out. Now, let's go home." He pushes her forward.

She grips the handle of the knife. If she could get behind him, she could use the butt of the knife to knock him out. Then, bust the tracker so someone comes to find him. Meanwhile, she'll make a run for it. The scenario plays out in her mind as they traverse the forest. Leaving would create a devastating hole in Nathan's life that could never be mended. The thought brings a smile to her face.

CHAPTER TWENTY-EIGHT

NOW

THE SUNSHINE ENTERS THROUGH the small gap of Victoria's curtains and urges her awake. She tries to ignore the call and curls up under her black and purple duvet. Moving her left leg sends a searing pain through it and up her back. She shoves the edge of the soft, plump duvet in her mouth to stifle her scream.

Resigned to the fact that the adrenaline coursing through her body won't allow her to go back to sleep, she sits up. The space beside her was undisturbed, as she made Finn leave after their foray into pleasure on the window seat.

A pair of crutches are leaning against the wall. Someone knew it was likely Victoria would refuse to spend the day in bed, no matter how much using her leg was torture. She hasn't let injuries keep her down before, and she won't now. Not when Nicholas is shutting her out and dismissing the idea that they may have been infiltrated.

If he won't figure out what's going on, she will.

Gravity pulls the towel wrapped around Victoria's shoulder length hair to the floor of her closet. She tosses on a sleeveless black shirt with a skull on the front and shimmies into some shorts. April's mild temperatures will be easier to endure than the pressure of pants against her wound. Besides, the bandages in full view will be a constant reminder of what Nicholas put her through.

Hand hovering over the doorknob, she takes a deep breath. Only a few more days to find this rat and get out of here. Anything more than that and the walls will become unbearably close. As it is, she finds her breath getting caught in her chest, and her muscles becoming tenser as the days pass.

She can't be trapped here again.

Aidan rests against the banister to the right of her room. A piece of white tape bridges his nose, where the swelling appears to have calmed. The ridge of a tattoo Victoria can't make out peaks out just above the collar of his white dress shirt, which is mostly hidden under a dark blue suit jacket. Nathan liked how professional sports players showed up to practice as though heading to a business meeting, and had the same rule for his employees. The creak of the door opening diverts his attention from his phone to Victoria. "Sleep alright?" He winks. The house may be grand, but the walls are not soundproof. The only exceptions are Nathan's office, and the panic rooms. Hence, those nearby could not have missed Victoria's overemphasis of her time with Finn.

"Not bad," she says with little emotion. Her anger about yesterday's events reawakens, and adding to it the allegation that Aidan isn't all that he seems, she's not in the mood for light-hearted jokes. She has half a mind to flip him over the banister and have done with him. It's doubtful that he'd break his neck, but she would definitely have a physical advantage over him, perfect for an interrogation.

He interrupts her thoughts, "I'd offer to carry you down the stairs, but I suspect you'd refuse."

"I can't trust you not to get me shot. How can I trust you to get me safely downstairs?"

"Well, if you don't need my help, then I'll leave you to it. My only excuse for being late for training is ensuring your safety. You look pretty safe to me." His elbow pushes him off the banister, and he rubs the back of his neck.

"Besides the bullet in my leg and the scraps of body parts I'm still pulling out of my hair, ya, I'm fine." She retorts, thrusting out the crutches at him. "Take these. No point in me trying to juggle them, and the steps if I don't have to."

Aidan tips his imaginary hat, does what she's asked and is out of sight before she has hobbled down three steps.

Hopping like a one-legged bunny, she makes it down the stairs with only one incident when her foot slips on the edge of a step and her ass takes the brunt of a fall. Thankfully, her grip remained on the railing, so there was no forward momentum.

Victoria's crutches thunk rhythmically with each step as she trails Devin carrying a plate of chicken and waffles, and a pot of Earl Grey tea, out to the back porch. The savoury southern chicken has her salivating and wishing she could take Devin with her when she leaves.

Brigitta turns to the irritating sound and her disdain for her make-believe daughter is evident behind the long draw of her cigarette.

Victoria pulls herself up to one of four high top tables spread out over the large veranda. She keeps her crutches close, in case she needs a weapon. Brigitta shuffles herself off the couch and leaves the comfort of her space on the opposite side of the porch. Sitting across from Victoria, she nods to the teapot while flicking cigarette ash over the railing.

Victoria grits her teeth as she pours her new companion a cup. She purposefully shoves too much food in her mouth to prevent forced conversation and stares out at the view.

It's not just the spring colours of the forest coming to life after winter that draws her attention. A couple of re-fortification efforts Nathan made in the last ten years brought the combat area to the other side of the pool, in full view of the balcony's occupants.

Half-dressed men and women punch, kick and tackle each other as they finesse their hand-to-hand combat skills under the tutelage of Rufus. His shaved head now stubbled with grey instead of brown hair.

"Do you have to stare at him in my presence?" Brigitta's shrill voice drills into Victoria's ears.

Without removing her eyes from the fighters, Victoria responds. "I'm not looking at him." Which was true. Nicholas' well-built body was distracting, but it was the muscular and tattooed body of Aidan that was drawing most of her attention. The cool spring morning air did nothing to calm the heat flowing through her body.

"I don't believe you. You stay away from him for the few days you're here. You got that. It took a while, but he's finally gotten over whatever twisted emotional games you two played with each other. He's found himself someone Nathan and I approve of joining our family."

Victoria's chest contracts, the fingers of her ribs gripping her heart. The air around her feels thicker than her lungs can handle. No one unexpected was with Nicholas at the wake or at the funeral. Victoria dismisses the comment and assumes Brigitta's trying to rile her up, but she isn't quick enough to hide her astonishment.

"Oh, he didn't tell you about Tessa? Oops. I didn't realize I gave away a secret," says Brigitta with a satisfied smile. "Tessa's sweet, but not make-you-want-to-vomit-sweet. She knows her place and makes Nicholas happy." Brigitta stabs Victoria's hand to the table with her ferocious nails. "Don't mess it up or I'll bury you in the back forest." She slides off her chair and rides the satisfaction of the hurt she's caused back into the house.

Victoria bites her lip and wills the tears welling up in her eyes to subside. When Nathan visited her, he never mentioned Nicholas' potential relationship. Was he understandably focused on himself and his feared death? Or was he afraid Victoria would return home intending to destroy a relationship that he hoped would keep his children apart? She resigns herself to the fact that Nathan withholding the information was probably best, even if it doesn't make his and Nicholas' deception hurt any less.

Victoria turns back to the arena below. Aidan and Nicholas are facing off. The others sit along the sidelines, bruised and battered. Both men's determined faces are shielded by a raised fist to block their opponent. They dance around the circle and each other. Punches make their marks with resounding grunts. Aidan gets a few quick swings past Nicholas' defenses and knocks him, stumbling backwards.

He recovers quickly, but Aidan is toe-to-toe. He blocks Nicholas' left hook with his hand. All he needs to do is twist his arm and Nicholas will fall to his knees.

Aidan lets go.

Nicholas capitalizes on the mistake and grabs the other man's sweaty neck, knees him in the stomach, and throws him to the ground. A few more kicks for good measure, and Aidan collapses. Drops of blood litter the field.

Clapping, handshakes and shouts of congratulations filter up to the balcony and drown out the birds. Nicholas catches Victoria's eye, smiles, and then stretches out a hand to Aidan.

"You let him win," Victoria pronounces.

"Excuse me," Aidan, dressed in nothing but a towel, whirls around, water dripping off his muscular body onto the cream marble floor. "This is my bathroom."

Victoria and her crutches take up the doorway, "technically, it's Nicholas' now that he owns all of this. And what's his is mostly mine, so, are we done arguing over whose bathroom this is and can you explain to me why you let him win?"

"I didn't let him win, and may I put on some pants before we get into this pointless argument?"

Victoria points a crutch to direct him out of the bathroom. Hangers shuffle in the closet. Aidan returns in black pants, fastening the buttons on his clean and pressed black dress shirt. "As I was saying. I didn't let him win."

"Nice try. Not only did you pull your punches, in the end all you had to do was put him in a Half-Nelson and he would have collapsed at your feet. I know that, you know that. You better hope Nicholas or any of the other soldiers don't know that. It would be humiliating."

Aidan blinks slowly and tries to hide a small smirk. "You have a keen eye."

"Yes, I do. There's not much around here that I miss." She searches the man for an unspoken response to her threat and finds none.

"You're telling me I should beat my boss to within an inch of his life next time?" Aidan fastens his watch around his wrist.

"How is he going to get any better if you let him win?"

"Do you think I'm the only one who lets him win?"

"Based on what I saw today, you are the best fighter out there. So, I suspect it's often the two of you in the final round."

"Look, sometimes he needs a bit of an ego boost, so a few of us let him win now and then. Not every time. As you said, that would be humiliating. With everything going on this week, I thought he needed it."

"What other times has he needed it?"

"We have a meeting to attend." Aidan opens his bedroom door and waits for Victoria to exit.

She stops in the doorway. "You may think you're helping him. But you're not. He'll trust you more if you don't hold back. Take the beating you'll get for embarrassing him the first time and then continue to kick his ass until he gets up to your level."

A calming light flashes across Aidan's dark eyes.

"Hey, you two," Louis calls from below the stairwell. "Lawyer's here and Nicholas is waiting. Mind you stop your bickering for a while so we can get this over with?"

"You heard the man." Aidan takes Victoria's crutches and tosses them over the railing to Louis.

"What are you doing?"

"Hop on." He turns his back to her.

"Are you crazy? I can make it down the stairs just fine."

"Sure, but it'll take you twenty minutes."

"I'm not climbing on your back."

"Alright then." He bends at the waist, hugs hers, and lifts.

"Put me down."

"You didn't want to go on my back, over the shoulder it is."

Victoria would kick him, if it didn't mean both of them tumbling down the stairs. So, she resigns herself to using her fists to pound on his back, but he doesn't yield. Not even when they get to the bottom of the stairs.

"I can walk from here."

"You're already up there. And besides, it's my job to keep you safe and on schedule. Now, I'm doing both."

Her fists continue until he flips her forward and down onto her good leg. She pushes her ruffled hair out of her face and is about to give him a piece of her mind when she realizes they are in the boardroom and everyone is staring at them. "You're lucky we are not alone," Victoria mutters as Louis secures her crutches under her arms.

Much like the dining room, there is a long, ornate wooden table in the center of the room, although this one is oval. With fewer windows, the room is darker and gives an air of doom until the mahogany walls are illuminated by the pot lights in the ceiling. Someone has left them at half power and shadows dance around the room.

The usual suspects take their assigned seats. Mr. Malarkey, the Townsend's lawyer, stands at the corner of the table beside Nicholas. Beads of perspiration emerge from the edge of his red hairline. A yellow envelope lies in front of him. He smiles at Victoria, then pinches his lips as if to hide it while looking away. Moisture drips down his temples and his hands shake.

Aidan notices it too and pushes his chair out a fraction, just in case he needs to react and take the man down. Although seated, Victoria keeps one hand on a crutch.

Mr. Malarkey says, "now that everyone is present, I will read out Nathan Townsend's Last Will and Testament."

Line after line, the property is divided between Brigitta, Nicholas, and Victoria, much to Brigitta's vocal disapproval. Nicholas keeps the compound, Brigitta the estate in the Dominican Republic, and Victoria the home in London, England. Frivolous items like vehicles and planes do not elicit as much of a response from the older woman.

Then the moment everyone, especially Nicholas, has been waiting for arrives. Mr. Malarkey licks his lips and reads, "As for my business, it's monetary and physical assets, I appoint, as my successor..." He inhales deeply and spits out the next words as though they taste foul. "Victoria Townsend."

Chapter Twenty-Nine

Then: October 2014

For hours, Emily and Nicholas walk in silence. The moon gives way to the sun. Strokes of orange and yellows highlight a voluminous forest of pines, maples and balsam fir trees, as they crest a hill. Birds, with their morning song, wake the other creatures of the forest. Squirrels scatter along branches in search of their breakfast. A few smoke trails billow up to the sky and identify the position of the other pairings.

Nicholas holds out a ration packet. Emily yanks it from his hands and tears it open. Odourless, brown slop falls into her mouth. A manufactured chocolate flavour allows the grimy texture to become bearable.

"Are you going to stay mad at me the whole time we're out here?"

"I have a lot to be mad about." She takes off her jacket and places it on a fallen tree near the edge of a cliff. She lifts her sweater to reveal a dark purple circle on her stomach.

"I'm sorry. But you frustrate me sometimes when you get stuck in a way of thinking and don't listen to reason. You may not be related to Father, but you sure act like him sometimes. And I'll keep apologizing for that bruise until it's gone if you want me to. I really am sorry." Nicholas sits beside her on the tree.

She recognizes the longing in Nicholas' eyes. It's often reflected in her own. His head tilts and the palm of his hand holds the side of her face. For the past five years, they've had to sneak in moments together. In the minutes when the tutors swap over and while doing chores around the property. Being alone in each other's rooms became impossible after their first kiss. Brigitta made sure of it. Until now, they've had very few moments without supervision.

They take advantage of their freedom.

Afterwards, Emily's left wondering if her first time matches up with those of others. Clothes refusing to come off without force? Did twigs and stones poke through a thin layer of a sleeping-bag? Did it hurt a little and their partner seem to get more pleasure out of it than they did? Was it over soon after it began?

They fumble to put the few clothes they got off back on. With the inactivity of the last few minutes, the cool morning air crawls into Emily's bones.

Halfway down the hillside, hand in hand, Nicholas speaks. "Do you want to talk about it?"

"Why would I want to talk about it?"

"I don't know."

"Do you want to talk about it?"

"Well, I guess not. I just wanted to make sure you're okay."

"I'm fine."

"Good." He lets go of her hand so he can pull out the canteen of water. They share a few sips before it's returned to its pocket. "Do you think you'll want to do that again?" He blushes with the question.

"Oh, um. Do you think we'll be able to?"

"I'm sure we can find a way." He winks.

Excitement swirls in her stomach.

Nicholas guides her down the rest of the hillside. "We're only a couple of kilometers out. We should burn the map."

"Won't that give away our location? We could see where everyone else was by their fires. And although I'm not worried about them, since I'm sticking around, I mean to get into the property unnoticed and win that $25,000."

Nicholas shields his eyes from the rising sun. "Maybe there's a cave or something around here. We can set it alight, and as soon as it's incinerated, we stomp out the fire, and no one's the wiser."

The Frogs call out as the stale air seeps into their clothes while they traipse through the trees looking for a covert place to destroy the evidence.

Finally, they come upon the mouth of a cave. Emily runs her fingers along the cold, wet, bumpy stone walls with fingerlings of tree roots growing through. Nicholas kicks away animal scat to create a livable space for the few hours they will be there.

They follow through with Nicholas' plan, and having not slept since waking in the cabin early yesterday evening, they decide to rest for a few hours before continuing on. If they want to foil Nathan's plan, they must remain alert. They sleep in shifts since they have no alarm clock, and no way of knowing whose home they may be inhabiting.

Emily takes first watch after refusing Nicholas' advances to spend his sleeping time recreating the events of earlier. He finally falls asleep. As his chest rises and falls to the sound of the rushing river below, the coolness of the stone cave opening calms Emily's desire to run. Nicholas was right. She'd never make it far enough to be successful.

Her eyes sting. It's been eleven years since she last saw her parents. She double checks Nicholas is asleep and turns her back to him. A stream of tears pulls memories forward from the back of her mind. The faces in her memories have deteriorated over time to featureless grey blobs. The sound of their voices lost to history. Her only connection the faded newspaper hidden away in her closet.

It took her years with the Townsends to realize it would be easier to push the events of her previous life to the outskirts of her memory. Now, she has a hard time figuring out where her old life ended and her new life began.

Nathan has become Father and Father is a synonym for boss.

There are days when Emily feels like Nathan is her real father, of sorts. The times when they're seated on the veranda, just the two of them discussing whatever topics come to mind. Or when he's working out different solutions to work problems, while she does her homework in his office, and appreciates her questions, which shed light on new perspectives and solutions.

As though Nathan thinks it will erase the life he stole, he confides in Emily about his concerns with Brigitta's drinking and wandering eye. Bonding them through their own hurt. Signs of the original Victoria are erased from his eyes when Emily is with him.

A snort catches in Nicholas' throat and he wakes himself up a few minutes before they are due to switch places. He shakes away the last trails of sleep, sits beside her, and tries to warm himself up by rubbing his crossed arms. "It's nice up here. We might have to come back."

"Ya. I'm not sure we can get this far away from the compound, though."

"I'm sure we can find a way." He bumps his shoulder into hers. "You should try to get some sleep."

"Right." She crawls into the sleeping bag, grateful Nicholas' warmth remains trapped inside. She doesn't know if it's because she is uneasy about what happened between them, or if she's nervous about the arduous task ahead, but she can feel every pebble under her. Rolling away from Nicholas, she stares at the shadowed cave walls and wonders what animals, or humans, may have found their place inside this refuge.

Grateful she and Nicholas had found it; she tells herself it's only a few more hours until she wins the means to secure her freedom.

CHAPTER THIRTY

Now

To Victoria it feels like the gasps from everyone in the room have sucked out all the air. Her heart throbs in her ears. She can't believe Nathan went through with it. Despite years of him alluding to it, she never suspected it would actually happen. She'd thought his comments were a twisted way of making her feel important so that he wouldn't lose a second daughter.

All eyes dart between Victoria, Nicholas and Mr. Malarkey.

Brigitta screams from the end of the table. "Tell me he didn't just say what I think he said."

Nicholas' stoic face reveals little, but his tense neck shows his fury. Without looking at Victoria, he rises from Nathan's seat, buttons his suit jacket and exits the room.

Victoria's crutches thunk against the floor as she tries to keep up, desperate to make whatever this situation is, right.

Before she gets to the end of the table, Brigitta steps in front of her. "You conniving little snake!" She slaps Victoria so hard across the face that Aidan has to step in to keep her upright. He ushers Victoria out of the room before her crutches are turned into swords.

They find Nicholas in Nathan's office. The neat towers of paperwork she'd built are demolished. Not a square inch of floor is left uncovered.

"Wait outside." Victoria instructs Aidan, who backs out of the door.

"No," Nicholas turns from the window. "He stays."

Aidan freezes, unsure of what to do.

"Why is he necessary?" Victoria asks.

"Because I'm afraid my anger may get the better of me and he may need to protect you."

"You're joking, right?"

Nicholas' glare mirrors the hatred Brigitta reserves for Victoria. She's never seen the two look so alike. It scares her. They have always trusted each other, and yet since she's been home, Nicholas is a different person. He's keeping secrets and overreacting to legitimate questions and situations beyond her control. It's soul-wrenching to watch.

"Do you honestly think I knew what Father was going to do? Why in the world would I want to come back to run...this."

"You've always had an angle. With Father, with me, all in the name of getting what you want."

Victoria stops her jaw from dropping. "That's not fair. I never had an angle with you. Now, can he please leave so we can have a proper conversation?"

"Technically, you're the boss." Nicholas strangles a flowered throw pillow and tosses it aside. "But no, he stays."

She rubs the bridge of her nose. If she's going to repair whatever divide Nathan has created between her and Nicholas, a man she doesn't trust is going to have to be privy to information she'd rather he not hear. Waiting until she and Nicholas are alone may be too late. She turns to Aidan. "Anything you hear in this room is never to be shared. Never. I will cut your tongue out if we discover any information being leaked. And that would be just the beginning of what I do to you. I don't care if someone ends up listening outside the door and spreads the information. I'll blame you. You got that?"

Aidan nods, sticks his head into the hallway to ensure there are no stragglers from the meeting, closes the door, and stands guard.

Victoria approaches Nicholas, but he holds out his arm. "It's best if you stay over there."

"Seriously?" He keeps his arm raised until she retreats. "You know, all I've ever wanted was to get out of here. Hell, live a different life if I could. I don't know why he did what he did, but I'll do whatever I have to in order to turn the business over to you. It's yours. Not mine."

"I don't know if I believe you. You were always Father's favourite, and I tried to ignore it. Rationalize that you deserved the extra attention given what you've been through. But this, this proves Mother was right all along and you toyed with my affection to distract me from your actual plan to get close to him."

Victoria can't believe what's she's hearing. "You ended the relationship, remember? And I left, which was as far away from him as I could get. That's the opposite of trying to get close to him."

"The damage to my future was done by the time you left. You had years to plant your seeds and turn him against me."

"If you think that's true, you don't know me at all."

"Maybe I don't."

On opposite sides of the room, they stand in silence, both trying to withhold their hurt from pouring out of their eyes and fists. Victoria turns to Aidan for his response to what's been said. His face is unresponsive and he stares straight ahead, out the window. She makes a mental note that he can put on a mask of indifference when it suits him.

Victoria breaks the silence. "I hope this reaction is the crushing disappointment of a dream being put on hold, and anger at Father for doing so. I understand you're upset. I would be too if I were you, but I promise you I had nothing to do with this, and I will do what I can to fix it."

"It's too late. Mother's anger will cause her to disclose everything to Paul. He won't remain silent for long. Once our partners, and especially our competitors, learn of it, no one will trust me. They'll presume Father believed I couldn't manage the business successfully, and we'll be finished."

"Well, then we have to make sure Brigitta and the rest of them don't talk. We can figure all of this out together."

Brigitta's voice hollers down the hallway. "Where's that little hussy? I'll claw her eyes out myself."

Aidan's body barricades the door until Nicholas nods for him to move. Brigitta comes barrelling in, but her drunken steps are no match for the obstacles littered around the office. She trips on some books and tumbles into a mahogany table behind the couch. Her half full martini glass shatters on the ground.

With Nicholas stepping between the women, Aidan remains at the door to prevent any other uninvited guests.

"Mother, this isn't her fault."

"Lies. She had your father eating out of her palm. How do you think she stayed alive so long? Or that cushy little protection job he, or should I say, she, came up with?" Her finger waves in Victoria's direction. "Don't think I don't know how you manipulated him to let you leave. I see right through your tricks."

Victoria ignores her taunts. If Brigitta knows, does that mean Nathan knew? Was he just playing along in the hopes she'd change her mind about wanting out? She'll never know now.

"Victoria doesn't want it, Mother. We'll get Mr. Malarkey to draw up all the paperwork we need to transfer everything to me. We'll finalize everything else named in the will, and then burn it. Nobody has to know what was said today."

"Oh, but I'll know. For twenty-one years this little shit-"

"Mother, ENOUGH." He takes a deep breath. "Aidan, take her to bed. And make sure she doesn't have her phone."

Victoria closes the door behind them, leans against it and watches Nicholas flip through pages of an old faded red-covered book as a form of distraction. Her gut twinges with distrust at the man across the room. She's tries to push it aside, but it grips her. Has Nicholas come under Brigitta's thumb? Or even Paul's control? Has his desire to prove he is just as good, if not better than Nathan, buried the man she fell in love with?

She can't bear the thought that her closest ally may have become her foe.

All she wants is to be as far away from the Townsend compound as possible. With him. Yet, she's not naïve enough to think they could sell the business to a partner and stay alive. Whoever took over would want to ensure they couldn't try to reclaim their place.

The police would likely refuse to give them full immunity and new identities. They're at the top of the food chain, the ones they are going after.

During the years of playing scenarios over in her mind, the only solution Victoria's ever come up with where she and Nicholas survive, is if they fake their deaths. But all Nicholas has ever wanted is to run The Family. He's so close. She'd be an idiot to pitch a plan to escape now. He needs to cool off, have a level head about everything, and then maybe he'd consider it.

Victoria focuses on the ticking of the Napoleon clock on a nearby shelf to center herself. If she is to leave, she needs to rectify their immediate problem. If they don't fix these unforeseen circumstances, Nicholas' reputation will be in tatters. The power of The Family needs to be in his hands.

Alone, she lowers her defenses and speaks with a kindness she would not show in front of others. "We can fix this."

"I sure as hell hope so, otherwise I'm ruined." Nicholas returns the unread book to the shelf.

Victoria steps toward him, stopping under the intensity of his glare. "First thing we need to do is make sure Brigitta doesn't tell Paul. Hopefully, once she sobers up, she'll realize the importance of keeping everything a secret."

"Yes, we do, as she almost blew the doors off your past."

"Ya, we don't need that right now, although I doubt it could do much legal damage. I'm sure Father's death prevents any actual legal retribution for what happened to me. The fact I was in Europe and England and never took the chance to run would only help Brigitta's case. Besides, you'd get dragged into all of that, and you know I don't want that to happen. It's been so long I doubt The Family would care. I'm sure some of them aren't who they say they are. Look at Janet. Right now, Brigitta is our biggest obstacle. If she spills anything about what happened tonight, Paul will feed her some story about him being better as the head of The Family than me, and I'm sure he'd convince her he'll hand the reins to you once I was out of the way. We both know that would never happen."

"Thankfully, Mother listens to me. Most of the time. I'll take Aidan off you and have him watch Paul."

Victoria nodded. She was hoping Nicholas would bring Aidan up. She knew if she did, he'd take it as her pestering him. This way, she didn't start the conversation. Even if the one he started was on a slightly different topic. "Why do you trust him? And don't say because he saved Father's life. Rumour has it, him being at Moonshine Cafe wasn't a coincidence."

"And do you trust the source of these rumours? Or have any proof to back up your claims?" His words are sharp as his anger flares.

"Do I trust anyone? I'll admit, the information came out a little too easy. And it implicated Janet as well. I have a feeling Finn's trying to make a play for position. It doesn't mean there wasn't an ounce of truth in what he told me. Even if I don't have proof. Yet." Victoria keeps her voice soft. She will not get the information she needs to determine who's on her side if she matches his tone.

"Well, you trust me, and I've done my checks and rechecks on Aidan. He's clean. I know you've read his file, so can we please drop this? I promise if you bring me something that proves he is against us, I'll believe you. But you and I both know hunches aren't enough evidence."

"Ignoring a hunch can get us put in jail, or worse, killed."

"And overreacting can sow seeds of distrust throughout the entire organization."

"Fine. I'll drop it for now." The hairs on Victoria's neck stand at attention. Something doesn't feel right. Whether it be Aidan, Finn, or even Nicholas, someone is lying.

Chapter Thirty-One

Then: October 2014

With the map's path to the Townsend compound memorized, Nicholas and Emily keep the knife and the binoculars, and ditch the backpack against a tree close enough to the perimeter of the property to fool people into thinking they were lying in wait. Meanwhile, they divert from the predetermined path towards the west side of the property.

They scuttle along the ground, almost on their stomachs, hiding behind the wide old tree trunks as they watch for their competition and guards. Moss and rotting twigs litter their surroundings. A few hundred feet away, the foot patrol makes their rounds. One man every ten to twenty feet. More than a normal day, but today isn't normal.

They finish the last of their water and regroup.

Nicholas assesses the situation. "The motion sensors will catch us before we make it to the fence. The panel to shut off the electric fence is inside the property. With the guards so close together, I don't think we can subdue two for their clothes, like we were hoping. Thoughts?"

"What's the likelihood we are strong enough to create a bridge with a tree trunk and walk over the fence without being noticed?" Emily jokes.

"It's nice to know you haven't lost your sense of humour on our little adventure. I'm losing the feeling in my toes after crossing the river, so, let's come up with a plan sooner rather than later. Otherwise, I'm just going to surrender."

"I hope you won't give up this easily if our enemies ever get their hands on you."

"This is just Father on a power trip. I'm not divulging family secrets by walking out of the forest, arms raised so that I can be warm, with Devin's pan-seared haddock in my stomach."

Emily glares at him and returns to surveying the patrol situation. "We can still use our clothes as a distraction." The late-night training call alerted their suspicions, and both had kept their black workout gear on underneath. "Now, leave your jacket here. They rustle too much. Follow me."

"Are you going to tell me what the change in our plan is?"

"No."

"Why not?"

"Because you'll think it's ridiculous and ruin it. Stop talking until we are on the other side of that fence."

Nicholas bites his bottom lip. "FYI, I'm only going to listen because you have that look of determination and excitement that tells me whatever craziness you've figured out just might work."

Slow and steady, they make their way to the southwest corner of the property. Shouts of "don't move," come from the north. Someone is caught. The disruption doesn't distract the foot patrol on the west side.

Storm clouds and the moon brush aside any last trails of daylight. Pulling down their night vision goggles; the guards prepare for action. The wisps of wind push leaves into the laser field and momentarily reveal its location. The alarm is set for a denser mass and doesn't go off.

Emily motions for Nicholas to remove his sweater, but he doesn't understand. The silence of the night allows any spoken word to travel kilometers. Her frustration takes over. She removes her own shirt and, with its arms splayed open, leans it against the trunk of a tree, as though someone is sitting there.

Hunched over, they quickly make their way around the south face of the property, staying in view of the sweater. A green military truck careens down the road towards the compound. Nicholas hangs and shakes his head with a smile. He's figured out the plan and wishes he'd thought of it.

They remove their pants and his sweater. They rub dirt on any exposed skin and hope the cameras don't pick them up. They only have one shot to make this work.

Three small red dots appear in the center of their decoy. Calls of "stop" and radio chatter fill the air. The men in the southwest corner leave their post.

The truck pulls up to the gate and Nicholas and Emily bolt behind it. The man in the gatehouse speaks with the driver and confirms the delivery over the radio.

Two people appear on the sidelines, yet to be seen.

Nicholas' hands become Emily's step-stool as she pushes herself past the canvas backing on the truck. She helps Nicholas climb in, his foot taking cover as men encircle the two figures only a few metres away from entering the property. Emily and Nicholas scramble to the back of the truck and crouch down behind two towers of crates.

Distracted by the commotion of competitors being captured, a flashlight travels overhead with a lackadaisical inspection of the back of the truck, then disappears. The gate chugs along its track and the truck jerks forward. After parking by the barracks, they'll have seconds to exit before anyone notices them. Neither of them are stupid enough to think they would achieve victory by simply making it onto the property.

They had to make it to Nathan.

When they pass by the bushes on the east side of the house, they jump out. They make themselves as small as possible and slink along the grass until they reach an old basement window. A few years ago, Nicholas had figured out a way to dismantle the alarm on just this window so he could sneak out of the house and play poker with the men in the barracks. Given Father knows everything that happens on the compound, Nicholas figures he knows about his Friday night escapades, but he's confident he doesn't know his means of escape as the alarm had not been fixed as of a couple of days ago.

He shimmies the knife between the frame and in unison, they hold their breath. Nicholas pushes the knife and the window pops open. No noticeable alarms go off, but they cannot guarantee a silent one isn't alerting someone. Victoria has him scout the situation, and he pulls himself inside the house, his shoulders almost too wide to fit through. He'll have to find a new way out of the house soon. Feet first, she joins him. Nicholas helps her down and they pause for a moment in each other's arms before moving on.

They scamper through what has become the storage room for all things unwanted. Rummaging through the shelves of a closet, they find some old clothes, and sneak into an old laundry room to clean up in the cast-iron sink. The guards are on the lookout for people in sweat-suits, and likely anything else out of the ordinary. Two individuals in regular clothes would require a double take. By then, they'd be gone.

Nicholas adjusts the tap of the sink to an excruciatingly slow drizzle to avoid keen ears of the inevitable patrol inside of the house. It takes a while to clean off the dirt, but they do their best and put on their new clothes.

Mostly, the house is silent. A few footsteps here and there, but security didn't appear to be as cumbersome as outside. They pass the bowling alley, games room, and private hospital room, before Emily manoeuvres up the basement stairs, their bodies pressed as close to the wall as possible.

She spies Louis stopping in the front entry and peering out the front door. Satisfied, he turns towards the kitchen. When his footsteps dissipate to nothing, Nicholas and Emily bolt down the hallway. Their socked feet don't make a sound.

Nicholas almost topples Emily over when she stops dead in her tracks a few feet from the dining room. The windows across the hall would reveal their position before they got there. On their stomachs, they slither across the floor. The mirrored reflection shows someone seated in Nathan's chair holding up a newspaper, their face covered.

Emily unbuckles the knife, and its sheath, from the belt. She doesn't want to stab the person in the chair, rather get their attention. She stands and throws it at the newspaper.

"Ah, what the...?" Devin lowers the newspaper, perplexed.

The kitchen door swings open and Nathan steps into the room. He reaches for the knife in its sheath on the floor and they make their move.

"Hello Father." Nicholas and Emily say in unison, their hands mimic guns.

Nathan rises to standing, knife in hand, and a sly grin escapes the corner of this mouth. "Looks like improvements to my security are needed." He taps on his phone.

Immediately, Louis slides in behind the children.

Emily lowers her arms, as does Nicholas. Given Louis' face resembles a stone statue, she is unsure if he is shocked by their success. She is certain that Nathan will be furious with the soldiers and someone will be punished. She hopes it's not Louis.

Nathan walks around the table towards the winners. "I suppose congratulations are in order." He firmly shakes their hands. "Now, sit and tell me how you did it."

Devin returns to the kitchen and clunks and clangs filter under the door.

Emily sits quietly as Nicholas retells their adventure, including their skillful detection of the tracking device, their decoys and ability to use other people's failures to their advantage. "And it was all Nicholas' idea.," she adds knowing that Nicholas rarely receives praise from his father. "Well, I remembered that today was delivery day, but he figured out how it could help us."

"Interesting. Louis, sound the alarm to notify everyone who isn't back that the game is over. Gather the team leads in the boardroom."

Louis turns to leave.

"Oh, and figure out how no one noticed the alarm on the basement window was disabled, and for how long." Nathan's eyes land on Nicholas, who lowers his chin to his chest. "As you both proved tonight, the house had a major vulnerability that could be exploited. That is unacceptable."

Emily feels the urge to take the blame, but Nicholas' demeanour gives away the truth. She'd only be getting herself into trouble.

"We'll deal with your punishment later. For now, stay here and eat while I debrief with the crew."

"We get the money, right?" Emily's shocked at her own courage to inquire.

"Yes, you'll get the money. But, I'll control how you use it." Nathan doesn't allow space for debate before he departs.

Both are famished and take only moments to enjoy the succulent garlic halibut, maple carrots and rice pilaf. With a wink and a promise not to tell Nathan, Devin removes their dirty dishes for them.

"I can't believe we actually did it." Emily yawns, torn between exhaustion and excitement.

"Me either." Says Nicholas.

Exhaustion wins. "I'm going to go to bed."

"Can we talk before you do? Maybe in your room? With Mom visiting family in Sweden, I'm not sure anyone will notice since Father will have them working to ensure no one else can sneak in here."

"As long as talking is all you want to do, as for one, I am about to pass out, and two, the other thing will never happen in this house."

"Get your mind out of the gutter girl." He chuckles. "Just talking, I swear." He crosses his heart.

Seated side by side in Emily's window seat, she wraps herself in a blanket, and notices a squirrel spotlighted in the yard by the moon. They watch as it tries to get through the shell of a chestnut.

She relates to the animal bashing, gnawing and clawing to get at what it wants. The money was supposed to help release her from her prison. Now, with Nathan controlling the funds, she won't be able to bribe anyone to let her leave the compound. Or have someone tuck her into a trunk when they go into the city.

She's stuck. Still.

Emily's lost in thought and Nicholas jabs an elbow into her side to get her attention. "You okay?"

"What? Oh, ya."

"Why'd you tell Father the plan was my idea?"

"You deserved the credit. I'm sorry he didn't even acknowledge it. One day, he'll realize how skillful you are."

"Am I? You're the one who came up with the entire plan. You wouldn't even tell me digging under the fence was out and truck jumping was in for fear I'd ruin it."

"True. But that was only because I selfishly wanted the money. We were so tired I didn't want you to think we couldn't do it and talk me out of it."

"Fine. Promise me next time we have to come up with a covert plan, you'll tell me everything."

"Promise."

They cuddle close until she asks, "how come you never call me Emily anymore?"

Nicholas rests his elbows on his knees, chin in his hands, and looks out at the forest. "Because you're not her. You haven't been for years. Today's the first time I've seen any sign of the tears she used to shed." He takes her hand. "When you stopped talking about your past, I thought it was best to stop reminding you of it."

"You thought it was best, or he thought it was best?"

"Both."

"Naturally. Isn't it weird, especially now, to refer to me as Victoria?"

"I know you're not my sister and you never will be. There are thousands of Victoria's in the world and you are another one. No weirdness attached to it." He wraps an arm around her. "Well, maybe a little, but I can get over it if you can."

"I'm sure I can manage." She kisses his cheek, leans her head on his shoulder, and leaves him to watch the dark clouds rumble across the sky from the west as her eyes flutter. A chill runs up her back as she says her own goodbye to Emily.

Chapter Thirty-Two

Now

Victoria's body is electric with a pent-up energy that could get her into trouble if she's not careful.

Someone is pulling the strings of her life in directions she doesn't want. The lack of control is frustrating and she must find answers. Before she's completely lost Nicholas' trust and he turns against her, if he hasn't already. Or worse. Kills her.

She avoids the verbal assault Brigitta is launching against those around her. The attack reverberates throughout the main floor of the house. Victoria cannot see the victims but suspects Mr. Malarkey is at the center.

She arrives in the kitchen unscathed and finds Devin sitting in the table nook reading the newspaper. He's lost some muscle mass since she went overseas, and his hair has more salt than pepper but his soft facial features remain. She's not surprised at the relic news source in his hands, unless using a contraband phone, internet access was restricted on the Compound. What she is surprised about is how calm he is.

He folds the paper in front of himself. "Hello, Miss Victoria. Would you like something to eat?"

"What I'd like to do is have a conversation. Please come with me." She holds out her arm to direct him through the kitchen door to the yard.

He does so without complaint and stands beside an antique white cast iron patio set awaiting further instruction.

She pulls a chair away from the table. "Sit. Now, tell me why you are so calm when the world around you is falling apart?"

"My role has always been the chef and only the chef. I don't get involved in your family matters. No point in letting them stress me out." His hands rest on his legs, not a twitch in sight.

"How Zen of you. Yet, your reaction to what is happening in there is suspicious."

"I don't even know what's happening. I assume Brigitta has blown some trivial thing out of proportion. Like I said, I stay in my lane, but if you think I can help you with anything, I can try."

"Oh, you will do more than try. You are going to need to convince me you are not leaking information out of this house, otherwise those magical hands of yours will be removed."

Devin's eyes widen.

She realizes using threats might work, but may not be the best tactic in this situation. If it turns out he's not the rat, she may lose an ally. "I'm sorry. I'm a little on edge."

She pulls a chair out and sits opposite him, maintaining a clear line of sight on him, and the house. Her voice softens and she continues. "Over the years, you have been gracious to me and been one of the few bright parts of my life. I need you to continue with that grace and tell me what you know about the events leading up to Father's death."

"Oh, I'm not sure I know much. For five, maybe six, months, he started acting weird. Nothing too noticeable at first. A small unnecessary jerk of a hand or finger. He drank more water than usual, but I figured he'd finally realized hydrating himself with more than whiskey and coffee was required for a lengthy life. Then he began forgetting things. Where he put his glasses or phone. Instructions he had given me, or those that were not delivered. He got hostile about it and I informed Nicholas and Mrs. Townsend of what I saw. I felt it wasn't my place to pry and left it with them."

"When did you speak to them about this?"

"Oh, about two, maybe three, months ago, I think."

Her mind won't block the thoughts of son turning against father. Or wife against husband. What if one of them had a long game plan but when the evidence became noticeable, took steps to bring about the intended results at a faster pace? They'd still have to bide some time to avoid detection by the medical examiner, but it would be doable. If Paul had gotten into Brigitta's ear, who knows how much damage she's caused.

Or has Devin cooked up the perfect ruse? Set them up to take the fall. But, to what end and on whose instruction?

She wants to throttle the answers she seeks out of the man before her. Instead, her fingers tap the arm of her chair and she calms her rapid heartbeat. "Food would be the perfect weapon of attack if someone on the inside was after Father. You are the only one he ever trusted with his food. Was his trust unfounded?"

"Never. He painfully questioned me about how I was preparing his meals. He thought I was poisoning him. Messing with his head. I had to cook with one hand while my broken wrist healed and I never want to see the inside of that barn again. He had that Finn kid test his food before he would eat it. I can't tell you if that's how I proved my innocence, but in the end, Mr. Townsend believed me. I hope you do, too."

She wants to, but has to follow every angle. "You could be a Michelin star chef with an award-winning restaurant, and yet," she lowers her voice, "you've been here longer than I have. Why?"

"I have no ambitions of stars or awards. Never have. You know Louis and I grew up with Mr. Townsend. Mr. McKinnon's tutelage has many schools of knowledge. Not everyone conducts illegal business. Some of us go into the service of those who do. I had an aptitude for food science and here I am, content with my insignificant life."

His eyes are an open book with no shadows hiding in the corners. Ruled by her gut, it's telling her to believe him. "That's what bothers me. If you were the only one with access to his food, how could he have deteriorated? He wasn't on any medication."

Devin runs his fingers along his goatee.

"What is it?"

"I don't want to step out of line, and I doubt what I'm about to say is something you wouldn't be able to find out anyway, but Brigitta kept his whiskey glass full."

"You think Brigitta's behind this?"

"I'm saying she had the opportunity."

She rests her elbows on her knees and her head in her hands. "You may go," she says without looking up.

The Queen of this castle may have taken down her King. What else will she do to get what she wants now that Victoria's protector is gone?

CHAPTER THIRTY-THREE

NOW

THE OCCASIONAL BURST OF anger breaks through the glass windows of the house. Brigitta's rampage is far from over. Victoria is surprised that the woman hasn't found her yet. Louis and Nicholas have been able to keep her somewhat tamed in whatever pen they've put her in.

A second run through of her conversation with Devin in her head, and a replay of her last conversation with Nathan fuels her forward. She won't approach Brigitta directly, with accusations. All she would get would be denials, and Nicholas wouldn't stand for it. He'd think it was another useless spat and it would show her hand before she was prepared to defend it.

Her cell phone out of her pocket, she places a call to a woman who specializes in blood analysis. With Nathan's body blown to pieces, he can't be exhumed if needed. Unsure what faith she has in Nicholas and Brigitta's man, she will feel more confident if her own person provides her with the results.

"Hi. I need some work done." Familiar with each other's voices, there is no need for introductions. "It'll be tricky given the body doesn't exist, but I know where you might find the sample. If I send you some addresses, can you coordinate an extraction of enough of the specimen for analysis?"

"No promises, but I'll do what I can." The husky voice of a chain smoker replies.

"Great."

"What are we looking for exactly?"

"Anything that shouldn't be there. More specifically, anything that could cause a person to lose their memory and/or kill them."

"Noted."

"How long do you think that will take?"

"I'll know better once I know where the sample is and get a team in place to retrieve it. Day or two tops."

"Sooner, if you can, please."

"Of course."

"The agreed upon fee will be sent to the usual account within the hour. If I have the results sooner, I'll send you a bonus."

She ends the call and makes another to have the payment made. Despite Nathan keeping a close eye on any accounts tied to the Townsends, Victoria has kept a nest egg off to the side for emergencies. A few contracts kept off The Family books, and cash withdrawals disguised as necessary spending money, means she could support herself and live a comfortable life without worrying about expenses. The funds were meant for her escape, but she won't be able to leave if she isn't alive, or doesn't get Nicholas in place as Director of The Family.

She follows the trail of screams towards the parlour. Two people dressed in black are posted outside the large arched wooden door. She wonders if they are there to keep people out or the occupants in. She can hear Nicholas trying to calm Brigitta down. Telling her he will fix the situation.

Everything goes silent.

Victoria steps in front of the doorway with an outstretched hand. One guard steps before her. Their eyes plead with her to stay where she is.

Before she can confront the person, the door opens and Louis steps out, Brigitta's body draped over his arms.

"What happened?" Victoria asks.

"A mild sedative."

"Mild? She was screaming one minute and now she's a rag-doll."

"She'll be fine."

"I don't doubt that."

Louis steps around her and heads towards a back stairwell. Victoria peers into the parlour, a room she's been ordered to stay out of for twenty-one years. The soft yellow hue of the walls and calming cream furniture are the opposite of the room's preferred occupant.

Nicholas cleans up some glassware. A syringe is wedged between his finger and a glass. He stops when he sees her. Without a word, he continues his task, and a guard closes the door.

Victoria isn't hurt that he's ignoring her. It wasn't him or Brigitta she wanted to speak with. She's after Louis.

She turns on her heals to catch up to the man and his unconscious companion. From the hallway, she watches as Louis places Brigitta on the bed with care. He removes her shoes and clip on earrings. She's amazed when he glides cotton pads effortlessly over the sleeping beauty's face to remove her make-up. How many times has he had to perform that task?

With the room and Brigitta in order, Louis closes the door and turns to Victoria. "I suppose you have some questions for me?"

She is not surprised by his usual bluntness. He may not speak much, but when he does, he gets to the point. "Shall we?"

They descend the front stairwell and convene in the classroom. The two student desks have been replaced by two columns of six rows of benches. Rather than mould the minds of children, the room is now used to debrief the soldiers on larger scale operational tactics. Unmarked maps of the Maritimes, Quebec, the northeastern United States, and a few European locations, cover some of the white boards and walls. The only secrets the maps reveal would be general locations of their business endeavours. Nothing law enforcement isn't already aware of.

The stress and shock of the day forms a headache around Victoria's eyes. She ignores the throbbing and leans against a bookcase.

Outside of a few wrinkles at the side of his eyes, Louis looked like he'd barely aged since Victoria was brought to the compound with his dark hair and beard without a sparkle of silver. He sits on a bench, his broad shoulders hunched forward. She knows it's been a long day for him as well.

"Did you know about Nathan's plan to name me as the successor instead of Nicholas?"

"Yes."

A response she wasn't expecting. "What? Really? I..." She takes two deep breaths and starts again. "When did you learn about this?"

"Nathan hinted at it once you proved your prowess in weaponry, combat, and analytical thinking. I assure you I cautioned him against it, but you know how he got stuck in his ways."

"When did he get stuck in this way?"

"I'm not sure. I know he visited Mr. Malarkey a few times in the last six months regarding business matters, but I've been assigned to Brigitta in order to monitor Paul. I'd lost touch with the inner workings of Nathan's mind."

Victoria hadn't yet seen a copy of Nathan's Last Will and Testament to know when it was dated. If it was before Nathan deteriorated, Nicholas might think she's been working to gain power behind his back. If it's after, she might be able to have the document voided because of Nathan not being of sound mind when it was signed. A glimmer of hope emerges from the darkness. Provided, her name wasn't also stated as the successor in the previous version.

"Do you think Nathan made the change recently, or has he always decreed it be me?"

"The last one I signed as a witness for was seven years ago. At that point, it was Nicholas."

"Why didn't you witness the one that was read out today?"

"You know how secretive Nathan can be. He must have found someone he trusted more."

Victoria's ears perk up and she walks towards him. "Why did he lose trust in you?"

"In the end, I don't think he trusted anyone. I know you two didn't always get a long, considering...well, all I'll say is it was painful to watch him fall apart."

"Would that pain, and your friendship with him, push you to do something about it?"

"It might have if it got to where he risked exposing his illness to beyond those closest to him. He still held his own, mostly, in inner circle meetings. As far as I know, there were no concerns with The Family. At least nothing Nicholas let on about."

"Did you usually get reports on Family meetings from Nicholas?"

Louis pinches the bridge of his nose. "I know where you are going with this. Nicholas and I aren't particularly close, but I look out for him the same as I do with you, Nathan, and Brigitta. Occasionally, he confides in me. I will say that the closer he has gotten to Tessa, the less he has relied on me."

"We will come back to her another time. Unless you think she's involved in all of this?"

"I feel she's a chameleon who can turn into whoever the person opposite wants her to be. Could she be a cold-blooded killer? Possibly. Then again, can't we all if the circumstances are right?"

"If someone killed Nathan, and I'm not saying they did, would you retaliate?"

"Depends on who it was. If it was someone on the outside, definitely."

"And on the inside?"

"I wouldn't make any rash decisions but would let Irving decide what steps need to be taken."

"I see. I have to ask; did you kill Nathan?"

"No."

They hold each other's gaze until their eyes become dry. Each not wanting to be the first to blink. Victoria breaks first. She has more investigation to do before she scratches Louis off her list. For now, he doesn't appear to be an immediate threat to herself or Nicholas.

"You can go, but if you see Nicholas, tell him to come to my room. Emphasize it is very important that I talk to him."

"Will do." Louis stretches his arms behind his back and departs.

The room around Victoria spins. Seated on the bench, she puts her head between her knees. There are too many moving parts. How can she be certain the people she's talked to today aren't a rat or a killer? Add in Tessa, a person she knows nothing about, to the mix and there are more variables to consider.

Her breathing becomes heavy, and she closes her eyes until her head stops swirling. She tells herself to focus on one problem at a time.

First, revoking Nathan's Will. Once Nicholas sees the succession problem can be fixed, they can work together to find the rat.

She heads upstairs and stops in front of Nicholas' bedroom door. He's talking to someone, but the lack of response tells her he's on the phone. She decides against angering him further by barging in. She texts him to come next door when he's done.

In the meantime, two painkillers ease her headache. With heavy eyelids, she fights off sleep for as long as she can. A blanket of relaxing muscles and exhaustion tries to pull her into the depths of dreamland. After an hour of nodding off, she gives in.

CHAPTER THIRTY-FOUR

NOW

A BANG ON VICTORIA'S bedroom door jolts her from sleep. Without waiting for an invitation, the door flies open before she can grab her gun from her bedside table.

"We have a problem." Nicholas is wearing yesterday's clothes, minus the suit jacket. His usually pressed grey suit is creased with wrinkles. His shirt collar and two top buttons are undone, his hair is dishevelled and the rolled-up sleeves reveal a compass tattoo on his left arm.

"And I have a solution." She rubs the sleep crust from her eyes and pushes herself to seated against her firm pillows. "If Nathan wasn't mentally sound at the time he signed the Will, then we can have it revoked. Put everything back the way it's supposed to be."

"It might be too late for that."

"Why?"

Nicholas tosses a piece of paper at her. Given its minuscule mass, it lands on the floor between her bed and him. Distracted by his thoughts, he doesn't notice.

Adrenaline from being startled awake doesn't hide the pain pulsing through Victoria's wound as she bends to pick up the paper. The letter is brief and contorts her face to mirror Nicholas'.

My Dear Friend,

If you are reading this, I'm dead and a successor for my place in The Family has been named. Victoria Townsend.

Posthumously, I would appreciate your support for my decision. I believe Victoria is the best way forward for us, and, as you know, I'm rarely, if ever, wrong.

Kind regards,

Nathan

P.S. As usual, please burn this letter.

"Where did this come from?" Victoria asks.

"I received a call this morning from Ms. Yang asking to confirm its authenticity. When I didn't know what she was talking about, I had her send me a copy. I immediately spoke with Mr. Malarkey, who informed me that Father's directions were to send one of these letters to each leader in The Family."

"And he didn't think to tell us any of this last night?"

"Apparently, Mr. Malarkey left the list of whom to send them to, and a sample letter, in the envelope with Father's Last Will and Testament. After our abrupt departure from the dining room, he didn't think he should disturb us. I checked the envelope, and it's not there."

"Does Mr. Malarkey have any reason to lie to us?"

"Not if he wants to live."

"Father was right, we have a rat." Victoria rests on the bench at the foot of her bed and watches Nicholas pace around the room. Making Nicholas the Director wouldn't be as easy as she'd thought.

Distressed, crows' feet extend from Nicholas' eyes and get deeper by the minute. Nothing in his life has been easy and now mountains stand before him and his inheriting The Family. He keeps it to himself that a provision of Father's Will was that Victoria was to remain in control of The Family, if they voted to confirm Nathan's request, for a period of no less than five years. After which, if she steps down, she may appoint the next successor. He didn't want her to feel more trapped than she already did.

Nicholas desperately wants to punch something. Someone. He always tried to deny Nathan's preference for Victoria, making excuses she deserved the extra attention given her past. It wasn't until she left, Nicholas saw just how much of Nathan's heart was held in her hands.

It only took three months for the paranoia and neurotic behaviour to start. Nathan was constantly worrying if Victoria was safe. His concern for her then turned to The Family itself. Not Nicholas, or Brigitta even. But the larger family. The organization. His third child.

With all the computers, except those in the safe rooms, removed from the house, the papers piling up in Nathan's office, and his dishevelled appearance, Nicholas had to admit Nathan wasn't the formidable leader he used to be. He never thought his father's madness would take his dream away. He never thought he'd give it to someone who so desperately wanted out. Now, here was one more piece of evidence that he could not surpass Victoria in Nathan's eyes.

He watches Victoria's fingers tapping the bench as she thinks, and un-clenches his fist. Hitting her would only bring him temporary relief, fol-lowed by immediate guilt. She didn't choose this. It's another manipulation game Nathan's playing. He may have seemed to lose a lot of his faculties, but he never lost focus on bringing Victoria home to stay. Even if he wouldn't be the one to see it.

"Have you watched the security footage?" Victoria asks.

"With Father's insistence of not having surveillance recordings of the conversations in the boardroom for our own protection, we have little. After you went upstairs, I went back to re-read the Will to see if there was more we didn't hear. There wasn't, by the way. Louis had dismissed everyone, so there was a twenty to thirty-minute window where the envelope was accessible to the group, other than Aidan, who was upstairs with Mother."

Victoria didn't like how the evidence was pointing away from Aidan being the rat. Her gut tumbled with doubt of his innocence; or was what she was feeling jealousy?

As much as she wanted out of The Family, it was ingrained. It is who she is, and now Aidan seems more than able to take her place. A person Nathan said was irreplaceable. Integral to the organization. To him. Nicholas de-fending Aidan as wholeheartedly as he has always defended her makes her feel as though her absence wasn't missed as much as she hoped.

Now with Tessa joining the picture, she feels obsolete. It should propel her to leave. Find her freedom. Yet, as she watches the worry form new wrinkles on Nicholas' face, she can't help but let her heart strings suffocate the thoughts of getting out. At least until they can fix the mess Nathan has made.

They pace the room with each going in an opposite direction.

"It's highly unlikely the inner circle are all working together. Too risky and we would have seen signs." Victoria says.

"Exactly, so last night the hallway cameras capture three people entering the room between the time everyone is dismissed and I retrieve the document. Erik, Louis and Brigitta. I've spoken to Brigitta - about everything. Despite her desire to see you burn in hell, I've persuaded her that informing Paul of our issue would not be to her, or my, benefit. She also voluntarily allowed me to go through her cell phone to ensure nothing had slipped out during her drunken debacle last night."

"Then, Erik or Louis? That doesn't feel right. Have either of them set off any red flags lately? Done anything somebody could use to turn them against us?" A sense of grave concern had not arisen from her conversations with either of them. Had she been wrong?

"Not that I know of. But things have been crazy here for a while. I had to manage Father, Mother, and the business. It's possible I missed something."

Nicholas replays key events since Victoria had left in his mind to see if there was something he hadn't seen. Erik spent his time bulking up, as per Nathan's orders, hours spent at the gym built into the workers' quarters. On days off, he didn't head into town like most everyone else, but remained at the compound. Otherwise, he was with Nicholas. There was no way it could be Erik.

Louis traipsing all over with Brigitta caused some alarm. Could Paul have gotten to him? Nicholas doubted after knowing his father for over forty years he would turn that easily. Paul, on the other hand, has only worked for The Family for a decade. Maybe, over time, Louis got caught up in something? Nicholas deflates at the idea that a man he's known his whole life may be treacherous. He can't bring himself to say it out loud and prays it's anyone but him.

Victoria's urge to tell Nicholas about Nathan's visit before his death almost pushes the words out of her mouth; but whispers of distrust halt their escape.

She stops pacing to give her underarms a break from being crushed by the uncomfortable bridge of her crutches. "Let's think this through. What advantage would they, or anyone, get from delaying us finding out about the letters?"

"They could try to prevent me from taking Father's place." Nicholas replies.

"What difference does it make if it's me or you? There is still someone running this place and The Family."

"Perhaps they want to seed some distrust in me. But I don't see how that helps, when Father hasn't even named me as successor."

"Distrust in you could mean distrust in Nathan - given I'm sure everyone knows you've really been running the show for the last while. And distrust in Nathan-"

"Equals distrust in you." Nicholas finishes her thought. "Which could give credence to a need for a change in leadership and cause our partners to vie for being the Director of The Family."

"Someone's trying to make a move." Victoria glances over at him and wonders again if it's Nicholas. Was the explosion at the burial really intended to create an opportunity to kill Paul? Or was it a means for Nicholas to cause some disruption and assert some power by taking out a self-made threat? Was what he was telling her now the truth? She needs to find out just how much she's lost him. "Could it be someone at the burial? Your explosion may have other members of The Family, or our enemies, feeling targeted?"

"Anything's possible. Which is why I tried to keep the timing to when most of the guests had left. Damn it!"

"Damn it, is right. You didn't look past your immediate goal with your actions."

"Stop. I don't need you berating me about my lack of leadership skills. Not now."

"If not now, when? Not only do we have an internal threat, the pool of external suspects has grown. All because you didn't think to have Paul taken out in private."

"Let's find the traitor closest to us, and then maybe we can figure out who they are working for. Our rat removed our copies of the documents. Whoever they are working for may not be a member at the table, as having the information is a powerful card. They could do a lot in eight hours."

"We better find them, and quickly. We'll need to fortify this place in case the move is a big one." Victoria tosses the crutches aside so she can move as freely as possible. She refuses to show weakness. Not today. She pulls her pistol out from the bedside table and checks the rounds. All are accounted for. After getting dressed in black pants and a t-shirt, she secures the gun and her switchblade to her legs. With her black backpack from her trip over her shoulder, she heads for the door.

"What do you have in there?" Nicholas asks.

"Hopefully, the means to catch our rat."

Nicholas places his hand on her shoulder and stops her in the doorway. "You know what Father did changes everything, right?"

She squeezes his hand. "We'll fix this. Everything will be fine." She reassures herself more than him. Nathan's move has shifted her choices. She must take the helm of the ship to protect the man who supported her through the most trying times in her life.

Her dreams, like Nicholas' crushed by the stroke of a pen.

CHAPTER THIRTY-FIVE

NOW

MUTTERINGS FROM THE HALLWAY announce the inner circle's arrival before Victoria sees them enter the boardroom. Whether it's the residual effect of sleep or genuine confusion, each person does a double take when they see a laptop set up at her location and Aidan standing at the entry holding an empty plastic container with a single cell phone in it -his.

"Cell phones in the bin," Nicholas announces.

Victoria scans the crowd for a twitch, flighty hand movements, or facial tics that will tell her they're having a hard time parting with their devices. Nothing.

Cell phones thump into the bin.

For the moment, Brigitta has turned her scowl from Victoria to the crowd. Nicholas will have reassured her that the person she loathes can find the rat, and she'll have to put faith in her son. It's the only way to put the crown on his head, instead of Victoria's.

Aidan places the bin beside Victoria and takes his seat across from her. He eyes her closely as she pulls the first phone from the pile and connects it to the computer. Her fingers rapidly tap on the keyboard, her technical prowess evident to all in the room.

She retrieves text messages, photos, calls and internet search history, even those the user believed had been deleted. Most have followed the rules of not taking photos of themselves or other soldiers. They all have a unique voice and she can pinpoint which phone belongs to which person without having to ask.

Uninformed as to the purpose of the phone search, the group sits militarily-still and stares over the head of the person on the opposite side of the table. A few close their eyes when Brigitta's glare reaches them. Her high-heels click and clack like a clock counting down to death as she circles the room.

Phone by phone, Victoria finds no evidence of the mole. She learns Erik may break you in half with his hands, but the softer side of him enjoys cast and knitting videos. Louis doesn't use his phone for anything but communicating with Nicholas and Brigitta. The only exciting piece of information Victoria gleans from Aidan's device is a deleted conversation with Finn.

> **Finn:** *Hope we didn't keep you awake last night ;)*
> *1:12 a.m.*

> **Finn:** *Look mate, we've all got unique skills. Mine are making women scream with delight.   1:14 a.m.*

> **Aidan:** *Go to sleep. I don't care or need to know about what skills you think you have. Besides, what I heard didn't sound genuine.   1:15 a.m.*

Victoria's stomach retracts as she stifles a laugh and tosses the phone across the table to its owner, just as she had with the others.

The next phone lights up all the metaphorical warning lights on her computer. Deep within the hidden depths of the device are the secrets they've been looking for. Conversations in code. For someone trained in deception, it doesn't take Victoria long to realize they are using a Caesar Cipher. In her mind, each letter is shifted to the right in the alphabet and she can decipher what was said.

The phone spins as it slides to its owner, who catches it before it falls into their lap. Two more to go. As the last phone is given back, the air in the room becomes heavy.

Victoria turns the laptop screen to Nicholas, who couldn't stay still and was pacing behind Nathan's chair. Victoria gives Erik's leg a quick tap under the table to alert him to be vigilant.

Nicholas' jaw tightens as he decodes the text messages, views photos of the compound, gun, drug and cigarette shipment manifests and Nathan's letter to the members of The Family. His eyes widen as Victoria presses play on a video she'd rather not have him see. The sound being turned off saves his ears from further discomfort. He runs his hand down his face, hoping to wipe away his frustration. At no point had he suspected this person would step a toe out of line.

He moves in front of Brigitta as she passes the head of the table. "Mother, may I please have your phone again?"

A stone face conceals her confusion, and she holds out her phone. Nicholas passes it to Victoria. "Why don't you take your seat?" he says.

Victoria revisits Brigitta's text messages.

Nicholas taps the back of Victoria's chair, searching for words. He'd love to scream and solve the problem quickly and violently. Instead, he practices Nathan's calm yet threatening demeanour. How he reacts in this moment will impart to his soldiers what type of leader he'll be.

He leans over the intricately carved back of his chair, hands folded together. "One of you finds yourself in a very precarious situation." He slowly walks around the table, passing Aidan first. "Occasionally, I'm a reasonable man and will allow a perpetrator to plead their case before they die. What I'm having trouble deciding, though, is if I let Victoria get her hands on you. She doesn't take too kindly to people invading her privacy."

On his second lap around the table, Nicholas stops behind Brigitta. He places her phone in front of her and slowly unravels the black scarf she has wrapped around over her head and neck, revealing her beautiful blond hair. He kisses the top of her head.

Like a flash of lightning, he steps to the right and wraps Brigitta's scarf around Finn's neck. He drags the young man out of his chair. Finn grips the fabric, trying to create a pathway for breath as his face turns a darker shade of red. Everyone stands; but only Erik moves to Nicholas, who kicks the back of Finn's legs so that he buckles to his knees.

"Give me one good reason not to kill you right here?" he says.

Finn gurgles, but his words are inaudible. Nicholas lets go of the scarf and Finn falls to his hands, coughing. "I can get you Paul."

"We can take care of that ourselves."

Victoria watches as Brigitta tosses her chair back and rips a high-heel shoe off her foot. Louis holds her as she struggles to escape his muscular arms, her shoe positioned as a weapon. Screams of "let me at him" fill the room.

Finn pushes himself away from Nicholas and stands upright against the wall. "If you kill me... you'll die tonight."

Nicholas' fist pounds on Finn's face until blood pours out of his nose and eyebrows before Erik steps in and pulls him away.

Unable to stay on his feet, Finn collapses to the floor.

Taking a moment to compose himself, Nicholas runs a hand through his hair and addresses the group. "This morning Victoria and I found out that Father has put this family on a different trajectory than we had planned. He had letters sent to our associates in The Family announcing Victoria's ascension."

Around the room, confused faces meet bewildered looks.

He picks up Brigitta's chair and nods for Louis to place his mother on it. She reluctantly gives in, but does not let go of her weapon. Her shoulders heave and she squeezes her eyes tight. There is no room for tears. Not right now.

Without instruction, Louis stands behind her to stop any additional attempts to go after Finn.

Nicholas continues, "We don't know what compelled Father to do such a thing, but legally transferring the business to me will no longer rectify the situation. Father's decision sent up a flare showing that I am not capable of running things. Although I have received phone calls from our associates expressing disbelief and support, there are bound to be questions and schemes being formed behind the scenes."

"Thanks to our friend Finn here, Paul, someone who did not receive a letter, knows about this hurdle we face. With Finn's eagerness to save his own ass, we know that Paul, likely in collaboration with others who would wish us harm, will attack The Family meeting we have scheduled tonight to confirm this family's new leader."

"What if we reschedule?" Janet asks.

"We could. It would give us time to regroup. But by then, our enemies will know we are on to their plan. No, we take them by surprise tonight. You will each pair up with another soldier and without telling them what is going on, visit our associates. Question them nicely about Father's decision, and if they give you reason to believe that they are involved, take care of them. Otherwise, you spend the day with them and accompany them to Maxwell's restaurant. No one speaks to, or meets up with, anyone else before this meeting. And keep an eye on who you bring with you. There may be more traitors amongst us."

Nicholas tosses Finn's cell phone to Victoria. No new messages. She digs her boot heel into Finn's chest. "When's your next check in?"

"Eleven o'clock."

With the use of his fingerprint, she changes the unlock code to the phone so she won't require her computer to access it. She sets the phone alarm for three minutes before eleven and sticks it in her pants pocket.

Nicholas continues his instructions. "Aidan, I was going to have you watch Paul, but we don't want to tip him off, so you and Erik will stick with Victoria and me. Louis, as usual, you're with Mother. If Paul's making a play, I doubt he'd want her around to ruin it. In fact, he might go after her first. Take her to the cabin."

Brigitta stands. "I'm not going to that stupid cabin. It's my fault Paul got this close to us, to you. I want to be there to finish him."

Nicholas cups her face in his hands. "I understand you're furious, and if I can take him alive, you can enact whatever torture you want on him. But for now, we need to keep you safe. And that means the cabin." Nicholas looks to Louis. "If one of the four of us doesn't knock on the cabin door tonight, you take her out of the country."

Louis nods and ushers Brigitta out of the room. She looks back with solemn eyes, doubtlessly wondering if it's the last time she'll see her son alive.

Erik uses Brigitta's scarf to tie Finn's hands behind his back and leads him out of the house. Nicholas, Aidan, and Victoria trail behind until they are all ensconced in a black SUV.

Nicholas is laser-focused on the purple-and-blue-face of the young man Father insisted on mentoring. He curses himself for being blind to Finn's scheme. Had he been too worried about his father finding out about the money he'd lost? Or more concerns Nathan's instability would cause their business to crumble? Perhaps, he'd been too preoccupied with Tessa to see what was right in front of him. Nicholas wonders if Father was right. Maybe Victoria would be a better leader than him. She didn't question Father's concern about a rat. Although, she hadn't seen how erratic Father became. He licks his lips and takes in Victoria from the corner of his eye.

Victoria's blood boils with a desire to torment the traitor in the seat facing her and Nicholas. Her anger seethes through her eyes and her rapid finger tapping on the leather armrest. She's itching to make Finn pay for recording their night together.

Beside Finn, Aidan sits with a gun rested on his knee. Is that the hint of a smile trying to creep out of the corner of this mouth?

Nicholas rolls and unrolls his sleeves over and over on as they drive to The Barn.

Victoria recalls the last time Nicholas fiddled with his sleeves. He was hiding something back then. What is he hiding now?

Chapter Thirty-Six

Now

Aidan opens the reinforced door of The Barn and disinfectant wafts through the air. The newly arrived occupants do not need to be told death is near.

Finn looks at those around him. "Please. I'll tell you anything you want to know. Just don't-"

"You'll talk when we want you to talk." Nicholas nods towards the center of the room.

Aidan and Erik push Finn forward before tying him to an old metal office chair.

Nicholas takes out his anger at himself on Finn's face. When he's done, the young man is almost unrecognizable from the blood and swelling, and his own hands are battered and bruised. Nicholas speaks above Finn's whimpers. "Now you may talk. Tell us everyone who is involved in Paul's plot and we'll make your death quick."

Finn spits out some blood. "I don't know who Paul is working with. I just know that anyone in The Family that is not aligned with him, or has not seen fit to promote him into the organization, is not to make it out of the meeting alive."

Victoria steps forward, and flips open her switch blade. "What is Paul's plan if we cancel the meeting?"

"His army will systematically eliminate his targets overnight." The group has to listen closely to understand the words escaping his swollen lips and cheeks.

"How was he planning on getting past security?" Nicholas asks.

"I don't know. If I received a text saying 'the cat's out of the bag', I was supposed to take you two out. That's all I was told."

"And you thought you'd actually be successful?" Victoria chuckles. "Fat chance that was going to happen. Why would Paul trust you enough to pull the job off by yourself? Unless you aren't by yourself?" Erik and Aidan are within her eyesight and neither reacts to her question.

"If Paul has someone else in your crew, I don't know about it. I was supposed to make it quick and easy. Gunshot with a silencer to your heads as you slept. Then get out before anyone found your bodies."

Victoria pricks Finn's throat with her knife and a trickle of blood escapes. "What was Paul's play if Father hadn't died?"

The sweat dripping from Finn's forehead does nothing to wet his dry lips. "Paul was getting impatient. He would have made sure Nathan died sooner rather than later."

"And was sooner seven days ago?" asks Victoria. Longing for confirmation that her suspicions are true.

"I don't think Paul has seen Nathan in months, so I'm not sure how he could have. I wasn't given any instructions about killing Nathan."

"So, this plan is recent?" Victoria hopes Paul's sudden change of tactic results in further errors in carrying out his plan. Errors she can capitalize on to save herself, and Nicholas.

Nicholas rests a bruised hand on Victoria's shoulder, and she steps backwards. The soldiers need to see him in charge. Nicholas signals to Erik to execute another blow. The behemoth of a man takes a metal rod to Finn's leg, who wails as crushed bones pierce through his skin.

"How and when did you inform Paul about the explosion at the funeral?" Nicholas asks.

"They same way I always kept him updated. We had our own cipher for our texts. After the final debriefing, I gave him the information."

He grips the young man's throat. "What else aren't you telling us?"

"Paul was going to make a move against you after the funeral, but your botched attack didn't allow him any space to enact it." Finn grits through the pain. "He wanted to wait until Victoria returned home. He knows if he doesn't kill both of you, the survivor will not rest until he's dead. Brigitta told him there would be a family dinner at Maxwell's in the coming days in memory of Nathan, and Paul updated his plan to kill everyone there."

Victoria and Nicholas exchange subtle quizzical glances. There was no plan for a family dinner. Brigitta avoids being seen with Victoria in public. Victoria wonders if Brigitta had suspicions of Paul and was planting false information to test him.

Finn continues. "Then tonight's opportunity arose with the meeting to affirm the new leader of your family and vote on the new Director."

Nicholas releases his grip and nods to Aidan, who pulls out his phone and makes some calls to inform the others of the developments.

Eager to continue the interrogation, Victoria moves back to the prisoner and sits in his lap. Her weight sends bolts of pain through his broken leg. She runs her blade along the side of his face. "That was pretty clever of you to hide your phone behind the curtain the night we were together. I assumed you were clumsy, and yet you made a move right in front of my eyes. How foolish of me not to suspect something more. At least I can get my revenge, but before I do, tell me, who have you shown the video to?"

Finn's phone activity didn't reveal him sending it to anyone, so the video itself was contained but, they'll need to do some damage control if the phone was passed around the soldiers, or others.

"No one. I thought it might come in handy if I needed something from you."

"You thought you could blackmail me with a sex tape? Oh, darling, you are so young. Shame you won't get to make any more videos." She stabs Finn in the leg and uses her knife to raise herself off his lap, ignoring his screams.

"One last question. When did you begin working with Paul? Or have you always been on his payroll?"

"I...well. You have to understand. He threatened my mother's life. He told me the only way to guarantee her safety was to do what he said and get Nathan to notice me. All I ever did, climbing the ranks, supplying Paul with information, it was all for her. To keep her safe." The last of Finn's tears careen down his cheeks.

Victoria feels a slight pain in her heart, but she mustn't weaken. He's obviously a skilled enough liar to have fooled both Nathan and Nicholas, so it's probable he's just trying to save his own life. She looks at Nicholas. "Can we please kill him now?"

Stoic, Nicholas replies. "Yes."

"No wait, please-" Finn's begging falls on deaf ears.

"Do you want to do it or shall I?" Moving closer to him, she offers Nicholas her knife.

"He's all yours."

Victoria steps behind Finn. As much as she'd like to make his death slow, they have a bigger problem to solve. With one hand on his forehead, she pulls his head back and places the cool metal against his neck.

Finn scrunches his eyes shut and holds his breath.

Victoria purses her lips, and is about to release Finn's soul, when she changes her mind and lowers the knife.

Finn opens one eye and exhales.

Everyone else stares at Victoria.

"You do it." She flips the knife handle toward Aidan. She wants him to prove that he's part of this family and will do whatever it takes.

Aidan looks from Victoria to Finn and back at her. His slow steps echo in the silence. He takes the knife, folds it in on itself, and pulls her into his chest. Their eyes lock, and he places the knife into her back pocket. He reaches between them, pulls his already cocked gun from his shoulder holster, and fires.

Chapter Thirty-Seven

Now

Once Finn's body and clothes are thrown into the incinerator inside The Barn, and the tidy up is complete, Nicholas, Erik, Aidan and Victoria change into the clean clothes that are kept on-site.

Nicholas pulls Victoria out of earshot of the others. "Are you satisfied now? Can you finally move on from the Aidan thing."

She glances over to the handsome man pulling a shirt over his head. "Yes, and I'll back off Aidan."

"Good." They return to the group and he continues. "We don't have much time before the meeting. Erik, you do one last sweep and turn off the incinerator."

"Yes, boss."

On the way to Maxwell's restaurant, reports filter in to Nicholas regarding their associates. After Janet and her partner applied a little alcoholic libation to one of Mr. Laurel's men, he opened up like a flower desperate for sunshine. Mr. Laurel then confessed to defecting to Paul's side after he was promised he would be second in command of The Family. Janet removed him from the equation.

Everyone else appears to be loyal. They will know for sure after tonight.

A few blocks away from the restaurant, Victoria's phone rings. Shocked, she stares at it a moment and rubs the new Peter Rabbit sticker on the back. Everyone knew to contact Nicholas. No one should be calling her. She looks at the man beside her, who nods for her to answer. Aidan looks around outside the car for anything of concern.

"Hello?"

"Victoria, Irving here."

Victoria mouths his name. Aidan is visibly less concerned while Nicholas' jaw tightens.

"Earlier, Nicholas informed me of The Family meeting and what Paul is up to. I would normally want to be there for the vote. Ensure what I want happens. With the likelihood one or more deaths will occur tonight, I can't take the chance. Given the speed with which everything is happening, I cannot ensure media or law enforcement won't show up. The fewer photos of us together that I have to locate and destroy, the better. The vote will proceed as planned. I trust you'll handle Paul. I'll call you later to discuss the results."

"Understood. Any chance you can send reinforcements?"

"Not this time. Anyone I could spare is on another job. I can't exactly have my personal protection detail left in the vicinity if they're killed. This is an excellent test for Nicholas. Prove his father made the wrong choice. Tell him to keep his temper in check and not to mess this up."

"Will do."

"Talk soon." The call ends before she can respond.

Victoria replaces the phone in her jacket pocket and looks at Nicholas. "For his own safety, he won't attend. He's unable to send reinforcements and will contact us to discuss the results later." She doesn't want Nicholas to feel overlooked by another powerful figure and hopes the 'us' is reassuring. "He did request that you keep your temper in check. I know, I know, we talked about that, and you will. I'm just passing on the message so that you know what he said." Not wanting to add another boulder to the mountain of stress Nicholas is under, she also keeps the test to herself. She's confident he'll prove himself tonight.

Nicholas rubs his hands along his pants a few times.

The hand-carved wooden sign for the restaurant swings in the blustering wind. The Townsend crew, shoulders up, brace themselves as they hurry into the restaurant.

As per usual, the different families arrive at intervals just before seven in the evening. Those who enter the meeting room hand over their weapons to the guards from each family outside, and nearby, the door. Nicholas has received reports that there's no sign of any snipers or suspicious characters within a two-block radius. A search of the premises has found no bombs, which convinces the group that whatever's being planned will happen mid-meeting or when they exit.

Everyone takes their places around the large circular table in the back room, permanently reserved for the group. Aidan, Erik and one member of the associate families stand guard at the door.

Normally, the table is covered with a plethora of fresh scallops, cod, lobster bisque and all the trimmings; but with an impending fight and potential deaths on the horizon, Nicholas made sure Maxwell Junior didn't waste the food before he and his staff were sent home.

Out of respect for Nathan's wishes, and to prevent the immediate ruffling of any feathers before the ownership of power can be discussed, Victoria takes the intricately carved seat reserved for the head of The Family. Like the other seconds, Nicholas teeters from foot to foot behind his leader.

Victoria commences the meeting with a cough. "Thank you all for joining us. Especially under the current threat we face. As you can see from the empty chair, we've identified Mr. Laurel as a problem and have taken care of it. Are there any objections if Nicholas takes a seat at the table until the vote reveals who will officially sit in this spot?"

Although Nathan has posthumously shared his wishes, and Irving McKinnon will be the ultimate authority on the decision, a vote will be held for The Family to select who will head-up the Townsend clan, and therefore show who they trust to follow. Mr. McKinnon will then decide if he agrees, or wants to restructure his entire criminal empire.

The associates exchange glances and Mrs. Harris, paying no attention to the law against smoking indoors, takes a long drag on her cigarette. Soft white clouds of acrid scent billows around her head. "I understand the uniqueness of the situation and I was surprised when I received the letter announcing you as the new head of the Townsend family, Victoria, but you know that we've never had our seconds sit at the table, and I don't see why there should be an exception now."

Victoria can hear Nicholas' nails dig into the back of her chair, but knows his face is a blank slate. "We understand and respect your decision. Our families have worked together for a long time. With our enemies nipping at our heels, it should be acknowledged that any words spoken in this room tonight won't be held against the speaker or their family." Heads nod in agreement. "Our goal is to move through the transition quickly and smoothly. That being said, what are your thoughts on installing Nicholas as the head of the Townsends and me stepping back to second? Our family feels that is how it should be."

Victoria indicates to Mr. Tanner, on her left to start the round table. His soft voice is the opposite of his rotund physique. "Is your plan to return to your role outside of the country or stay home?"

"Would people have a preference?" Victoria asks.

Those around the table shrug their indifference.

Mr. Tanner continues, "We can't ignore the unsaid reasons Nathan had for choosing you to run your family. He was a consummate businessman and never took decisions lightly. Is there any reason why we shouldn't trust his decision?"

Revealing the deterioration of Nathan's mental state in the months leading up to his death was off the table. It would unhinge any confidence the other families had in the Townsends. Victoria also knew she couldn't allow them to learn that Nicholas did nothing to remove him from power.

"Nicholas and I were as surprised as everyone else with Father's decision. He left no record for his rationale, and Mr. Malarkey was not privy to the information. The only thing Father's appointment of me would ensure is that I would remain in Nova Scotia. You've been working with Nicholas since he was nineteen. You've seen how he handles disputes with suppliers, and keeps the information flowing through The Family. Our contact has been indirect and intermittent. As such, is there anything about me that stands out to you as to why this group should heed Father's decision? Or, do you have more faith in working with someone you know and trust?"

Mr. Bendale, a forty-something banker-turned-money-launderer, speaks, "Nicholas is an adequate leader. Despite Paul's yearning for power and turning against us, Nicholas has done exceptional work with the employees and management at the Port of Halifax. With his relationships, your brother has ensured smooth transportation of our goods, and keeps the payoffs low. However, your reputation precedes you. Nothing and no one intimidates you. Your expansion into private security has been very lucrative. An ingenious mind like that is what we need if we are going to remain relevant."

Victoria's head feels heavy, but she refuses to let her chest support it. "That's very kind of you to say. But the flip-side of nothing and no one intimidating me, is that I don't always have a filter for my opinion, which will get us into trouble. On top of that, I'd rather use force to come to the agreement I'm looking for. Whereas, Nicholas is the experienced negotiator who can keep his cool in a tense situation. Isn't that who you want sitting in this chair?"

Mr. Metcalf, the oldest of the group at eighty-one, raises his voice, "Your Father was the same way, at first. With time, he learned how to use intelligence over a verbal lashing to get what he wanted. Unless, the situation absolutely warranted it. There was never anyone else I wanted on my side. Of course, that meant, if we were working one on one, he always got the better deal." He smiles and a soft chuckle travels across the room.

Victoria rises from her chair. "We don't have time for this. The longer we sit here, the more time Paul has to ensure the vote is of no consequence. There is no reason for you to think I want this job, I'm better on the outside of this room, not on the inside. Now, the Townsends support Nicholas for this chair, as do I. So, let's vote - and be thoughtful about it."

Seated in front of each person sits a pine box with the symbol of each family. The Townsends have a compass to represent how tides and directions may change, but the True North is always home. A ship's wheel to represent the Metcalfs and their family heritage of generations on the water. The box of the Yangs displays the Chinese character for courage. A Triquetra sits upon the box for the Tanners and crossed spears appear on the box of the Harris' - both symbols of protection. The Bendales chose an owl for their intelligence and nocturne preferences. The Laurel's box sits alone with a sly fox staring up at the ceiling.

All boxes contain two coins, a black one to represent a vote of 'No' and a gold one to vote 'Yes'. The box positioned in front of Victoria also contains a red coin, which allows the leader of The Family to veto any decision.

Nathan always told his children that it should only be used in extreme circumstances and he cautioned against its use when a vote didn't go the way he, and now they, wanted it. The decision to use the coin had to be weighed carefully, as one didn't want to be seen as petty, or someone the group could not rationally work with. If that happened, they would lose the respect of the group. Risking everything had to be worth pulling that coin out of the box.

The leaders pass around a royal purple pouch and cast their votes on whether Nicholas should ascend to Nathan's position. With Mr. Laurel's spot vacant, Nicholas requires three people to support him. Victoria has no vote, given the chair she occupies is in question.

The vote complete, Victoria reaches into the pouch and pulls out the first coin. Gold; yes. The second, black; no. As is the third. The fourth coin is gold. Victoria's hand trembles inside the bag as it clings to an object that will decide her fate.

A battle of destinies plays in her mind. If she becomes leader, she will have access to money, with the possibility to hide some away, dismantle everything, and start a new life. She's pretended to be many people in her life, and wonders what difference another name would make. Then, she thinks about the cost. She's still unsure if she could leave Nicholas behind. Although, knowing Brigitta, and now this mysterious Tessa person, will be around, she isn't convinced it was worth taking him with her.

If Nicholas is voted the leader, everything stays the same.

Victoria is wise enough to know that if the vote favours Nicholas, she'll lose the opportunity to dismantle the system that took her from her parents. Nicholas' desire for power, for the group's approval, and eagerness to make Nathan proud of him, even in death, would force him to come after her if she ever became a turncoat.

Victoria's fist emerges from the bag. Palm up, she opens her fingers.

The Family has chosen.

CHAPTER THIRTY-EIGHT

NOW

GRUNTS AND SIGHS FLOAT around the table. The black coin feels hot in Victoria's hand. She places it on the table and massages the base of her skull, where a headache is forming. She reaches for her box. Nicholas' hand stops her.

She's confused by how calm his eyes are. All he's ever wanted was to be the Director, and now it has been snatched from him. Some in The Family have just made a play for power, and it will be up to both of them to figure out the next move before someone uses this vote to suggest an overall change in leadership.

Victoria speaks the words Nathan would have spoken. "As is our way, we will abide by the vote at the table."

Unsure if those who cast the black coins actually support her, she eyes the table's occupants. Mr. Bendale's statements about needing to be relevant, and the slight smile creeping out of the corner of his mouth, puts him as a vote for her.

Mr. Tanner appears smug as he takes a long drag on his cigarette. He's pleased with the result. Victoria will have to watch him.

Even seated, Mrs. Harris's six-foot-three figure towers over everyone around the table. Her face is stern and calm. Victoria has always had a hard time reading her, and tonight is no different. But she's logical. She'll go along with everything for a while and see how it plays out. That causes Victoria to think she voted for Nicholas. The fewer ruffles created by the quick change, the better for her. Her son's debacle in Japan three months ago has brought that family enough attention lately. She wouldn't want more.

Mr. Metcalf looks longingly at Nicholas, so she's confident he didn't vote for her. So that leaves Ms. Yang. As Nathan told her, Ms. Yang's a risk taker and enjoys trying new things. She also wasn't appreciative when Nicholas blamed her son for not being able to track down the proper container in the Port of Halifax for a gun drop. He escaped arrest by a meager ten minutes, when the police arrived at what they thought was the exchange location. Thinking about it now, Victoria feels Paul likely had a hand in the mix-up, but Ms. Yang is probably still stung by the incident.

Cognizant of the impending attack, Victoria moves the schedule along. "Next on the agenda, Father's death. The medical examiner and Nicholas' secondary expert have confirmed Father died of natural causes. A heart attack."

While the medical reports being passed around the table seem accurate, she knows only her results will satisfy her concerns that his death was not natural. Her suspicions will not be shared with The Family at this point.

"At least we don't have to worry about an assassin being in our midst." Mr. Bendale says. "Any other concerns within your family, aside from Paul, we need to be apprised of?"

Victoria takes a slow deep breath as she ponders what information Mr. Bendale has. All their associates were made aware of Paul's treachery. If Mr. Bendale knows Finn was working for Paul, and Victoria doesn't bring it forward to the group, no one will trust her or Nicholas again. If Mr. Bendale is also working for Paul, it's unlikely he'd reveal his knowledge, knowing it would blow his cover. It's also possible he knows nothing and is trying to pry and create instability. She decides to monitor him during the next few hours and months, but keeps the truth hidden. "Nothing other than we promised Brigitta that we'd try to take him alive so that she can play with him before she kills him."

Heads nod around the table.

Victoria continues, "This brings us to our last item for tonight. Getting out of here alive and taking as many of Paul's people out as possible."

Nicholas opens the meeting room door and ushers Erik in. One other member of each family enters the room. Aidan and another man remain on guard.

The additional personnel return the weapons to their owners.

Mrs. Harris stands and casts a projection of a map of the area on the wall. Her experience as a former commander in the armed forces has her formulating most of The Family's larger tactical endeavors. "The pins mark the places where we've identified Paul's people have set themselves up since the meeting began." She runs through the plan.

"The Townsends and Bendales will exit through the tapestry at the back of the room. The Metcalfs and Tanners through the painting at the front, and the Yang's and my family will depart through the bookcase. Then, we split up according to our assigned colours on the map and take down Paul and his crew. Any questions?"

No one speaks. Mrs. Harris nods to Victoria so she can retake control of the meeting.

"Okay. We all know what we have to do. Good luck everyone."

Chairs tucked into place and their weapons ready, Mr. Bendale bows his head and prays over the group. "Lord, we know we falter in many aspects of the qualities you wish for all people to embrace. We are sinners, and we humbly seek your protection tonight as we fight for our lives. If that is not your will, we accept our fates. In the loving name of Jesus Christ, Amen."

Everyone replies with their own "Amen", some forming the cross over their bodies. Nods and tipped hats signal their imminent departure as they approach their respective masked exits.

Before they can raise a tapestry or open a hinged painting, the double doors connecting to the main eating area of the restaurant smash open. The group swerves on their heels, the number twos swiftly step in front of their leaders. Everyone aims their guns at the entry.

Two men the size of giants drag Aidan's limp body into the room. Another one drags the other guard by their collar. A scantily-clad woman in a red, knee-slit dress follows them. She steps in front of the men and nods to each side of the room, where the men toss the bodies like trash.

With Nicholas shielding Victoria, she squats down to inspect the prone figure beside her. Aidan's face shows no evidence of a struggle. His pulse is slow, but it's there. At least these strangers left her the opportunity to kill him for failing to alert them to the intrusion.

Whistling past the three arrivals, Paul saunters into the room, twirling a pocket watch. He places a brown briefcase that looks like it's travelled from the 1990s onto the table. A group of people crowd in behind him. All have gas masks attached to their hips. The only people without one are Paul and the lady in red.

The Family isn't outnumbered, but a fight will be too close to call.

Paul smirks, and glances at the nails on his right hand. "Don't tell me the meeting is over already. We have so much to discuss. The first being that everyone needs to give my lovely Alicia, here their weapons, otherwise," he pops open the gold latches on the briefcase and reveals the contents. Two tubes of a red liquid sit in a metal contraption, intricately connected with wires. "I'll have no choice but to detonate our friend here. The air might get a little toxic, and I'm sure none of us want that. At least not yet."

Alicia, with a black bag held out, stops in front of each person, each of whom obeys Paul's orders. Another of his crew pats everyone down to make sure all weapons are accounted for. Alicia gives the bag to one of the other nameless men and returns to stand in front of Nicholas. "I need to pat you down again. Just to be sure we missed nothing." She takes her time, running her finger along the scar down his face and neck, and then sliding her hands all over his body, her eyes never leaving his. She winks. "Hey, boss, I like this one. Mind if I keep him?"

Victoria's muscles tighten as she watches the woman's roaming hands. She looks away. She needs to focus on getting them out of the restaurant alive.

Nicholas smiles. "I'd be amenable to a little one-on-one time." His fingers twitch for the cold metal of the gun he no longer holds.

Paul chuckles. "I'm sure you would. Let me assure you, you would not be disappointed. But, I'm not here to have your needs satisfied, Mr. Townsend." Paul makes his way to Nathan's chair and sits in it. The bomb remains on the opposite side of the table.

The veins in Nicholas' neck throb at his arrogance. Victoria restrains herself with difficulty.

Paul gestures at the floor. "Everyone on your knees, side-by-side. No human shields." Alicia goes and stands beside Paul, like a queen beside her king.

Nicholas and Victoria are on either side of an intricately carved antique hutch. Flowers and vines hide another secret.

The table blocks Victoria's view of Ms. Yang, but she trusts they've assessed the situation the same as she has. One man stands on guard between every two people, including Alicia and Paul, with the giants by the door. She has to guess at where the detonator is for what she assumes is a poisonousness gas inside the briefcase. They can't make any move without getting their hands on it.

As steady and stealthy as Victoria can, she presses the tips of the fingers on her right hand against an inset frame of wood on the hutch beside her. Millimetre by millimetre, the wood moves in on itself. Nicholas' shoulder rests against his side of the sideboard and she suspects he's doing the same thing.

With a penchant for hearing himself talk, Paul continues. "I was going to wait until you were all lined up on the sidewalk to take you out, but then I thought, what would be the fun in that? Drawing out this life and death torture fest would be more amusing." Paul twirls the watch between his fingers. "The question is, who do I start with? I mean, the obvious choice would be little Victoria. I presume based on Nathan's instructions; you've voted her in as Director." His disgust for her stains his face. "Then again, having her watch what I do to her brother would cause much more pain than I could ever have inflicted." He gets up, and a man moves aside to give him more space in front of Nicholas.

Nicholas pushes out his chest to give off the allure he won't back down from Paul, but in reality, he's hiding the opening in the cabinet. He's not yet ready for catastrophe to erupt.

Paul stares down at Nicholas. "For seven years, I've watched your father treat you like nothing more than an errand boy. Yet, you kept going back for more. Took your licks, biding your time, helping him become more powerful, and now look at you. Side stepped by the very man who was supposed to take you to the top. Instead, he chose her. That's gotta hurt."

Nicholas' nostrils flare, but he stays in position. He taps the face of his wristwatch twice.

Kneeling beside him, Mrs. Harris gives a faint nod in acknowledgment of the signal.

Paul turns on Victoria, but he stops when Mrs. Harris coughs. "Something on your mind, Melinda?"

"I was thinking we can make a trade. My life in exchange for the weapons inside the cabinet and revealing how to get out of the room without using the door."

CHAPTER THIRTY-NINE

NOW

VICTORIA IS AGHAST AND Paul's face turns a multitude of colours, from white to pink and finally red. Before he can move, she looks on as Nicholas has pulled Paul's feet from under him. The men wrestle like school children.

Mrs. Harris lunges for the cabinet and pulls back with a weapon in each hand.

Victoria kicks the legs out of the man in front of her, takes his gun and his life. Another bullet finds its mark in the closest enemy to her. With both of them out of the way, Victoria grabs a pistol from the cabinet and tosses it to Ms. Yang. She grabs another and tosses it to Erik, who has subdued their personal guard.

Bullets from both sides careen through the air, some hitting their marks, others making their homes in walls and furniture.

Mrs. Harris takes down her man, and bodies tumble along the floor, table and walls as each fight for their life. Mr. Bendale closes the briefcase as the fists of his number two, and bullets from Erik, prevent anyone from getting to him. He tosses it out into the empty restaurant and it slides along the stone floor until it stops by the front door.

Alicia knocks Nicholas off Paul and climbs onto his back, putting him in a headlock. He falls back against the table, but even the thump of her head on the hardwood does not cause her to release her grip.

Victoria's bullet does. Turning from Alicia, she raises her gun to Paul, who backs himself into a corner. Victoria's associates, now armed with the weapons of the dead and those from the secret cabinet, create an arrow of black metal hovering before their target, waiting for permission to fire.

Paul smiles. "This is why Nathan decided against Nicholas to lead you. Nicholas just got you all killed with his cabinet trick." His palm opens, and he catches his pocket watch by the chain, letting it swing from side to side. He slowly retracts the chain with his fingers until his thumb hovers over the latch release.

The side of Victoria's mouth twitches. Just one bullet and she would never have to hear Paul speak again. Without looking at her associates, she asks, "Mr. Bendale, would I be correct in my assumption that with its current location, we will exit before whatever toxin that is in those vials reaches this room?"

"Correct, Ma'am. The people near the door might feel some remnants of it before we do. There's nothing to worry our lives over." The people by the door step to the side and use the walls as a shield.

Victoria smiles. "Your plan wasn't half bad. Less damage and witnesses if you killed us all in here. Where you faltered was underestimating how much Father would have planned for a potential attack in the meeting room. Rules may dictate that weapons may not be brought into a meeting, but it doesn't mean they couldn't be acquired if needed."

"You also underestimated our knowledge of chemical explosives. The moment you opened that case, at least two of us recognized how low impact the bomb would be if kept at a distance. I suspect you did it on purpose to make sure you weren't hurt making your getaway. Nicholas, would you care to explain to Paul how you figured out where the detonator we are after is?"

Nicholas steps beside Victoria. Half-dried blood sticks to his temple, his hair is in disarray and his gun remains pointed at its target. "You've always had a propensity for showmanship, extravagance, and tall tales. Reasons Mother liked you. You think you're smarter than everyone else, and couldn't help but dangle the answer right in front of our noses. Within our grasps and yet out of reach." He snatches the golden pocket watch from Paul's grasp, passing it to Erik who follows Mr. Bendale out to disarm the bomb.

Nicholas rests his gun on Paul's chest. "Just so we're clear. You will die tonight. Unfortunately for you, it will be by Brigitta's hand. You remember what she did to the maid who tried to sneak information to the police, don't you? It'll be ten times worse, so I hope for her sake you can hold out long enough for her to have some fun. But for now-"

The man collapses in agony as a bullet pierces his knee.

Two men grab Paul and drag him out as everyone prepares to leave the restaurant.

A group of six exits out the back. They scout the locations where Paul's crew was thought to have been, to check if there were any stragglers or lookouts. When they return without the echo of gunshots or more prisoners, The Family knows it is safe to depart.

The street is empty. Paul is hog-tied and put into the trunk of the Townsend's SUV. Two others put the dead weight of Aidan across the backseat opposite Nicholas and Victoria. As Erik drives away, Victoria looks to Nicholas.

He rests his head against the headrest and closes his eyes. The veins in his temples pulse to the beat of his heart. Other than foiling Paul's plan, tonight didn't turn out like either of them had hoped. Exhaustion wraps its arms around him, but he doesn't give in. There is still too much to do yet tonight.

Victoria breaks the silence. "What next?"

Nicholas keeps his eyes closed. "You're the boss, you tell me."

"Let's not do that right now. As far as I'm concerned, you're in charge."

Nicholas sits up, rubs his eyes, and runs his fingers through his hair. "We'll hand Paul off to Mother and Louis. Hopefully, that will dissipate some of the anger she has over being trapped up in the cabin for the last few hours. Then I suppose we should deal with him." Nicholas uses the toe of his shoe to raise Aidan's arm and it falls dead when released.

Victoria takes in the unconscious man before her. His tattooed arms tell a story she had previously paid little attention to. A little girl walking a dog on a leash hides within the vines of flowers. Lines of music wrap around words in a language she doesn't recognize. She thinks he looks peaceful, but, takes some pleasure in knowing it will be short-lived. "Are you coming around to the fact he's not everything he says he is?"

Nicholas doesn't want to admit he may not have noticed two rats in his house. Once again, he wonders if Father was right and that Victoria is better suited to run The Family. "I agree he needs to explain why he didn't tell us Paul had arrived, not to mention, how they took out a well-trained military man."

"All a little too convenient, if you ask me," Victoria says.

"We'll soon find out what he's hiding. For now, let's rest. It's going to be a long night."

The trees of Highway 103 pass by outside the windows as Nicholas ponders how to tell Victoria a secret, one he's been wanting to get off his chest since she called him from England. Fear she will do something drastic has prevented him, but he's running out of time. If she finds out before he tells her, he'll lose her forever.

Chapter Forty

Now

THE FULL MOON BLANKETS the land in a light so bright the stars are afraid of it and hide behind wisps of clouds. The rolling forest below the Townsend's cabin dances with the soft warm breeze of spring, refusing to let summer move in, while the hoots of owls bounce along the tree branches in a melodious rhythm.

The song does nothing to drown out Paul's screams filtering from the elegant log cabin behind Nicholas and Victoria.

They sit on the back of the handmade log bench in the yard, overlooking the playground of their youth. Still unconscious, Aidan lies tied up beside the blazing fire pit. Victoria could not reach anyone in Mr. Bendale's crew to hear what story their unconscious guard provided about the ambush.

Nicholas avoids the difficult conversation that is on his mind and focuses on the inevitable one. "Does the vote mean you'll stick around for a while?"

Victoria picks at her cuticles. "I don't think I have much choice, unless I can somehow convince everyone that you saving our lives back there deserves a promotion."

"They've made their choice. Anyone who changes their mind now looks like a coward. A second vote won't change anything."

She hates to admit it, but he's right. "I'm sorry this is happening. We'll have to devise a foolproof plan to facilitate your takeover."

Nicholas' eyes focus on the flames.

Victoria senses something is off with him. He's quieter than normal around her and his eyes are distant. "Are you okay?"

"As okay as I can be given the situation." He runs his fingers along the back of this neck. "I'm confident we'll find a solution, but how long until the rest of The Family agrees? I think we need to step back and make sure everything's stable with you taking over before we create another big change."

"I understand. Leaving is probably not the best thing for you. The last thing I want is to install you in control and then get a text like the one you sent me." She tries to console him. "You know it's not your fault."

"What isn't?"

"Him." She nods towards Aidan.

"We still don't know if he's a problem. But if he is, then it certainly is my fault. Which means you've found two issues I didn't."

"Your hands were full with Nathan's instability. Had life been normal, you would have caught on."

Nicholas runs his finger over his brow. "I have to tell you something."

"That sounds ominous," says Victoria griping the back of the bench.

"Well..."

"Oh, god, is Tessa pregnant?"

"What? No," he pauses. "Would that be the worst thing?"

"Right now, yes. It might look like we have our family's position secured, but it's holding on by threads. Having a child, let alone bringing a stranger I haven't vetted into our fold, creates opportunities for them to be used against you or leverage to manipulate you."

Nicholas chuckles, "You sound like Mother."

Victoria despises being compared to Brigitta, but recognizes her intelligence in selecting Townsend clan members. She couldn't stop Victoria from joining, but Victoria knows Brigitta will sure as hell make sure anyone else joining has her approval. She wonders how Finn got past her and if Brigitta had dug deep enough into Aidan. "Let that be the only thing we have in common."

Not wanting Brigitta to be the topic of conversation, Nicholas tries to steer them back on track. Before he can, Aidan moans.

The man uncurls himself the best he can with his hands tied behind his back. His eyes fight with him to stay closed, but he wins and, seeing the fire beside him, rolls away from the heat and scrambles to sitting. Seeing Nicholas and Victoria, he relaxes, a little.

"Hello sleepy head." Victoria says, hopping down from the bench. She opens a canteen of water and gives him a taste. Not enough to quench his thirst, but enough to loosen his tongue. "Anything you'd like to share with us before your lifeless body rolls down that hill?"

Aidan licks his lips. "It looks bad, but it's not what you think."

Nicholas reaches out and pokes the fire with a large stick. Sparks dance along the air like fireflies. "Then you have about five minutes to change our minds, otherwise those sounds you hear coming from the cabin will also come out of you."

Aidan tries to get to his knees, but Victoria kicks him back on his ass. "Don't move."

He obeys. "Right, well. First, I'm not working with Paul. I know it looks that way, but I swear I'm not. A man, or more accurately, a teenager, whom we had positioned outside, came into the restaurant to announce an ongoing disturbance between a woman and a man. The teenager was uncertain if their intention was to cause a distraction or if they were in the wrong place at the wrong time. He wanted help to figure it out. I confirmed the time. By then, following the plan, everyone should have been in the tunnels. When the people he mentioned reached the restaurant window, the other guard and I had to act fast."

"No time for a simple knock or a quick glance to check if we were gone? Yelling 'Stay Alert' would have taken seconds." Victoria says.

"There wasn't. You gotta trust me on this. We got outside, and the fight broke up before I said a word. I knew I'd messed up when the woman smiled. I turned around to warn you, but before I could return, everything became fuzzy and went black. Was the other guy in on it?"

Nicholas' fists open and close in frustration. "The other guy's story is none of your business. I'm supposed to believe the young man got the jump on you? Someone with years of surveillance experience?"

"Either him, or the other two, but yes."

Nicholas grabs Aidan by the neck and pushes him down into the dirt, "You can take down every man in my employ in training, but a kid can sneak up on you? I'm finding that hard to believe."

Aidan inhales the dirt and chokes before he speaks. "I would too, but it's the truth. I let my guard down when I became concerned the two people out front were working with Paul and stopped paying attention to the other one."

Nicholas looks over his shoulder at Victoria. "What do you think?"

Her head tilts to one side as she considers Aidan's argument. "What does this kid look like?"

"Shaved head, dressed in black like the rest of us. The back of his left hand has a skull tattoo."

Victoria recalls the bodies littered on the meeting room floor. "Erik killed him in the fight, so that part of your story lines up. But I just don't know. It would be a good move for Paul to have two wolves hiding in our midst, just in case one got caught. It would explain why you had no issues putting Finn down. The current problem is that Paul is with Brigitta, and has only a few hours left to live. You would be smart to act like a sheep and return to the herd."

"My willingness to kill Finn was out of no loyalty to Paul, but to your family. Even if he hadn't been a rat, he was a cocky troublemaker. If he hadn't caused a problem now, he would have in the future. I was happy to do it."

"A convenient story, given he can't refute it."

"I'll prove I'm loyal. Just tell me what to do."

Nicholas lets go of Aidan's throat and stands over him. "The thing is, we're not sure what you could do to prove it. Any information you may share about our enemies that we don't have would prove you're working for them. Your disregard for life proves nothing. I'm just not seeing a scenario where we can risk keeping you around."

Gasping for breath, Aidan pushes himself up to sitting. He scrambles to come up with something that will keep him alive. When ideas fail him, he hangs his head. He knows he's a dead man. A scream causes his head to pop back up. "Ask Paul."

"Paul would say anything right now. Unless Brigitta has removed his tongue." Nicholas replies.

"Please, I swear I'm not working for him or anyone other than you. He approached me once last year, but the way he asked me about my loyalty to you was so nonchalant I thought he was joking. I ignored the question, and he didn't ask again. I assumed he wasn't serious. Ask him about the thirty-year wedding anniversary party. That's when he came to me."

Nicholas and Victoria move out of Aidan's earshot, but keep their eyes on him.

"What difference does it make if Paul backs up his claims?" Victoria asks.

"I hate to say it, but loyalty is limited right now and, if he is telling the truth and we kill him, we are killing a very talented worker."

"Why do you have such a hard-on for this man? I mean, I know why I would if I wasn't so suspicious about him, but I've never known you to play both sides of the field before. Seriously, what's happened that has you dismissing the risk we'd be taking in letting him live?"

"He got me out of some trouble last year."

Victoria's eyes widen. She pinches her lips, in frustration. Nicholas always has a soft spot for people who help him with a serious problem. He was like Nathan in that way. "For Christ's sake. What did you do?"

"I lost one million dollars."

Victoria chokes on her own tongue. "I'm sorry you did what?"

"Without Father's knowledge, I took a chance on black market lobsters and it didn't pan out. My colleagues failed to follow through. Aidan gave me the money to cover the accounting tracks so it would look like a bank error."

"Where did Aidan's money come from?"

"His savings."

"Bullshit." Victoria walks over to Aidan. "No way you gave Nicholas that money out of the kindness of your heart. What was your angle? And how the hell did you get one million dollars?"

"No angle, I swear. With room and board covered, I squirrel away the rest of my pay and bonuses from specialty jobs. Nicholas said he'd pay me back, and I finally found a place I felt I belonged. Why wouldn't I help? I know you don't believe me, but this is my family. Family helps-"

"Shut up." Victoria kicks Aidan back against a tree. Specialty jobs could earn up to one hundred thousand dollars each, so saving one million wasn't unreasonable. She still doesn't like it. Shaking her head, she returns to Nicholas. "Do you think you owe him his life for helping you?"

"I'm saying we should exercise caution. If we keep picking off our own soldiers, people will notice and attack us when we are weak."

Victoria kicks at the dirt. She wants to shake some sense into Nicholas; instead, she punches Aidan in the jaw. He grunts but doesn't object. An ounce of anger released, Victoria gives in. "This is absurd. But fine, you go talk to Paul."

"I might return to find Aidan dead 'by accident'. You go."

"You know me too well." Victoria glares at Aidan and heads to the cabin.

The scene inside the building would give a horror fan a chill. Hours of hard work have dishevelled Brigitta's ponytail and matted her bangs to her face. Her gloved hands are no longer white, but a deep red. A plastic tarp below Paul prevents the floors from being tainted by the enemy, but the walls have not gone unscathed. Louis sits by the table, letting the master work.

"What do you want?" Brigitta barks.

"I need to ask him a question." Victoria says.

"Why should I let you do that?"

"It would determine the fate of the man outside. And if that's not good enough. Nicholas wants me to."

"Nice to see he's calling the shots." Brigitta steps back and twirls a knife between her fingers. "Fine, but be quick about it."

Normally, not one to shy away from the mess the Townsends sometimes have to make, Victoria decides it's best to stay by the door, away from Brigitta and her knife. "What's Aidan's role in your organization? And don't think Brigitta won't know if you are lying. I'm sure after playing with you like a field mouse, she's figured out when you're not telling the truth."

Paul spits out some blood and tries to catch his breath. "He...he," Brigitta sticks the tip of a knife into a shoulder wound and twists. Paul hollers. "Nothing. Nothing. He didn't take my bait."

Brigitta twists the knife again and gets the same results. "You wouldn't just be telling us that in the hopes he'll keep working to destroy my family, would you?"

"No, no, I swear. He's clean."

Brigitta pats the side of his face. "That's a good boy."

Victoria clenches her jaw. She still isn't convinced the good-looking stranger outside isn't hiding something, but questions if her distrust in everyone around her means she'll never be satisfied that Aidan is who he says he is.

"Another thing." She ignores Brigitta's glare at going beyond the agreed upon one question. "What do you know about Nathan's death?"

His eyebrows squish together. "So, it wasn't natural causes after all?"

"I'm just checking out all the hidden corners of recent events."

"Which is what I was doing before you came in here." Brigitta's eyes flash with an unspoken warning to leave her with her prey.

Paul gives a short, stiff chuckle with what little breath he has left. "Priceless. I should have held out a little longer and let you tear each other apart from the inside. Maybe then, AHH!!"

Brigitta's knife slashes his chest. Not deep enough to kill. Not yet.

Victoria decides to leave the information gathering to the person with the knife. Louis knows what she's searching for. If anything useful results from the cabin's torture-fest, he'll tell her.

In a rare move, Victoria gives Brigitta a nod of thanks and departs the cabin.

With the creaking of the screen door, Nicholas gets up from the bench seat. Victoria shakes her head, and Nicholas steps towards Aidan.

"Wait." Victoria says. "I'm not finished with him yet."

"Vic?" Nicholas asks.

"You may not be working for Paul, but what about Mr. Singer?"

Aidan's brow furrows. "I wasn't working with him either. I didn't even know he existed until Nicholas briefed me about what happened at The Bellamy Hotel."

"Another convenient fact." Victoria squats down in front of the dark-haired man and holds his stare. Is he showing a genuine fear of death, a fear of being found out, or both? "Let him go," she says with some reluctance. "Needless to say, Nicholas is not repaying that one million, and if I find any evidence you were involved with Mr. Singer, or I get a whiff of anything else that makes me question your loyalty, I won't be looking for his permission to kill you."

Nicholas cuts the ties off Aidan's wrists and he stumbles to his feet. "I understand."

"Good." Victoria turns to Nicholas. "Any objections to going home? I've had enough of Brigitta's torturous symphony and red isn't my colour, so a shower would be nice."

Nicholas smiles and wraps an arm around her for the short walk to the car. When the car doors open, Erik wakes from a restless nap. Aidan slips into the passenger seat and massages his tender wrists.

"Looks like Paul didn't have a hand in Father's death. He seemed genuinely surprised when I asked?"

Nicholas holds the door open as she climbs into the vehicle and pulls on the cuff of his shirt. "I figured if he was involved, he'd have either botched it like tonight, and we wouldn't be here. Or Brigitta's revenge would have been louder."

"Louder than that?"

"Love can push your rage to a whole new level."

Victoria caresses his hand on the door. She's familiar with how closely love, hate and vengeance can become intertwined.

The low roar of the engine and subtle rumble of the car careening down the road almost puts Victoria to sleep. Nicholas' face becomes blurred as she fights to stay awake. "You realize your one-million-dollar-mistake cost you Father's seat at the table, right?"

"I know. I didn't think he found out, but the latest version of his Will was dated a week after I returned the money."

"I'm sorry," Victoria says.

"Me too. Now get some rest. You have a couple of hours before we get home." He turns on her heated seat and she melts into dream land.

A whisper travels the airwaves to her ears, and she swears she hears, "It's my fault you had to come home."

Chapter Forty-One

Now

AFTER THE EVENTS OF last night's attack and massacre, the Townsends and their soldiers are sore, tired, and running on adrenaline. A few scrapes, bruises and minor flesh wounds hidden beneath their suits. The loss of one of their own weighs on their minds, but they are thankful it was their only loss.

The smell of sausages carries Victoria into the dining room. She squints as she realizes that breakfast has become the new meeting time for the inner circle. Finn's chair remains empty, but the rest of the group is intact. Brigitta looks like she slept a solid eight hours.

Unprepared for a morning meeting, Victoria is in the t-shirt and pajama shorts she had slept in. The stitches from the funeral bullet wound are visible to all.

"This is how you show up at a business meeting?" Brigitta scowls.

"Only once has breakfast been a meeting. I wasn't expecting it to be a regular occurrence." She puts her unbrushed hair into a stump of ponytail in a pathetic attempt to appease Brigitta. She stands behind her regular seat, and places her hands on the occupants' shoulder, "You're in my spot."

"That's your seat now." Nicholas points to Nathan's empty chair.

"No, it isn't. I've sat in this chair for..." She stops before revealing too much. "All my life. Now please move."

"At least she hasn't lost all sense, and knows her rightful place. Even if she looks like a ragged mess." Brigitta says from the opposite end of the table.

Victoria bends and whispers into Nicholas' ear, "Please let me toss a knife at her. I promise to hit nothing important, maybe just a shoulder."

He chuckles and stands up. Victoria steps aside to let him out. Before she can take her place, he puts his hands on her shoulders, moves her behind Nathan's seat and swaps the two chairs. "Since you want your chair so badly." He jokes.

Everyone but Brigitta chuckles. She stares at Victoria like an ice queen, seated on her throne.

The view of the room from Nathan's spot is eye opening. A full perspective of the crowd gathered, despite the table being rectangular, rather than a circle. The large windows beyond the room's entry arch reveal the driveway. She would know if anyone was approaching before the rest of the group did. The perfect spot for a ruler.

Victoria lifts the chair and moves it to the edge of the table closest to Aidan. "If I must sit here, I'm not doing so alone. You are the commander of this family. Even I have to be the figurehead outside of this place. Does anyone disagree?"

A chorus of "No Ma'am" fills the room. Brigitta grins and sips her coffee. Her long nails tap her cup.

With a smile, Nicholas moves his chair and place setting to beside Victoria, joining her at the head of the table.

Victoria raises her coffee cup to her lips and looks to Nicholas. "Well, Mr. Townsend, what are your orders?"

"First, let's eat. Then we'll discuss business."

Plates are scraped clean following round after round of Devin's world class cooking, leaving everyone more energized than when they first came in.

Nicholas pours himself another coffee and, with the porcelain cup held below his chin, speaks, "We have a drug shipment coming in today and with everything that's happened this week, we need to revise the plan. We have to trust Finn disclosed the details to Paul, and although both are dead, we haven't yet confirmed if some of Paul's crew were left out of last night's endeavours in order to continue their work. We can't risk an ambush. Nothing, and I mean nothing, can go wrong with this. If it does, the Townsend's will face ruin. Thanks to Janet's stellar interrogation skills of Mr. Laurel yesterday, we found the remains of some of our stolen gun shipments, that Paul had yet to move from a warehouse near the port of Halifax. She, Erik and I will make the arrangements for their movement and decide how we are reorganizing today's meeting."

Nicholas continues, "Vic, you'll then call our associates with the update and make sure everyone agrees."

A huff at the end of the table turns everyone's heads to Brigitta. "You should be the one making the phone calls, not her."

Nicholas goes to speak, but Victoria's hand on his thigh silences him, so that she may address Brigitta's defiance. "I would ask you to keep your comments to a minimum during meetings. Your role as observer and soldier hasn't changed. The Family voted me as Director, as such, having Nicholas fill the roll outwardly would only tarnish our reputation and strength."

Brigitta looks at Nicholas, who says nothing. She opens and closes her mouth, but no sound comes out. Instead, she purses her lips and crosses her arms.

Nicholas finishes his coffee and stands.

Those around the table mirror his actions.

"Everyone suit up and be ready for your orders. Janet and Erik, I'll meet you in the boardroom. Aidan, wait in the hall."

After everyone departs, Nicholas takes Victoria's wrist and walks her to Brigitta. He pushes Victoria into Finn's old chair and he sits in Louis's on the other side of Brigitta. "Hate each other all you want. Have your war of words. But right now, until everything has stabilized around here, please be on your best behaviour. I trust our people, but people talk and we don't need our associates or enemies feeding off your grudge."

"Things will be so much easier once Tessa is living here," Brigitta says.

Victoria's heart jumps to her throat. "I'm sorry, what?"

Nicholas runs his hand over his face and glares at Brigitta, "Tessa was supposed to move in last week, then Father died, and you came home...it didn't seem like the right time."

"Hold up. You hinted the relationship was serious, but you did not mention it was a move-onto-the-compound-and-learn-all-our-secrets serious. She wasn't even at the funeral."

"It didn't seem like the right time to tell you. I knew there would be questions if Tessa attended the wake or the funeral. Sue me for trying to not give you a reason to get back on a plane immediately."

"Right time?" Victoria pushes herself from the table and topples the chair. Footsteps echo down the hall. Victoria calls out, "Aidan, we're fine, go away." The footsteps dissipate in the distance. "Is there a ring on this mysterious woman's finger?"

Nicholas is speechless.

Brigitta is not. "Not yet, although we have it all planned out, don't we, darling?" She pats her son's hand. "Her first night here, they'll be out on the veranda of his room, overlooking the forest. And he'll get down on one knee. She'll say yes, of course. I've already made sure of that. No need for an embarrassment to become front page news of The Family gossip columns. Oh, it will be so nice to have a like-minded person around here."

Victoria moves to the window to put some distance between herself and the others. A gloomy sky threatens a storm outside like the one raging inside of her. She has so many words she wants to say, no, scream. Mostly, questions about how Nicholas could keep this from her and let Brigitta hurt her like this. With everything they've been through, what she was hearing should come from him. Brigitta's gotten her claws into him while she's been away. She knew it was likely to happen, but prayed he'd be strong enough to resist. She will have to pry each claw out of him if she has any hope of maintaining some semblance of sanity around this new woman. Tessa. Even the sound of her name gives her a headache.

Victoria's decision to extend her stay at the Townsend compound evaporates with this latest announcement. It'll be two, maybe three, against one. Torture worse than Nathan's beatings. She wants out, but she'll play Brigitta's game until she can devise a plan that ensures her survival. "Do I want to know what you mean by like-minded?"

"Oh, Tessa agrees Nicholas deserves Nathan's seat and that nothing, and no one, should stand in his way. I updated her about what's been happening around here." She turns to Nicholas. "I hope you don't mind, darling. I thought it best she knew what she was coming into."

Victoria swallows her anger and steps nose-to-nose with the woman. "What do you mean you've told her what's happening?"

"Don't you dare think because Nathan thought you were good enough for this family that you actually are."

Nicholas weasels his way between the two. "Mother, you have put us at risk by sharing things with Tessa that's best she not know." He grips Brigitta's wrist, and she wriggles in pain, "What did you tell her?"

"That you two have a past and for her to monitor Victoria."

Nicholas huffs and releases her.

Victoria senses he only did that out of a fear he'd hit his own mother for her recklessness. "Anything else?" she asks.

"She knows you were foolish teenagers who needed to be taught boundaries, but nothing that would disgust her and turn her off Nicholas."

"Great." Victoria turns away. "I can't listen to any more of this. Nicholas, you deal with her."

"That's right, run away when the walls close in." Brigitta retorts.

Unable to punch the woman, Victoria pushes her arms out to her sides. "UGH!" She stomps out of the room to the sound of Nicholas' enraged words behind her.

As she approaches Aidan, he pushes himself off the wall and waits for instructions.

"Follow me," she says. She's given up paying attention to the pain of her wound and takes the stairs two at a time. A battle between her, two women, and an army of enemies is forming. She needs all the ammunition she can get.

Chapter Forty-Two

Now

Victoria busts into her bedroom and sends hangers flying as she rips clothes off of them. For once, she wishes Nathan was here. He'd be able to put everyone in their place. Her grip tightens around a black shirt and she realizes this engagement wasn't coming out of nowhere. Nathan's death put a wrench in the plans, so he had to have known about it and supported it. Even if he was alive, one of her nightmares would still come true.

She pulls her phone from her back pocket and requests an update on the blood work she requested.

Bouncing dots appear on the screen, followed by, "I just received the vial. I should have something soon."

"Good." Victoria replies and exits her closest.

Aidan stands by the door, waiting for her next instructions.

Victoria turns on the shower and once it's warm and steam billows to the ceiling, she steps inside. "Bathroom now." She hasn't forgotten her vow of retribution for Aidan's mistake at Maxwell's, but there are more pressing matters on her mind. Plus, she wants to come up with the perfect punishment and watch him squirm while waiting.

Aidan likes his doorways, and stands awkwardly in his second one in a matter of minutes.

Victoria leaves the steamed-up shower door ajar and sticks her head out. "Sit," she orders and points to the tiled encasement of the bathtub. "Now, tell me everything you know about this Tessa person. Starting with her last name."

Aidan diverts his eyes from her fogged-up body. "Braeman."

"As in, Ewan Braeman, the Scottish politician I worked with two years ago?"

"Yes."

"Goodness gracious. Well, tell me everything and don't hold back on account of your loyalty to Nicholas. Love, or whatever this is, could be blind, and I will not let him get dragged into another debacle with a woman." Victoria returns to washing herself.

"They met in Paris," Aidan says.

A knife to her heart. That was the last time they were together.

"Nathan and Nicholas were debriefing with Mr. Braeman after you got the photos of him with the twenty-year-old daughter of the Minister of Finance. And those of him with the thirty-year-old son of the Prime Minister. Ewan brought along his daughter in the hopes they'd take pity on him, and her future, and keep the photos hidden. Nicholas obligingly accepted her invitation to the Opera and they've been flying back and forth across the Atlantic ever since."

"I must have soap in my ears, did you say the Opera?"

"If it makes you feel better, he didn't enjoy the show."

Nothing about the situation made her feel better. Victoria turns off the taps and steps out of the shower. "Who did the background work on her?"

Upon seeing her naked body, Aidan stands and whirls around. His instinctual military background places his hands behind his back, one wrist held by the hand of the other. "I did."

"You'll forgive me if I don't feel reassured by that. Is no one concerned we are blackmailing her father to ensure we can operate smoothly in Scotland?"

"We have discussed that at length. Ewan and Tessa have assured us they have no ill intentions and are more interested in getting into our lucrative line of work. We have found no evidence to suggest they are lying."

"No one has concerns they are making a power play by marrying into a powerful and wealthy crime family? That doesn't bring me any comfort. You can turn around now." Victoria's reflection in the mirror has improved since breakfast. Back in her usual tight black pants and t-shirt, she brushes the tangles from her wet curls. "No one has any concerns about this relationship at all? Nathan approved?"

"It was Nathan's idea." If Aidan recognizes Victoria hasn't referred to Nathan as Father, he keeps it to himself.

"Really?" Victoria ponders if Brigitta manipulated Nathan's senility, hoping to replace his affection for a long-lost daughter with Tessa. "What kind of schooling does Tessa have? Job? Are we working with a pretty, yet dumb, person I can manipulate, or should we have concerns she can influence Nicholas' decisions?"

"I like the insertion of 'we' into that question," he smirks.

"Don't get excited playboy. It was a figurative we. You and I are not on the same team."

"I'll earn your trust yet."

"We'll see about that. Now back to Tessa."

"Didn't you do all this research on her when protecting her father?"

"Yes, but my brain can only hold so much. I remember what she looks like from a photo, and that I didn't take her as a threat. But, for her safety, Ewan kept her away from him while I was with him. We never met. Once the job was done, I deleted the information from my mind. Now, stop stalling and fill me in."

"I'm not stalling. I was just curious. She comes from a middle-class family, but when Ewan became a politician, he made some connections. An illegal one, gave him the money necessary to ensure Tessa went to a top university. She majored in chemistry and law."

"Great, she's smart and could probably kill me without leaving a trace. I don't know if I like her, or am even more wary of her."

They make their way back into the bedroom. "How friendly is she with Brigitta?"

"I'm not sure Tessa actually likes her, but she's smart enough to get on her good side."

"So, she can play the long game." Victoria says to herself, "Something we have in common." Victoria doesn't need her leather jacket, but feels more like herself with it, so she tosses it on. "You want to earn my trust? You watch Tessa once she gets here. See if she takes a liking to you."

"You want me to seduce my boss's soon-to-be-fiancée?"

"Technically, I'm your boss. But yes, I might."

"If she's playing the long game, like you believe, I doubt that will work. At least not that quickly."

"Hmm. You're probably right. We'll have to keep that in our back pockets."

"The more you refer to us as a team, the more I think you like me."

"Ooh, you are a terrible judge of character. Now, I definitely don't trust your assessment of Tessa." She walks out of the bedroom. "There's an office that needs to be cleaned before the stacks of paper make me lose my shit on more than just Brigitta."

"Note to self. If I want to get under your skin, make a mess."

Victoria glares at Aidan. "Not funny, and for that, you get to help me."

Chapter Forty-Three

Now

Twenty banker's boxes later, Victoria and Aidan have only organized half of the paperwork in Nathan's office. Open windows and fresh spring air cannot clear the dust that is thick enough to taste.

"He really lost his mind in the end, didn't he?"

Aidan knows better than to respond or speak ill of his former boss.

Victoria collapses onto the couch, her eyes dry and she refuses to try make sense of another piece of paper. They have boxes for general business, blackmail, accounts payable, accounts receivable, assets and miscellaneous. In the brief lull, Nathan's leather captain's chair swivels on its own. "Did you see that?" Victoria asks.

"See what?"

"I swear the chair just moved." She wonders if this office makes people crazy.

"It was probably just the wind."

"Right." She rubs her eyes. "When Brigitta was on a rampage, or Nathan wanted to monitor me, I'd watch him work as I tried to make sense of my school work. He'd make calls I didn't understand, and put plans down in nice leather notebooks, only to burn them when the deal was done. I can't explain it, but this room was once peaceful."

"Is that why you want to get it organized? Try to find one area of peace in your life?"

"Hello Mr. Psychiatrist, I must say it's a little unnerving that you may have accurately assessed my motivations. Where'd you pick up those skills?"

"Years spent with diverse individuals in the military, jail, and surviving in a life with more corpses than living beings."

"Well, let's turn off that ability around me, shall we? I don't want to know the actual reasons I do things, and I don't need you highlighting their significance." To ensure Aidan doesn't assess her mental state any further, she changes the subject. "Pass me the humidor on the shelf over there."

Aidan places Nathan's cigar humidor on the now-clean table in front of Victoria. She sits on the edge of the couch and types in the security code Nathan had given her during his last visit. The lock releases. Aromas of tobacco, wood and spices waft up from lines of cigars. A wave of memories wash over Victoria and her chest tightens. She pushes back the tears, and focuses on the contents of the box.

Composing her face to hide all emotion, she pulls a smooth brown cylinder from the pile and offers it to Aidan. He accepts and leans against the desk, one ankle crossed over the other. She releases the cutter from its casement in the drawer below the cigars and chops the end of hers, before tossing it to Aidan.

White clouds waft into the air as they try to keep their cigars lit. Victoria relaxes back into the couch. "I had my first cigar when I was fourteen after distracting a man on the street, causing him to be late for a crucial meeting. I didn't know it, but as a result, Nathan won a very large contract for Mr. McKinnon. It was what set things in motion for his installation as Director of The Family. In celebration, we sat out by the pool and he gave me my very own cigar. I hated the taste of it. I still do."

"And yet you're smoking one?"

"Remember how we are not reading into my actions?"

"Right."

Victoria's phone vibrates on the table. Cigar between her fingers, she unlocks it. Her face remains calm as she reads the text, *'Definitely murder.'* And opens the link to the full blood analysis. She pays no attention to the ashes that fall on her knees, or the astray Aidan places in front of her, as she scrolls.

Before she can find the results that say how Nathan was killed, the office door opens behind her, and Nicholas enters. "Okay, we're ready…what are you doing?" Nicholas grabs Victoria's cigar and tosses it across the room.

She flings her phone aside and jumps to her feet. "What the hell? I was smoking that." She retrieves the cigar, stomping on the pile of paper it had landed on before it catches fire. Her eye twitches at the photo of a familiar property. Her heart skips a beat. She picks up the paper to make sure her tired, dry eyes aren't playing tricks on her. It looks like the same large, blue home along the coast of the Bay of Fundy that Mom and Dad took her to in Harrod's Harbour for two weeks every summer. She wonders if it's the same place and why Nathan would have the property details.

Temporarily off kilter from the text and Nicholas' unexpected action, she asks, "What's this property?"

"Forget the property," Nicholas says. "How many cigars have you had?"

The concern on his face forces Aidan to take her cigar, put both of them out and toss them into the garbage.

"Just this one. Why?" She frowns at her phone on the couch before returning her attention to Nicholas.

He closes the office door and looks at Aidan. "And you?"

"Same, just that one."

The paper secured in her hand; Victoria walks up to Nicholas. "What's wrong with the cigars?"

Nicholas rubs the scar on his neck and lowers his voice. "Please know that this is not how I wanted to tell you."

"Tell me what?" She hopes if he doesn't say it out loud, it won't be true.

"It had to be done."

"For the love of all that is holy, tell me you didn't." The veins in her neck pulsate.

"I…look…I…They're laced with cyanide."

Victoria blinks rapidly. "Poisoned?"

"Yes."

"You-"

"Yes."

"You told me the blood work came back clean. Your paperwork supported…" The room was spinning around her. Among all the secrets that surfaced after her return home, she had hoped this wouldn't be one of them. "Are we...?" Victoria points between herself and Aidan.

"If you only had the one, you'll be fine."

Victoria's body temperature rises, and she fans herself with the paper in her hand. She turns to Aidan. "Did you know about this?"

"No, Ma'am."

She considers if he'd risk a small dose of the poison to get closer to her. She decides she can worry about that later. "Wait outside."

He hesitates, but does as he's told.

"Look, I-"

Victoria tosses the paper in her hand at Nicholas' face. "Stop. I need a minute." She retrieves her phone and finishes reviewing the analysis.

"What are you-?"

She raises her hand and his question goes unfinished. The report confirms there was cyanide in Nathan's blood and it was what slowly killed him. She closes her eyes and lowers her head. Putting the phone in her back pocket, she bites the inside of her mouth. Then turns on Nicholas and pounds his chest with her fists, disregarding the volume of her voice. "You better explain everything to me. I'm sick of all these secrets you've been hiding."

Nicholas grabs her wrists. "I wanted to tell you. I tried to, at the cabin, but then Aidan woke up."

"We sat there for three hours. There was enough time to tell me under the mask of Paul's screams. The guy you were getting to verify the medical examiner's findings, did his wife really die, or was that a tactic to stall me finding out what really happened?"

"She really died. It was just...luck isn't the right word...anyway, it gave me time to figure out how to tell you."

"And you didn't think I'd take matters into my own hands to find the answers when the world is falling apart?"

"Did you undermine my authority and go behind my back?"

She tries to free herself, but his grip is strong. "Let's not talk about sneaking around. Your secrets are adding up to be more volatile than me having the blood work rushed with a trusted source. It's not like I would have shared the report I received with anyone but you. I thought we were a team. Yet, you keep this big thing from me."

"I know, but I was afraid of how you would react."

"To what you did? That you didn't tell me beforehand? Or that you didn't let me help?"

"All the above."

"Our life is complicated," she admits. "Our relationships with Nathan were convoluted, but that doesn't mean you can exclude me from this. I feel like I don't know you anymore. You're making poor business decisions. You're apparently marrying this Tessa woman, and now, Nathan's death, or shall I say murder. What's going on with you? You used to tell me everything."

He releases her wrists and backs away from her. "We've barely spoken in five years. How was I supposed to tell you how bad things were getting, when it's hard to find time for myself?"

"Yet, you can get away to be with Tessa?" Victoria disliked how petty she sounded, but what he was telling her wasn't adding up.

"I don't know what to say. I thought I was handling it fine on my own. That I was protecting you, if the truth comes out. Knowing these walls really had ears, and not just Father's, I did the right thing."

"Oh, don't patronize me. You didn't tell me because you wanted to be the hero." She pours herself some of Nathan's whiskey, but before she gulps down the amber liquid, she assesses the contents and decides it's probably safer not to consumer it and returns the crystal glass to its tray.

"Father was making decisions that would have a negative impact on The Family, on us. If I hadn't intervened before they were put into action, we'd be ruined."

"Like the decision where you lost one million dollars?"

"That was different. If Father kept going, our associates would have noticed. It was hard enough keeping them in the dark for the last few months. We'd have lost everything."

"You mean you would have lost everything? All you ever wanted was to run this family. The Family. The power. The money. The prestige. How did that work out for you?"

"Don't."

"Don't what? Perhaps he made the right choice to alter his Will. It appears you've lost your freakin' mind, too." She needs to do something with her hands to expunge the energy coursing through her. Once again, she starts stacking papers.

"You weren't here. You don't know what it was like."

"Yes, I do." Victoria can't be outraged at Nicholas for keeping a major secret when she had one of her own. "He came to see me three months ago, in England."

Nicholas runs his palm over his face. "He told us he was going up to New Glasgow."

"He came to me instead. He warned me someone was trying to kill him. Maybe even messing with his mind. Making him forget things."

"Cyanide doesn't make a person go crazy."

"Maybe not, but after a few days with me, his mind seemed to clear up a bit. He was called back before we could really test our theory."

"I swear if you say another person infiltrated this family, I will burn this property to the ground." Nicholas says.

"Other than your murderous revelation, I have no evidence anyone else was after Nathan, now that Finn and Paul are taken care of. Maybe the cyanide messed with him more than you thought. Or, like you said, his paranoia returned. No matter what it was, you should have told me. You could have sent an S.O.S. Had Don fill in for me for a while. Hell, you're flying to Scotland all the time. A brief diversion to fill me in wouldn't have been so hard."

"Not that simple."

"Are you kidding me?" Victoria says.

"I thought you might tell him my plan."

"You trust me that much, do you? Why would I tell Nathan you were planning on killing him?"

"To avoid returning home."

"Maybe if you kept me apprised of what was happening, I would have trusted that you were doing the right thing. Hell, after everything he put us through, I might have come home to help make it happen."

"No, you wouldn't have. It was a tense time, and I didn't want you using the information to facilitate your staying away forever."

"You don't know what I would have done. Even if I hadn't returned, I wouldn't have told him. I wanted him dead just as much as you, apparently."

"But can't you see why I couldn't take the chance?"

"I suppose." Victoria's blood starts to cool. It's impossible to change the past. Nicholas did what he thought was best and there is no way to reverse it. "How did you know the code to the humidor?"

"The day you were brought here, 11-12-03, wasn't very hard to guess."

"I suppose. What about the cigars? How did you figure to use them?"

"Now, don't get mad."

"Oh, you did not tell Tessa you were seriously considering killing him." Furious, she hurls books at Nicholas. All her work organizing Nathan's bookshelves was for nothing. "How could you?"

He ducks, shielding himself with his arms. "I'd trust her with my life."

Victoria can't believe what she's hearing. Someone has replaced her. She's not sure what she expected after being away for so long, but the pain didn't hurt any less. "After two years seeing her off and on, you trust her with your life? What else have you told her? Does she know about me, the real me?"

"No. Although, she noticed from some photos you don't really look like the rest of the family."

"Great, we have a detective on our hands. If she's making comments like that, it means she's looking for something. Loose threads to pull, trying to reveal secrets."

"Not everyone is out to get us. It was just a normal conversation."

Victoria glares at Nicholas. She can't believe he's ignoring the red flags. "How long had you been poisoning him?"

"Not long, couple months tops."

She wonders if Tessa had used her knowledge of chemistry to add another ingredient to the concoction that killed Nathan to mess with his memory. "You need to get rid of these cigars before someone else smokes them. Or worse, figures out what's in them and you become the target of blackmail. Thankfully, I doubt anyone would be stupid enough to go to the police." Victoria thrusts open the office door, her leather jacket over her shoulder.

"I need to go for a walk to process all of this. Get my head on straight, then I'll come discuss the plan for tonight."

Aidan pushes himself off the stairs. "You okay?"

"Hmph." Victoria storms off in the direction of the backyard and he dutifully follows.

The crisp night air does little to sooth her. It takes everything inside Victoria not to breakdown. She's been kept in the dark and Nicholas acts like it's acceptable.

Before coming back to the compound, she'd told herself it would be a quick trip. In and out. Now, Nicholas' plan has backfired and she sees no way out. Not even being tethered to The Family from afar seems to be an option.

She's circled the expansive yard twice, Aidan a few metres behind, and the same questions keep rolling around in her mind. How could she trust Nicholas to keep any other secrets? Hell, if he could kill Nathan, how does she know he won't try to kill her so he can finally have his rightful throne?

CHAPTER FORTY-FOUR

NOW

THE NORTH-EAST CORNER OF the cleared land, just before the tree line, houses a temperature-controlled, black, double-wide, bunkie. Like The Barn, it appears to be a standard building, but within its walls is anything but normal.

Victoria turns on her heels and Aidan stops on his tiptoes to prevent plowing her over after speed walking to keep up with her pace.

"You stay here. This conversation is not for your ears." Victoria instructs.

"Yes, Ma'am." Aidan stands at ease, legs shoulder width apart and hands behind his back in the field between the barracks and the armoury.

Victoria cringes at the use of Ma'am; however, it creates a hierarchy and a semblance of respect. Both are imperative if she is going to keep everything together until she has time to analyze her situation and make a plan that is best for her. For now, it is business as usual.

She knows Janet will be taking an inventory of their weapons, and rather than go back to the house and speak with Nicholas, she decides to kill two birds with one stone. Find out the plan for tonight's shipment and figure out if the woman can be trusted.

At the unexpected footsteps, Janet looks up from a crate of weapons, puts a check-mark on the paper on her clipboard and nods, her face calm and collected. "If we have a few people with grenades and rifles around the perimeter, on top of our handguns, no one is taking this shipment."

"Agreed. Thank you for stepping into the Strategic Coordinator role. I'll discuss it further with Nicholas after tonight, but we may need you to fill in on a more permanent basis for a while."

"Anything you need." Janet's mouth does not give away any jubilation she may feel at the opportunity to move up, but the twinkle in her eyes reveals all.

"Now, don't go getting excited. You are not jumping up the ranks with the shit-show that the last few days have been. I just need to assess a few things, and make those who made mistakes pay for them. If I'm satisfied Aidan has done his penance, it's possible he'll be back." Victoria runs her fingers along the barrel of a rifle hanging on the inside of a secret door. The other side contains gardening tools to fool a quick search. "I don't trust you. Not one-hundred percent. I know you want to prove yourself, so I'm not worried about tonight. It takes a lot to earn my trust. Moving up will not be easy. I've learned a lot about you since my arrival, and I suspect some is true and some is not. What you tell me now, will determine if you stay or if you have to find refuge with your aunt."

"I understand," Janet says.

All the secret compartments along the walls of the bunkie and underfoot are open. The soldier continues taking her inventory.

"How has the return rate of weapons been? Given Finn's allegiance with Paul, do you think he's been syphoning out anything?"

"No, not that I can tell. We've only had a few damaged or lost items but they had valid explanations. Nothing that resulted in the prescribed gruelling punishments for losing a weapon. Come to think of it, I'm not sure any of those were used by Finn."

"Right. I see we've made some updates to our building."

Janet looks around. "A bit. With some of our weapons becoming sleeker, we optimized the storage space. Constructed even smaller, thinner compartments inside the building. It takes a bit more time to unload and reload, but hopefully it helps them go undiscovered in a search."

"I'm confident if law enforcement get's the opportunity to access our land, they will tear open more than walls. Let's hope it never comes to that or, by chance, what they find are the legally registered ones." Hands behind her back, Victoria steps in front of Janet. "Tell me about your relationship with Aidan."

"Aidan? There's no relationship there. It's strictly work."

"Is that so? And what about late-night talks about your strategy to get ahead around here?"

The freckles on Janet's cheeks are hidden by a red hue. "Is that what he's telling you? He's lying." The pencil in Janet's hand snaps in half, and a crate of weapons feels the brunt of her steel-toed boot. She regains her composure. "There have been no talks about that. Hell, we barely talk about anything outside of work or joking when we're playing poker. Which he rarely does. Look, I'm just thankful that your father took me in. I wouldn't jeopardize that. I swear."

Victoria wonders if she's vexed because she's been caught, or because someone has attacked her character. "What about your time with Nicholas? What was that about if not an attempt at upward movement?" Victoria asks.

"Well...that was...gosh, people really know everything that happens around here."

"Yes, we do. Now talk." Victoria's patience was already thin, and there was no room for skirting around the truth.

"I guess it was loneliness."

"There are a multitude of men around here. Women, if you want, as well. Why Nicholas? And I don't have all day." Victoria picks up a handgun and cocks the barrel.

"Right, well. I...uh. It wasn't a power move, I swear. I liked him. He helped me transition and get settled here in Nova Scotia and on the compound. We got close. That's it, I swear. But it's over now."

"I know. The problem I'm having is, I don't know how I'm to believe that you aren't in an alliance with Aidan to better the position of the Harris family. Strategically, it makes sense. It would be what I would do." Victoria rests the gun on Janet's chest.

Janet raises her hands in the air. One still clings to the clipboard. "I'm not sure what else to say, but I promise, on my life, I'm not working with anyone but your family. I don't even talk to my aunt much, and when we do, she doesn't ask about what's going on here. We are both loyal to the Townsends. To you."

Victoria's eyes bore into Janet's. There's no proof of Finn's allegation, and Janet's shaking body and trembling lip do not appear to be an act. Victoria lowers the gun and steps back. "Alright. I'll leave it for now. But, if I hear anything else that leads me to think you just lied to me, I won't hesitate to pull the trigger."

"Understood."

Victoria tosses her next question as nonchalantly as she can muster to mask her annoyance, which isn't much. "What do you know about Tessa Braeman?"

"Not a lot. I've seen her with Nicholas a couple of times, but they keep to themselves. I didn't get a good feeling from her when I was introduced to her. None of us women did. The way she glares and talks down to us, it feels like we are all her enemy. I stay away from her as much as possible."

"Hmm. Okay." She wonders if she could come to rely on Janet. Perhaps the two could work to remove a common problem? "Well, we better prepare for tonight. Fill me in."

Twenty minutes later, Victoria is up to speed, and ready to head to the meeting location outside of Bridgewater. Janet sends a text and within moments, people are loading up vehicles with the weapons. The armoury locked; Janet finally notices Aidan standing alone in the grass. "Ma'am, do you mind if I re-break Aidan's nose for spreading those lies? I'm not one to let someone get away with sullying my name."

Victoria grins, "As much as I would love to see that, he wasn't the one who was telling lies. At least, not that one."

"Who then?"

"Finn."

"Oh, well, I guess the punching bag will have to do. Unless, we run into trouble later." Janet smirks and pats the gun in her shoulder holster.

Victoria smiles at the thought of Janet using physical violence to soothe her anger. Her reaction would usually be the same. She nods for Aidan to follow as the group attending the meeting piles into vehicles. Before she can join them, her cell phone rings. With almost everyone who would call her at the compound, her stomach churns.

"Hello?"

"Victoria, Irving here."

"Hello Mr. McKinnon. How are you?" Victoria walks away from the vehicle to keep the conversation private. "Is there something I can help you with?"

"I have a plane waiting for you, under the name Sally and Trevor Watkins, at our private airfield. I need you on it in an hour. We must discuss the fallout from The Family meeting."

Victoria swallows hard. "Of course. I'll have someone else handle tonight's shipment. Shall I bring Nicholas along?"

"No. Just you and whatever bodyguard you choose. It won't be a long meeting. You'll be back in a few hours, so no need to pack a bag."

"Right."

With his instructions delivered, Irving McKinnon ends the call.

Victoria looks at the time. The group needs to leave in ten minutes if they are going to get to the location and set up before the vendor arrives. "Janet, I want you and Rufus to take everyone to the rendez-vous point and get ready. I'll be sending Nicholas along to handle the meeting in a few moments."

"You're not coming?" Janet asks.

"Not anymore."

She turns and bolts into the house as the whirring of engines dissipates in the distance. "Nicholas, front door, now!"

With rosy cheeks and the click of his dress shoes, Nicholas appears as beckoned. He opens his mouth to speak, but Victoria won't let him. "You're going to the meeting."

"I thought you-"

"Irving called. I need to go to New Brunswick."

"Shit. Wait, why am I not going with you?"

"He said to leave you here."

"I really fucked this up, didn't I?"

"Not necessarily. But we don't have time to talk about it. The vendor will be at the location soon, and I need to get on a plane. There's no point in upsetting Irving with me being late. The last thing we want is him meddling.

Once the meeting's done, call Aidan with an update. I'll let you know how the trip went when I get back. I won't be long."

Nicholas squeezes Victoria's wrist. "Thank you."

Still angered by his secrets, she pulls away. "Just get to the meeting." Before she returns outside, she looks back. "And don't screw this up."

Nicholas watches as Victoria's car passes through the gate. Her being mad at him was never a good thing. Even if he knew she'd come to understand what he did, eventually.

He wants to scream. Instead, he balls his hands into fists as tight as he can to release his tension. It doesn't work.

Nothing was going as he and Tessa had planned. The only good thing to come out of it was that Victoria was sticking around for a while.

But now, Irving wanted to meet with her, alone. He was being cut out, and if Irving didn't want him at the top, he never would be. It would be like the King of England telling the world his first-born child wasn't good enough and skipping to his spare. Banished from the life he knew. The life he desired and deserved.

He didn't want to think about what he'd have to do if he and Victoria couldn't work their disagreement or the situation out.

CHAPTER FORTY-FIVE

NOW

THE LUSH, GREEN LANDS of New Brunswick are saying goodnight to the sun when the small private jet transporting Victoria and Aidan touches down on an airstrip in the middle of nowhere. Bringing Aidan along, allowed her to keep up the charade of her position within the Townsends and she can monitor him. Even if she was coming around to the fact that he appears to want to protect her.

As exasperated as she is with Nicholas, she'd never forgive herself if Aidan is a turncoat and kills him. Or worse, if given the time, the two of them worked together to plot against her. She scrunches her eyes closed and inhales deeply. She's been in power for two days and the paranoia is already setting in. Silently, she vows it will not eat her alive like she saw it do to Nathan over the years.

Before they can step off the plane, Irving McKinnon steps onto it.

"Good evening, Victoria." They shake hands and he motions for them to sit on the cream, leather couch at the front of the cabin. "You look...well. I see you still don't conform to our request for business attire."

Victoria bites her tongue. "Makes it easier for an enemy to underestimate me."

"Touché." Irving looks Aidan up and down a few times before taking a seat across from them. "Nice to see you again, Aidan Fraser. Nathan spoke highly of you. Too bad you couldn't save his life a second time."

Aidan bows his head and stays silent.

"I also hear you allowed our Victoria here to get shot. You're not doing so well these days. What explanation do you have for that?"

Victoria pinches her lips together as the veins in Aidan's neck throb. Perhaps Irving will deliver Aidan's retribution and she can simply enjoy the show.

"Sir, I take full ownership of my mistakes. If I could have prevented Nathan's death, I would have. Regarding Victoria, I will say that I tried to steer her away from the bomb. In hindsight, I should have dragged her to safety."

"Oh, I would have liked to have seen that. Victoria is not easily moved, now, are you?"

"You should have been at the compound the other day. Aidan wasn't afraid to toss me over his shoulder that time."

"Under Nicholas' orders, of course," Aidan adds.

"Ah yes, Nicholas. The reason we are here." One of Irving's three body-guards saunters to the back of the plane and fixes three drinks, hands them to the passengers, and returns to his position at the open door, while the others remain at the bottom of the steps.

Before Irving can continue, Victoria speaks, "Perhaps this conversation should be contained to the two of us?"

"Do you not trust your man here?" Irving stares at her over the top of his glasses.

"I haven't been back long enough to trust anyone."

"Well, if you brought him along, you trust him enough. And if he's going to ensure your safety, he should hear what I have to say." Irving directs his next comment to Aidan. "However, if I find out a word about this conversation leaves this plane, you will pray for the torture Nathan's men enacted on his enemies. At least it was swift. I take my time, years even, if necessary."

Confident of his audience's attention, Irving continues, "I was the one who approved your father's Will, after he had it updated to name you his heir." He sips his drink. The revelation hangs in the air.

Victoria grips the arm of the couch she sits on. She shouldn't be surprised Irving would be involved in the decision of who his closest ally in The Family would be. Yet, her chest tightens, and she pushes back the tears of frustration and hopelessness threatening to break through after a day of skeletons being released from closets. One mistake, and Nicholas was pushed out. Once again, she's forced into a life, a role, she doesn't want.

She wants to beg him to reconsider but she knows her efforts would be fruitless, so she stays quiet.

"That reminds me, thank you Aidan for bailing Nicholas out; if there's a next time, let the boy learn his lesson."

"Yes, Sir." Aidan nods.

Victoria assesses the older man in front of her. She hasn't worked with him much directly. Nathan had overseen the management of The Family, with little interference from Irving. But she knew that he had a handle on almost everything that was happening within his organization. He was also one of the few privy to the fact that her real name was Emily. Nathan had known better than to keep that large of a secret from the one man who could ruin someone's life with the snap of his fingers.

The way Nathan had told it to Victoria, was that Irving was furious a kidnapping plan was formulated without his knowledge and it took three years of repentance and reduced percentage of earnings for Nathan to re-gain his trust.

Now this kind-eyed man held her life in his hands. What would he do with it?

"Victoria, you should know that I recommended your appointment over Nicholas."

She blinks a few times and uses the liquor to release her dry tongue. "But why?"

"We needed you back. Nathan saw it, and I saw it. Yes, you've done great work on the other side of the Atlantic, but the criminal landscape here is changing. Politicians aren't as easy to buy as they used to be, and rumour has it multiple branches of law enforcement are getting ready to make a move on the Townsends. It doesn't look like they can connect anything to me, but we need to protect what we have. Nicholas is ready to take over the status quo. You're a fighter, and I need you to steer us into the future."

If only he knew how much of a fighter Nicholas really is, Victoria thinks.

Irving continues. "Nathan and I were collaborators. We may not have seen or spoken to each other frequently, but together we always decided what the best course of any major action was. I hope you and I can get to that point in our relationship. For now, you will have a direct line to me for any significant decisions." He hands her a cell phone. "The only number programmed in there, 'Nick's Donair', goes directly to me. Not my soldiers, but me. The shipments and endeavours already on the books continue as you see fit. If you want to open the doors up to a new venture, new partnerships or extend existing ones, you will run everything by me. That includes any thoughts you have for filling the vacancies in your inner circle. We can't have another Finn situation. With the loss of Gus, during the gunfight at Maxwell's, God rest his soul, you have two vacancies to be filled. I will approve of them both. Questions?"

Victoria clears her throat. Her head is buzzing with questions about The Family, her power, Nathan, but she doesn't want to come across as questioning Irving's authority or ignorant of the full picture. Instead, she sticks to the topics brought forward. "Do you know when the police are coming at us?"

"No, but as soon as I do, I'll call. In the meantime, I recommend destroying or moving anything incriminating."

Victoria nods in agreement. "Nicholas and I were planning on running things together. Partners, but with me as the public figure, in adherence to Father's, and I suppose your decision. Our goal is to get The Family's trust in Nicholas back. Most, if not all of it, has been taken away. I suppose you are not in agreement with that approach?"

Irving finishes his drink and places the crystal glass in the mahogany-ringed cup holder. "It's not a dangerous plan. We need people to trust Nicholas enough to work with him. He can be your number two, with all the power that affords him, but your crew and The Family need to see one leader."

A headache forms at the base of Victoria's skull. Her plan is falling apart. As much as she wants vengeance for being kept in the dark about Nicholas' plan, she wouldn't take it as far as removing his power. Irving's orders will crush him. A delicate situation that she will need to massage to smooth over. "I know you are aware of my...unique relationship with Nicholas. I want to ensure his anger and disappointment at the outcome doesn't turn into a mutiny. Do you have any concerns if I tell him we've altered course on leadership? I'll have to disclose the potential law enforcement threat so we can prepare, but your involvement in my leadership will be kept secret. He knows I'm here and he'll know we didn't meet to talk about the weather."

"That's fine." Irving stands and buttons up his suit jacket. "Look at us collaborating already."

Victoria and Aidan mirror his upward movement. "Tessa Braeman, do you approve?"

"Ah, Nicholas' soon to be fiancée. Nathan and I both had our concerns about her, but nothing we can substantiate. On paper, it looks like a good business decision. You keep an eye on her and if anything, and I mean anything, comes up, you contact me."

"Yes, sir." Victoria decides to try her luck with veering outside the lines of controlled conversation. Her, and her people's lives, were under threat by more than the police. "Any chance you know anything about the Mr. Singer that attacked my client in England?"

"All indications are it was a well thought out alias. My best people haven't been able to track down who he worked for. Or if his intended target was only your client. I haven't heard of any rumblings of an international threat coming our way. There haven't been anymore attempts on Mr. Conrad's life, so you could consider bringing Don, and your crew home. We will keep our eyes open and ears peeled. I suggest you do the same."

"Yes, sir."

Irving takes Victoria's hand in his. "Your father was like a son to me. I may not have been much of a grandfather, but I'm definitely an ally. We can be unstoppable together, and I am here to protect you. I want you to know that. Provided you listen to me."

"Thank you," was all Victoria could muster. For five years, Nathan had minimal involvement in the protection racket, and she had made her own rules. Now, she was a bird in a cage to be let out when her master tells her. Her jaw clenches at the thought of confinement once more.

Chapter Forty-Six

Now

With the wheels of Irving McKinnon's plane back in Nova Scotia, Victoria heads for the warm glow of the blue and red neon lights in Trudy's Bar. You wouldn't call it a dive, but you wouldn't call it the finest bar in Nova Scotia, either. It sat somewhere in the middle and felt like home to locals and tourists alike.

Boots, broken bottles, chairs and canes have scratched the stain on the wooden floor. The deterioration adds to the charm, as does the squeak of the front door.

Victoria is hit with the smell of fried food and the combination of wheat, barley, and hops. She's grateful that it masks the stale perfume and sweat from the patrons.

Thuds echo from darts hitting the boards lining the wall of a room to the right of the entrance. Hoots and hollers cheer on those vying for another person to buy the next round of drinks. She can't help but smile at the familiarity.

She appreciates that everyone who walks into Trudy's is on the same level. Whether or not they are law-abiding citizens. No hierarchy. No power. Just good booze, music on the jukebox, and a place where everyone can avoid their problems.

Victoria's three tequila's-on-the-rocks in to Aidan's one, and he's been nursing it for an hour. As he's driving, she doesn't pressure him to consume it.

The warm yellow lights around the bottles of liquor cast an ethereal shadow on Aidan's bearded face. She leans over to him. "I don't think I've seen you drink anything since I've been home."

"That's because I don't drink. Too many times something bad went down and I was too slow on the draw."

She downs the remains of her glass. "Smart. Then I'll take that off your hands. Marcus, get my friend here some soda water. And toss in an umbrella fun." The bartender winks and adds a cherry on a sword and an umbrella to the bubbly water. Victoria laughs and steals the cherry. "I like to think that one really hard night of drinking, every once in a while, is good for a person. Let go of some steam and ensure any pent-up frustration doesn't get directed to the wrong person."

"I find other ways to release my frustration."

"Why, Mr. Fraser, are you hitting on me?"

Aidan smiles and takes back his cherry before Victoria can consume it. He uses his teeth to pull the cherry off the blade of the sword, places the plastic decoration on the bar and sticks the umbrella behind his ear. "I meant boxing."

"Right." Victoria admits she's slightly disappointed, which is alarming. Last night, she didn't trust an ounce of the man beside her.

Aidan's phone rings. He looks at Victoria, who nods at him to take the call. He scans the room for any threats, and not finding any, steps outside.

She'd texted Nicholas to advise they had returned and that she'd update him tomorrow on her conversation with Irving. In her current mood, she knew if the conversation was held tonight, she might reveal information that could get them both killed.

"Another tequila, my friend." She pushes her glass towards Marcus, who adds a couple of ounces of Victoria's favourite liquor.

"You're having a good night. Nice to see you around here again. Are you back long?"

"Not if I can help it, but I'm not sure I'll have much say in the matter, so you'll likely be seeing me again."

"I'll keep the good stuff stocked, then." Marcus' dark eyes have a mischievous glow that Victoria has a hard time resisting. The desire to relive her time with him is what drew her into the arms of bartenders around the world.

"I was sorry to hear about your father."

And just like that, she lost any lust she had for her old flame.

"Thank you." Victoria scans the room to make sure no one's listening. "I doubt I need to say it, but nothing about our arrangement changes."

"I appreciate that."

"I still have to review the books, but I suspect there will be no issues with the monthly payments. I hear the man responsible for your wife's death hasn't been having a good time in prison lately. Seems Nathan's annual apology to you went ahead as scheduled." Victoria couldn't help but admire Nathan's devotion to his community. As a teenager, she thought it was all an act, but over the years, she knew most of it was genuine. Especially when bystanders got caught up in the crossfire. Like Marcus's wife.

Although the forensic reports proved it was Nathan's enemy who killed Marcus's wife, Nathan took responsibility for the tragic death that occurred during a shootout between his soldiers and an enemy's.

"Anyone saying anything I need to know about?"

"Not really. Most people were shocked when Nathan died so young. Otherwise, they hope the Townsend generosity doesn't stop with him."

"It won't."

"Anyone new in town?" Victoria wasn't worried about tourists. They are common, but they move on quickly. Anyone new in town, and the Townsends need to know. Strangers could be completely innocent, or trying to set up shop, but Nathan, now Victoria, didn't want to wait long to figure out which one.

"No. Although I hear Nicholas' new friend will be a permanent installation."

"Where did you hear that?" Victoria's skin crawls at the thought. She wonders if there's a way she can postpone the engagement. Maybe play up the tumultuous times the Townsends face right now?

"Paul was in here a few times with his men. He can be a loose cannon, that one."

"Has he said anything else?"

"No, but I'll keep my ears open as usual when he comes in."

Victoria doesn't tell him that Paul won't be a patron anymore. Instead, she moves on to ensuring there have been no threats to Marcus, his family, or his establishment. "Have you had any problems lately? I can get a couple of people to reinforce our protection agreement."

"No one has tried to encroach on your area. I think any retribution for landing Trudy's killer in prison left the minds of that crew long ago."

"Things have a way of lingering and festering. We're here if you need anything. How are the children?"

Marcus's shoulders slacken and Victoria recognizes the weight of the grief he carries. "They're well. Getting big. We're grateful for the house that Nathan bought us. They've definitely outgrown our old one. Even if all the memories were there."

"Memories are in our minds, not a location."

He brushes some hair behind her ear. "When did you get all sentimental?"

She looks down at her drink. "I'm not."

He smiles and walks down the bar to a patron holding up an empty beer glass.

Aidan retakes his place at the bar. "The meeting went as planned." His eyes focus in on Marcus. "What's between you two?"

"Nothing."

"You just let anyone touch your face?"

The liquor has reddened her cheeks and hides her blushing. "Moving on. No more talking about business or my life. Let's play some pool." They walk over to the table on the opposite side of the bar from the dart throwing drunks.

"Are you any good?"

"Am I any good? Not really. But I need to keep my hands busy, or else I'll finish that bottle quicker than I'd like."

They split the wins, two games apiece. "Don't let me win, that's patronizing," she says.

"I didn't let you win."

"Right, and that eight ball just fell into the corner pocket of its own volition when I still had six balls to drop?"

"The lighting in here is terrible. I mistook it for the solid purple four."

"Sure you did. Unlike Nicholas, placating me only makes me angry. So, rack them up and don't play down to me."

"You got it."

The next game went by so fast Victoria had only sunk one ball before Aidan was done. "I see you've played a lot of pool."

"You said not to play down."

"Maybe just a little."

"So, you are like your brother."

"Oh, I'm not like Nicholas. You can still win the game, but it would be nice for me to play it," Victoria chalks the tip of her pool cue. "Speaking of Nicholas, what would it take for you to not hold back your punches and kick his ass in this week's training?"

"I thought we weren't talking business?"

"We aren't. We're talking about retribution. Or a comeuppance, if you will."

"Didn't he receive that when they named you Heiress of the Townsend Kingdom?"

"That's business. That's what we aren't talking about."

"Noted." Aidan racks up the balls "And if I take Nicholas down this week, what assurances do I have he won't enact his own retribution on me?"

"None." With the tequila bringing her guard down, she continues, "I seem to have lost my control over him. So you'd be doing it with the possibility that Erik, and a few others, wake you up in the middle of the night to teach you a lesson."

"I'm not seeing the upside to your proposal."

"The upside is, you make something actually go my way since I've been back. Maybe earn a little of my trust."

"Well, if that's the upside." He winks and then wipes his smile off his face while looking over Victoria's shoulder.

With a wobble, she turns on her toes to find Constable Jefferson in full RCMP uniform, hands on his hips and a large, knowing grin on his face. Beside him stands a scrawny young man who looks as though he's not old enough to have shaved.

"Constable. Or should I say Superintendent? Nice to see you and congratulations on your promotion. It's good to see decent people making it in this world."

"Victoria, always good to see you. Condolences for your father."

"Thank you."

"I hear you're the new boss."

"Is that what you heard? I see myself as just another hardworking member of the family contributing to the growth of our society."

"You always were the thoughtful one of the group." He steps so close their toes touch. "I sure am sorry I never got to put handcuffs on Nathan. I guess I'll just have to reserve them for you."

"This girl loves some silver bracelets, but I'll let you keep those. The last time we used them, you were stuck to the bed for hours before anyone found you." She looks around Jefferson's body and directs her next words to the young cop. "Be careful with those things. Probably best if you only use them for legitimate work purposes."

The young man's Adam's apple dances up and down while he blushes. Jefferson rubs the back of his neck. "We had some fun times back in the day, but don't think that's going to have any influence on me working to put you in prison where you belong."

"I appreciate the cordial notification of your intentions. Now, are you going to follow the rules of Trudy's and stop trying to intimidate the patrons, or do I need to call the couple at the end of the bar over here? I know they've been dying to get their hands all over you." Victoria winks.

Jefferson raises his hands as though someone is pointing a gun at him. "I said my piece."

"Thank you." Victoria retakes her place at the bar. "Three tequila's to-go please, Marcus."

"Are you sure you haven't had enough? You've had half of the bottle."

"It's just what the doctor ordered. Now, please don't make me beg."

He pours her a triple and watches her drink it in one gulp.

Victoria turns to Aidan. "Let's go."

"Where to?"

"Hell. I mean home."

While protected from the elements inside Trudy's, a storm has moved in off the east coast of the United States. Walls of water make the drive slow. The yellow paint on the roads is invisible. As Aidan avoids fishtailing and driving into the ditch, Victoria turns in her seat to face him. "What's your deal? I mean, outside of what's in your file. What was the turning point that made you decide the military wouldn't turn your life around?"

"Capitalism."

Victoria rolls her eyes. "Capitalism? Isn't that the entire world's problem?"

"That too. With my past, the path I was on, I wouldn't amount to more than 2nd lieutenant with a mediocre salary. Meanwhile, the rich get richer and they aren't sharing it with the poor. Why should I spend my one life working my ass off so someone else can profit off of it?"

"Isn't that exactly what you're doing with us?"

"At a very high premium. As you know, I found a lucrative opportunity to move some product while serving out my time with the military. Unfortunately, I didn't do the best job of covering my tracks. One of my partners figured out where I stored my supply and turned on me. They received an honourable discharge, while I spent three years in prison. But you know all of that and what came next."

"How lucky for us that your good behaviour got you out of jail early." Blame the alcohol, or Victoria's exhaustion at always suspecting the worst in a person, but she lets a part of her wall down. "Before you enter the code in the gate, what would you say to running away? Do you think they'd find us?"

Aidan retracts his wet arm into the vehicle, and turns to her while his left side takes a shower in the storm. "You don't like it here?"

Victoria reveals an artful smile. "You may have been trying to blend into the background this week, but I know your eyes and ears are always working." She leans over the middle console. Her vision is a bit blurred, but she's sure he doesn't slink away. She wants to kiss him, just to see if she can, but she stops herself and leans back in her seat. "If you haven't picked up on my disdain for this place, then you aren't as smart as I thought you were. How disappointing. Now, it seems, I'm stuck here for the foreseeable future. Unless, you want to take over? Pretend to be me. I'm sure no one will notice."

"Haha. I do look good in a Tragically Hip t-shirt, but I'm sure they'll notice you've grown a full beard overnight."

"Ah, right, that." Her guard back up, she waves her hand and Aidan unlocks the gate. The trip up the driveway is silent.

Victoria stumbles into a quiet and darkened house. The occupants having gone to bed; she knows Erik or Louis have left a few lights on to guide her path.

Aidan occasionally grabs her arm to make sure she stays upright. "I see those last drinks have kicked in."

"I'm fine." Victoria says as she pushes him away and eyes the painted Egyptian vase by the base of the stairwell. "Oh, I've always hated this vase. Oops," with a swift push it shatters on the floor and the sound reverberates up the tall entry way, bounces off the ceiling and echoes in their ears.

"Let's get you to bed." Step by step, with a few slips in between, Aidan ushers Victoria up the stairs.

Out of breath at the top, she feels like she's hiked a mountain. "We really need to put in an elevator."

Nicholas stands against the railing in his blue monogrammed bathrobe. The stern look on his face goes unnoticed by Victoria. Aidan shrugs and mouths, "I'm sorry."

"Had a good night, did you?" Nicholas asks.

With the help of the wall, Victoria stands upright. "Why, yes, I did."

"You know that vase was worth $25,000?"

"Pennies then."

"You're incorrigible when you're drunk."

"And you're a filthy liar when you're not."

A woman an inch shorter than Nicholas, with long locks of curly brown hair, steps out of Nicholas' bedroom. Her rose silk house coat barely reaches her knees. She places her left hand on his shoulder and an enormous diamond protrudes from a golden band. "Everything alright out here?"

Victoria thrusts out her chest and pushes her messy hair out of her face. Her eyes focused on the intruder in her life.

"Vic, this is-"

"Tessa. Otherwise, you have some explaining to do," Victoria sneers.

"Tessa, meet Victoria," Nicholas says.

"Pleasure, I'm sure," Tessa says.

"Pleasure? Oh, I know they've warned you I'm anything but a pleasure. Well, I'm not dealing with all of this right now." Victoria turns and Aidan has to catch her before she hits the floor. "Goodnight."

"Is she always like that?" Tessa's birdlike voice trails behind Victoria.

"Only when I hurt her." Nicholas guides Tessa back into his room.

Victoria stumbles around her room, tugging off clothing and tossing it haphazardly aside. She falls, sprawling, onto the bed. The room starts to spin. She inches towards the lamp on her bedside table to silence the light when a thin stack of paper catches her eye.

With both hands, she holds it above her head. She squints so she can focus on the words. It's Nathan's will.

Her mind is a flurry with alcohol, so she has a hard time concentrating, but she knows what she needs to find.

She confirms the document was dated a week after Nicholas made the bad lobster deal. They can't use a diminished capacity to negate the document as the error in judgement was before the poisoning started.

It takes a few pages, but then she sees it. Even in her drunken state, there's no mistaken what it means. "As for my business, it's monetary and physical assets, I appoint, as my successor, Victoria Townsend. She shall lead the family for a period of five years, no less a day, before she can name a successor in the event she wishes to make a change in leadership prior to her death."

Five years.

She wasn't sure if she could hold death at bay that long.

CHAPTER FORTY-SEVEN

NOW

Grateful for her metabolism, water, painkillers and a concoction of ingredients she didn't dare ask Aidan about when he brought her the cup of green liquid, Victoria's world ceases spinning and she feels more functional. She stands in her closet, considering the move she should make. She is determined not to be seen looking like a sloppy mess after the show she put on last night. Lord knows Brigitta would make sure Tessa looks her best.

Victoria considers a powerful business suit. With no business outside of the home to attend to, her outfit would be like waving a red flag of desperation. Brigitta would see how Nicholas and Tessa's engagement had gotten under her skin. There was no way she would let that happen.

Thankful for the unseasonably warm spring, she opts for a tight fitting, yet comfortable, pair of blue jeans with a black spaghetti-strap tank top. Classic yet alluring.

Kind-hearted as always, Devin offers to make Victoria anything she wants for breakfast, but she goes simple, with a bowl of Fruit Loops. Perfect for aggravating Brigitta with how unladylike she thinks eating them is.

With a mouthful of cereal, Victoria walks onto the terrace. Brigitta lowers her sunglasses to glare her disapproval with Victoria's attire. She favours fashionable over comfort. Tessa's white and yellow floral dress flows around her as she rises from the patio couch.

Brigitta, who doesn't care to move on Victoria's account, says, "This is Tessa. The newest member of our family."

Tessa steps forward and leans over the railing with a smile. "We met last night." She crosses her arms and her diamond dances in the sunlight.

Victoria refrains from acting on her impulses to rip it off the scrawny finger and hurl it into the yard.

"Well, then you met the real Victoria. The destructive member of our family."

Brigitta's comment ignored, Tessa points to a chair near her soon-to-be mother-in-law "Care to join us?"

"I prefer to watch from over here." Victoria pulls out a chair at the high top table, where her back is to Brigitta. She turns her attention to the soldiers below, who are gathering some rifles and heading for the outdoor shooting range.

Tessa pulls herself onto the chair beside Victoria.

Victoria recognizes the power move of not taking the chair opposite her. This way, Tessa can get right in Victoria's face if needed. "Nicholas tells me you're a pretty excellent shot yourself."

"I can hold my own. Haven't spent a bullet that didn't make its mark."

The women stare out into the forest. Flocks of birds scatter with the sound of nearby shots. Hunting season is in full swing, but not for animals.

Brigitta walks over and stops the spoonful of cereal Victoria's about to shovel into her mouth. "Must you eat like an animal?"

"Technically, we are mammals."

Brigitta rolls her eyes. "Has Tessa told you the good news?"

"Are you referring to the diamond ring on her finger?" She turns to Tessa. "Congratulations, by the way. I don't think I said that last night."

"No, you didn't, and thank you. Nicholas and I are very excited."

"I bet," Victoria says through a mouthful of Fruit Loops.

"Only four months until the big day, September sixth." Brigitta takes a long draw of her cigarette.

Victoria almost chokes with the news the wedding will occur on her real dad's birthday. "Anything special about that date?" Victoria chews vigorously.

"Brigitta called The Capital Club in Halifax, and that was the only date available in the next year. They'd had a last-minute cancellation."

"Is that right? How fortunate."

Victoria's aware that Brigitta's smile isn't painted on today. She's hit her mark and it stings.

Brigitta chimes in, "I thought about having it here. Safety and all, but then I realized Nicholas will only have one wedding, so we'd better do it in style. Make sure people know just because Nathan has departed this world, the Townsends aren't going anywhere. Well, I'll leave you two to get acquainted. There's lots of planning to do for a celebration this size. Victoria, be nice to your new sister."

The word dances like ants on Victoria's skin. Brigitta hums as she departs. Something Victoria has never heard her do. Alarmed, she picks up her dishes and goes to leave, when Tessa gently places a hand on hers. "We should talk."

"I suppose we should." She retakes her seat.

"Brigitta told me about you and Nicholas when you were teenagers. With no other kids around, I suppose it's natural. Perverted, but natural. She's also mentioned you've remained close. I'd be lying if I say I don't hope to come between you. I get that siblings have a unique relationship, especially yours. But I'm about to be his wife, and I don't need to worry that you'll be poisoning his ears against me. We don't have to like each other, but we have to live together. So can we agree to be affable?"

"What, no deep-hearted speech about how much you love him?"

"I don't think you'd believe me if I gave you one. You know the play my father is making by trying to secure our futures. But, yes, I love Nicholas, even if you may not believe me. And I'll do whatever it takes to ensure that he and I are protected."

"Do you have any idea who I am and what I've done for this family? For Nicholas?"

"I know you've lucked your way into running the whole thing. Although, if I have any say in it, it won't be for very long. I also know what you did during those late nights protecting my father, and how you got his enemy to back down. So, I know you don't shy away from the dirty work. But I don't mind getting dirty myself."

"I'm aware. Nice work with the cyanide, by the way. It was kind of you to help Nicholas with his problem."

Tessa's mouth gapes open.

Victoria smiles, knowing Nicholas hasn't told Tessa he'd shared their secret. She steps off her chair and Tessa mirrors her action. Tessa, taller than Victoria, hovers over her. Victoria clenches her fists. "I should not have to say it, but I will. You hurt Nicholas, physically or emotionally, and I will kill you. And you know that is not an empty threat."

Tessa doesn't back down. "You get in my way and you'll need some serious plastic surgery if you ever want anyone to look at you without revulsion again. I'm sure Brigitta would be happy to help me get you out of the way."

They stare each other down, each refusing to look away.

Victoria knew this woman would be trouble, but she did not expect a power-hungry viper. Victoria's going to have her hands full if she can't stop the wedding.

CHAPTER FORTY-EIGHT

Now

Infused with anger from her conversation with Tessa, Victoria is on the hunt for Nicholas. She's not hiding her emotions and those she comes across divert out of her way. She didn't expect Nicholas to remain celibate, or become a monk while she was away for an undetermined amount of time. But it didn't make the idea of him actually being happy with someone else feel less like a searing dagger through the heart. Especially, with someone who was clearly out for their own good fortune.

She locates her target in the alcove library at the top of the stairs. Like her, Nicholas was a voracious reader. She also suspects he was keeping his distance while the women of the house flashed their claws.

"We need to talk," Victoria says.

"We can use my room." Nicholas offers as he rises from his chair, draping his book over the arm.

The thought of being in the space occupied by her new rival made the contents of last night's revelry, and her breakfast, in her stomach swirl. "Let's go in there, where we know no one will be listening." Down the hall, towards the back of the house, she stops in front of a woven tapestry of the original Bluenose racing through Halifax Harbour.

With six short beeps, a large metal door silently swings open, and blue lights illuminate the floor to reveal the shadows of a panic room as large as Victoria's bedroom.

Nicholas follows her in, and with a push of a button, the door closes a lot quieter than she would expect for something so large and heavy. Clunks and clangs of metal bars lock them in. With the door secure, the blue lights turn white.

Victoria brings a large screen to life and reveals what is happening on all of the cameras on the property. She'll see if someone attempts to interrupt them.

"I've gotten to know your beloved a little more this morning. I can't say that I like her or her intentions."

"Do we need to do this right now? I want to know what Irving said."

"We'll get to that." She feared he'd shut down after that conversation and she needed information. "First, little Tessa wasn't shy about why she was marrying you. So, how is it you agreed to this charade?"

"Did she also tell you she loved me?"

"The word may have come up. But, a man's heart has been his downfall before. I want to make sure that's not happening here. I think we can agree that the last thing either of us wants is for Tessa to be the one pulling the strings of this family."

"She knows her place."

"How Edwardian of you. I can guarantee you she will not be content sitting in the background. Hell, take her hands-on approach to help you kill Nathan. What if she comes after us next?" Her hands shake and the freedom the confined room creates allows all the sadness, grief and stress to release itself. She drops into the bottom bunk of one of two metal bunk-beds that mirror each other at the back of the room. Tears stream down her cheeks.

Nicholas moves to join her, wrapping his arm around her. Despite her anger, she doesn't refuse his affection. They lean back and she curls up against his chest, massaging the lapel of his suit jacket. The smell of his coastal cologne brings her comfort.

She's reminded of how they stared up at the stars six years ago, when Nicholas was forced to break off their relationship. Back then, she had let her anger get the better of her. Tears stain her face as her mind wanders back to the memory.

The fire crackles and mesmerizes them as they lie on a blanket beside Rocky. The light to see each other was the fire's only purpose as their bodies provided each other with what little heat they needed on the warm, starry summer night.

Nicholas' arm is his pillow, and he watches the blinking stars dance in the clear sky. The soothing aroma of burning wood does not calm his nerves. He's glad he gave in to Victoria's idea to spend the evening together, away from the prying eyes of Father and Mother. An ache in the back of his throat forms at the thought of what he has to do.

He's dreaded this day for months but it's the right thing to do. For The Family. For him. And, he hopes, for Victoria.

She burrows further into his body. His cologne tugs at her heartstrings as she attempts to bury the trepidation dancing along her skin. Over the last few months, Nicholas has been brushing off invitations to spend time with her, when normally, he initiates their encounters. She wants to ask him about it, but is afraid of the answer, so she focuses on the rhythmic beating in his chest, noticing it's a little faster than normal.

As if he's read her mind, Nicholas' hand rubs her arm. As he raises himself on his side, his eyes fill with sadness, and Victoria wonders if she spots some fear. "There's something we should talk about," he says.

Victoria sits upright. "If it's something that would ruin this night, then let's talk about it some other time."

His shoulders slump forward. "It can't wait."

Her heart drops. "Are you sick?"

"No. I'm fine."

"Oh." Her eyes fall to her hands.

"Despite being discreet, our colleagues, and enemies, are talking about how close we are."

Victoria's jaw tenses, and she grips the blanket in her fists. "Let them. It's not like we act like anything more than brother and sister when we are with anyone else." The word brother leaves a foul taste in her mouth. "Business isn't being affected."

"Actually, it is. Not in the amount of money we are making, but people have somehow noticed the fact we are more than siblings. To everyone else, we are committing incest. The people we deal with like to keep things in the family, but not that much. They are thinking Father can't control his own children. If he can't control his family, what else can't he control? If people keep talking, Father will lose his seat as Director of The Family."

Hurt and rage fight for release from Victoria's rigid body. She stands and puts her clothes on in a frenzy. She circles the fire.

Nicholas buttons up his shirt but keeps his distance. He knows better than to approach her when she's angry. He waits for her to speak first.

"How do people know anything more than what we portray? It's Brigitta isn't it. She's done this."

"Maybe."

"Maybe? Who else would knowingly put Nathan's position in danger, risking their own life if he ever found out? She'd be able to convince him that her actions were for the best, and receive little to no punishment. She'd know how to rectify the situation before it would ruin him. Hell, he's probably in on it." She leans on Rocky and grips it so tight that, if she were Superman, she'd crush it.

Nicholas remains silent.

"I see you're not disagreeing with me. Are you in on this, too?" she asks.

"We have to be realistic."

"Great, just great." She swallows the tears welling up in her eyes and allows her fury to eat the sadness.

"Can you be serious for a moment so we can talk about this? I don't like it either, but it makes sense that whatever this is must stop."

"Whatever this is?" Unable to stop herself, she lunges at Nicholas. He stumbles backwards but catches himself. He clamps his hands around her wrists in the hopes she'll calm down and listen.

His actions have the opposite impact. The restraints fuel her rage and she tugs herself free. She wants to punch him but stops herself. She needs him to see reason, and beating the shit out of him won't help her cause.

"This hurts me too," Nicholas says.

"Bullshit." His eyes reflect pain, but she questions if he's learned the art of deception through Nathan's use of fake feelings. Is he now good enough to fool her? "If you loved me at all, we'd figure a way to make this work."

"That's not fair. You know I love you, and that's why we need to talk about it. You're an expert at boxing up your feelings when you want to, so can you please do that for ten minutes and talk rationally about this?"

Victoria is speechless at how effortlessly he disregards their love. As though it's a switch to be turned on and off. She stares at him in silence.

"Father said that if we don't-"

"Father said? Oh, of course you two have talked about it and decided without me. Why would my opinion need to be heard?" She finds some pebbles nearby and whips them at Nicholas.

He raises his arm as a screen. "It's not like I brought it up. But you know how Father is. Another test of my loyalty to guarantee I'm willing and able to do what it takes to lead our family, and the larger one. He's focused on how to rectify the growing concern of our reputation."

"Is this is the reason you've been acting cagey around me for the last few months?"

"It's taken me a while to accept what has to happen. I knew if I came to you before I was ready, you'd convince me not to end things. I want you to know that I don't want this, but it has to happen."

His lack of emotion punctures her heart. She wants to cry; instead, she uses the heartbreak to push her through the conversation. "Congratulations! You've become Nathan. No one else matters but yourself."

Nicholas runs his fingers through his hair. "Stop acting like a child and think rationally. You know this is the right thing to do."

Victoria boils over. If he thinks she's acting like a child, well, then he can get his wish. She sprints over to him and knees him in the groin. He topples to his knees, hands bringing little comfort to the throbbing pain between his legs. "You're a self-righteous bastard." Her desire for him to feel the same level of pain as she does in this moment causes her to do something she'd never thought herself capable of.

She pushes him into the fire and runs towards the house.

With his hands preoccupied, Nicholas can't prevent himself from landing sideways on the hot embers.

Fury overtaking concern, Victoria keeps going until a scream filled with so much pain jumps through the air. She turns and sprints back.

"It burns, it burns." Nicholas on his knees, is clawing at the air around his neck. Too scared to scorch his hands on whatever is causing the pain.

Victoria peers at his neck and sees his polyester/nylon mix shirt has melted to his skin, and continues to burn. Part of it is stuck under the remaining fabric of the collar. In a panic, she reaches for it with her bare hand, but Nicholas stops her.

"It's too hot," he says through gritted teeth and tears.

"I need to get it off." Victoria's eyes land on a bucket of water they have ready to dowse the fire with. She dumps it over his head. Sizzle and smoke travel to the stars, but the ember still glows. She splashes the water from the other bucket on his neck.

Nicholas pulls off the remnants taking with it some skin and tosses it into the fire. For good measure, he takes off the rest of his top, just in case there are any stowaways he didn't feel past the pain in his face, neck and shoulder. The freshly burned skin is red and has already blistered.

Nicholas stares down at Victoria, his eyes reflecting the flames in the pit. Will the bond between them shield her from his hostility?

Permanently marked by Victoria's outburst, Nicholas stomps into the forest without a word.

Retracted from her minds eye, Victoria can't help but feel karma has come to kick her in the ass for her actions that night. A bullet wound being the least of the scars she's received since returning home.

She silently curses herself of allowing Tessa, and Brigitta, to get under her skin. She'll do better to heed Nathan's advice and let the scorn of others fall off her back.

She clears her throat and pushes herself up on her elbow. "Promise me that there will be no more secrets. If we are going to keep this family in power, and get you into the Director's seat, I can't be worried that you're hiding things from me. We have to tackle this together."

"I promise."

"That means sharing anything important you and the future Mrs. ..." her lips refuse to let the Townsend's last name cross them, "talk about regarding the business. Or if she tells you Brigitta is conjuring something up."

"I promise. And you'll promise to be a little more trusting with Tessa. And others."

"You know the life we live right? Trust gets you killed."

"Stop being dramatic. The people around us are loyal."

"How about I'll say I try?"

"Fine. For now, but if you don't start trusting us, you'll go crazy just like father did."

She averts her gaze. "Right. We definitely don't want that. Have you spoken to Brigitta about her suspicions of Paul?"

"Briefly. The more ill father got, the more he started talking about their future, including marriage. Not wanting to cause alarm, she played along, while seeding misinformation."

"Did she tell you any of this before?"

"No. With everything else I was taking care of; she didn't want to worry me. She said she thought she was handling it."

Victoria's confident Brigitta wouldn't jeopardize Nicholas' succession, especially for the likes of Paul. A man useful to keep her occupied while Nathan was focused elsewhere, but not a person she'd position herself under outside of the bedroom. "I suppose if she had found something explicitly incriminating, she would have come to you. Enable you to exercise your authority to take him down."

Unsettled by what she has to tell him next, she pushes herself off the bunk, stretches and turns to Nicholas, who is hunched on the lower bunk with his hands clasped and elbows rested on his knees.

"The conversation with Irving?" he asks.

She licks her lips. "As it stands, he supports The Family's vote," she quickly adds, "but he agrees we need to reinstate their trust in you and the two of us leading behind the scenes is sufficient." The second in command was a de facto leader, anyway. She didn't need to tell Nicholas that Irving specifically relegated him to that role.

"And the future? Is he cutting me off from officially leading once your years are up?"

"He didn't say, and I didn't feel like it was my place to ask. Not this soon. But, we'll fix this sooner than that. We have to."

"Right." Nicholas rubs his face with the palm of his hands. He pushes himself to standing. "And how do we do that?"

"I'm still trying to figure that out. Everything has been happening so quickly, I've barely had time to think. We'll come up with something. Together. I don't want to stay in this role longer than necessary. You know what that will do to me."

He rubs her arms. "I know. I'm sure Mr. Malarkey can find a way around all of this."

"And if he can't."

"Then we adapt," he says.

"I'm happy to see you looking more opportunistically at the future. You had me worried you might never come around."

"I don't like it, but I understand it's my fault. Like you said, we'll figure this out together."

"Irving had some other news."

"Oh?" He steps back.

"In lieu of what happened with Finn, he'll vet and approve any promotions to fill the current vacancies in the inner circle."

"I suppose that makes sense. He'll want to assert some of his power over us to make sure everyone knows who the real boss is. Plus, we probably could use some outside eyes to make sure we are surrounded by people on our side."

"I thought you just said everyone around us is loyal."

"You know what I mean."

"Well, we'll worry about that over the next few months. I'm not sure we need to fill those spots immediately. Also, law enforcement might be making some inroads against us. He's heard some rumours about multiple agencies collaborating. We need to get rid of, or move, any evidence that could be used against us. He doesn't know when it might happen, but as soon as he does, he'll call."

"I'll have Rufus and Janet work on a plan to relocate the weaponry. We'll store the illegal weapons elsewhere. It's not ideal if we need to arm ourselves in an emergency, but we can make do." He taps a metal cabinet beside him.

"Good call." She takes Nicholas' hand before he unlocks the panic room door. "You'll get what you deserve. I promise."

He kisses the top of her head. "I know. I always do."

CHAPTER FORTY-NINE

Now

THE COLD DAMP AIR outside The Capital Club by the Halifax waterfront chills Victoria through to her bones. September wasn't known for it's winter like conditions; however, today, the hood of her jacket fights against the chill. She circles the vehicle in the hopes that she can generate an ounce of heat while waiting for the owner to unlock the building so they can proceed with the wedding reception of her nightmares.

Victoria doesn't feel like celebrating. She's focused on trying to figure out what's best for her and is frustrated that in just over four months she is nowhere closer to an answer. The voice inside her all these years telling her to run, still pokes are her. She now has the financial resources and skills to hide. What she doesn't have is the power to keep those who would want to eliminate the knowledge she has at bay.

She couldn't sit idle in the car. Not after standing at the alter of Saint Peter's Church and witnessing Nicholas vow to love and cherish her newest rival. She needs to keep moving. Keep her thoughts away from them and away from her dad.

Brigitta knew exactly what she was doing when she selected today for Nicholas' wedding. Victoria hasn't let on that her grief for her old life, and for her parents, returned like a waterfall during this morning's shower. And she won't. She's adhered the mask of fake congeniality and will push through. Brigitta will not win.

Victoria bites the inside of her mouth. She needs a distraction. She takes in the tall, dark, and handsome man, in his blue peacoat, leaning against their vehicle. His ungloved hands are deep inside his jacket pockets. If the weather is bothering him, he isn't giving any outward clues.

"I wonder if they'll take this weather as a bad omen. Like God's not smiling down on this union or something." Victoria takes to running up and down the stone steps of the iconic 1860s building to keep from freezing. And her mind from spiraling.

"If some clouds and water doomed every wedding in Nova Scotia, less than half the population would be married," Aidan says.

"Okay mister literal. Remind me why I agreed to be part of this charade?"

"Because you love your brother. Not to mention, you're sticking it to Brigitta by being his best man."

"Ah yes, must keep reminding myself of that. Maybe that will warm up my insides." The man isn't a satisfactory distraction. She puffs up her cheeks and blows on her hands. Her mittens only a thing barrier to the cold.

She tries not to think about the hoards of boxes full of Nathan's mess. She has dismissed Nicholas' suggestion to burn it. She wants to know what information built the paper towers. Needs to know. To appease him, and ensure they're protected from a pending raid, she's moved everything to a location only she, he, and Aidan as he rarely leaves her side, knows about. There could be more secrets at her fingertips that could help her or hurt her. She needs to arm herself either way.

Yet, everyday she makes excuses to avoid the pieces of a man, and his life, that took hers away. A man who transformed her from a sweet, innocent girl into a woman skilled at, and willing, to pull the trigger with little second thought. A woman engrossed in the tumultuous life of law breaking and death. Someone who enjoys the challenge that the Townsend life brings.

She squints away the tears forming in the bottom of her eyes. With the busyness of the transition of power, and at her own avoidance, she has evaded the confusing grief that came with Nathan's death. Pushed aside the waves that have come over at the realization that someone she thought was practically immortal, was slowly taken by the greed of others.

For her own protection, she shoves Nathan in the same locked box in her mind as her parents. A box that has remained closed for years. She knows opening it would force her to face fears and realities about herself that she'd rather stay buried. Right now, looking back would only hurt her. If she wants to survive, she needs to focus on the now, and the future.

A black and red Mini Cooper pulls into a stall marked Staff.

"Oh, thank goodness." Victoria paces on the first step to the club.

A ragged, bone-thin woman, in a sleek black suit, pulls a key-ring from her jacket pocket. "Sorry about that. I got a flat and it took a while for someone to stop and help."

Two Townsend soldiers, who were not ashamed to take cover inside the vehicle, enter behind Victoria and Aidan, and take their positions inside the entrance. It's taken a while for her to get used to constantly having a protection detail. Even when it's just Aidan. She used to be the one ensuring the safety of others. Never one to desire attention, the role reversal makes her uneasy.

The modern, yet traditional, décor of the entry brings Victoria back to a time when women wouldn't be allowed in such an establishment. The Merola tile floors show little wear from centuries of traffic. Antique paintings adorn the white walls and crystal chandelier provides much needed light on a dreary day.

They proceed into an elegant reception hall decorated in golds, oranges and deep greens. The chargers under the plates, and the rims of the stemware are coated in gold. Nothing but the best for Brigitta's baby boy. Victoria was astonished at the cost, but with other battles in process, and brewing, she had little energy to fight this one.

The woman addresses Victoria, "I hope everything you saw last night is still satisfactory."

"Ya. Sure. Where's the staff? Everyone will be here in less than an hour." She could smell the succulent roast beef filtering in through the vents, but there wasn't any sign of any one else.

"They will be here momentarily. Don't worry. We'd never, well, pardon my French, fuck up this wedding. We know who you, and your family are, and I assure you everything will be perfect."

"Good." As much as Victoria would love a disaster to erupt tonight, she didn't want to deal with the aftermath. It was better for her if things ran smoothly.

"If you want to head upstairs and get settled in the groom's suite, I'll bring up some champagne."

"I'd prefer tequila." It had been a long day and Victoria couldn't see an end in sight. She might as well enjoy what she can of it.

She and Aidan saunter up the grand staircase adorned with a brass railing on one side, and a dark wood banister on the other. The modern grey carpet elegant and understated.

The groom's suite has floor to ceiling cherry wood walls with worn centuries old panelled flooring. Victoria could see jolly men of the past, and present, gathered around smoking cigars in comfort while they shared secrets or made conniving business plans. Much like her and The Family do at Maxwell's. She unbuttons the jacket of her form fitting tuxedo, falls onto the modern cream coloured couch and sinks into the soft cushions. "Thank God Tessa didn't want me there for all of the photos. I'd need more than tequila to deal with that."

As if on cue, the owner of the club places a tray with a charcuterie board and drinks on the table in front of the couch. She nods as she departs.

Aidan removes his jacket, rolls up his sleeves and pours Victoria a drink. She downs it, he refills the glass and cracks open a sparkling water for himself.

She pats the cushion beside her, "Sit."

He follows her command.

"We've been pretty much inseparable since the funeral and yet, I don't know who Lucy is."

He looks at her quizzically and then at the inside of his left arm "Right. Just an old flame. Nothing exciting."

"Nothing exciting? A lot of effort has been put into that tattoo with the flowers, and music notes growing out of the name. If she was just some fling, I would have thought you would have covered that up by now. Unless, you somehow manage to have a woman outside this family I don't know about?"

He chuckles. "We both know there's only you."

"Funny." She holds his soft gaze and sips the amber liquid from her crystal glass. They've never been intimate, but that hasn't stopped her recent dreams from becoming scintillating scenes of them ravaging each other's bodies. She licks her lips and thanks whatever god overseas the universe that the club has allowed Marcus to run the bar, rather than just their own employees. At least she's guaranteed to get laid tonight without compromising her authority over Aidan.

She pulls her mind away from sensual thoughts. "No, really. Who's Lucy?"

"Honestly, she's no one. I couldn't bring myself to destroying the beautiful art by trying to hide it. It's not like she shattered my heart or I loathe her. It was a mutual break-up."

She doesn't believe him, but she has enough emotions running through her today, she doesn't want to delve into a pile of his. "Hmm. Right." She holds out her glass and he dutifully tops it up.

"You might want to slow down on that. Don't you have to give a speech?"

"Thankfully they changed their minds. Everyone agreed that giving me a microphone would not be a good idea. Tessa's Maid of Honour and Brigitta will do the talking. I get to sit there and try not to kill anyone."

"Ya, I'm pretty sure that's not the wedding present Nicholas registered for."

"Ugh. Don't ever become a comedian. You're not funny." She thought it was a little funny, but didn't want to encourage him.

There's a knock on the door. Aidan rises from the couch, hand on the gun in his shoulder holster.

Nicholas pops his head inside, then finding who he's looking for enters. Not a strand of his dirty-blond hair is out of place. His Armani suit tailored for his body accentuates his medium build. He may not have the muscles Aidan did, but he wasn't any less handsome. "I see you started without me."

"I needed to do something after I was kicked out of the photo party." She winks and pours him a drink.

Nicholas nods for Aidan to leave, who closes the door behind him.

"Is something wrong?" she asks.

"No. I just wanted to talk to you before dinner."

"How much more tequila am I going to need?"

"Vic, come on. I'm serious. We haven't really had time to sit and talk like we used to. I wanted to see how you were doing after the past few months.

Is being Director everything you thought it would be?" He restrains the playfulness, but it's present.

She wants to brush aside the topic, but he's right. Outside of the quick chat in the panic room, they haven't connected for more than business, or meals where Tessa and Brigitta were present. They need to lay everything on the table. "I understand why you killed him. We would have lost everything if Nathan kept deteriorating. I just don't like that you did it without me. Not after everything I, and we've been through. But I forgive you."

"Really?"

"Yes. Do I forgive you for including *her*? Not yet. And I can't promise that I will."

"What can I do to make it up to you?"

"Well, I'd say don't go through with the marriage, but look where we are." She half-heartedly jokes. "Seriously, I'll be fine. Provided she stays out of my way. And that you are careful around her. Irving hasn't approved her getting too close to our work. The last thing I want is to have to clean up after some loose lips start giving her the upper hand."

He puts a hand over his heart, "I'll be careful."

"Good." Victoria cracks her knuckles. She wants to tell him that the analysis conducted on Nathan's blood showed more than cyanide, but the information would shatter him. She's kept the information hidden for months, what's a few more days? Or Weeks? She might not be full of joy, but days like these don't happen often for Nicholas. He deserves to enjoy it. "That was a beautiful ceremony, by the way."

"Ya. Tessa did a great job with it."

She won't admit Tessa was good at anything. Instead, she nibbles on some cheese.

"Should I even ask if you are happy your stuck here for a while?"

"Five years is more than a while." Leaving isn't an option. Irving McKinnon has made that clear on multiple occasions. The reins that previously tethered her to Nathan have tied her to another monster. "Do I love it? No. Will I keep trying to figure out a way to put you in the position you belong? Yes. For now, I'll do my part. I won't go all destructive on you."

"That's good to hear. The Family seems to respect you, and not because Irving backs you, so that's one of the big hurdles overcome."

"Oh, I don't think they are done making me prove myself, but at least no one has challenged my position. I think knowing you and I are leading the charge together has helped us more than hindered us. Those who voted against you seem to have come around."

Nicholas swirls the tequila around in his glass. His face can't hide the scar that betrayal has left. "A united front is always a stronger one."

"When did you become so wise?" She playfully nudges his elbow.

He smiles and his soft eyes focus on her. "How are you doing about today? Like, really doing?" The question hangs in the air for a moment.

She squeezes her eyes shut as her chest heaves. "Honestly, today sucks." She grabs a tissue from the side table and daps her face.

He wraps his arm around her. "I'm sorry. I tried to get them to change the date, but they wouldn't budge. I couldn't tell Tessa the reason, so I didn't have much of a case to keep fighting."

"I know."

"Do you want to give a little birthday toast to him?"

Even with Victoria superseding Nicholas as the Head of the Townsends, and Director of The Family, he found a space in his heart to still care about her loss. She can't withhold the tears anymore.

After a few moments, and a tear-stained lapel, Victoria removes herself from his arms. "Why can't you be an asshole? It would make today so much easier." Her attempts to severe his relationship with Tessa were futile. She lost and she hates losing.

He rubs her back and stays silent.

"I guess you really love her then, huh?" She avoids his gaze. She doesn't want to see the truth. The words will be hard enough.

"I do."

She bites her lower lip. "So, then I guess this is goodbye, in a way."

"I suppose, but you know that I'll always be there for you. Whatever you need. And we'll still be in the same house for a while as the other one is built. You can't get rid of me that easily."

"I'm just glad we don't share a wall anymore. That, I couldn't handle."

"That was a bit awkward. Hopefully, your new place gives you the separation you need to not go stir crazy with everything."

"I hope so too." She finishes her drink, rises from the furniture, and looks down on the face of the one person who made her feel loved in a den full of beasts. "I should get cleaned up. I don't need Brigitta on a rampage because my make-up is a mess."

He stands before her and his soft hands cup the sides of her face. "One last kiss."

"One last kiss."

CHAPTER FIFTY

NOW

FROM THE HEAD TABLE, the guests look like a herd of deer in headlights. Their eyes glazed over and forced to feign attention. Tessa's speech started twenty minutes ago and no one but her knows when it will end. Victoria hopes it's over soon. Even Nicholas, seated beside her, has had to stifle a yawn.

With the two bottles of wine on each table empty, Victoria observes the guests twitch as they consider if it's worth risking the bride's wrath to go to the bar for a refill. They restrain themselves.

Ms. Yang, elegant and poised as normal, pulls out a golden flask from her red clutch. She passes it around to other members of her family. Victoria wishes she'd thought of that.

Mr. Tanner's chin bounces off his chest and startles himself awake. He looks around to see if anyone but his wife noticed. Victoria smiles at him and he puts a finger to his lip. She winks her reply.

Mrs. Harris and Mr. Bendale, at their family tables, pay more attention to their laps than the bride. Victoria assumes cell phones are involved and for a moment wonders if the two of them are having an affair. She chuckles to herself at the thought, followed by a good for them. Their partners aren't winning any spouse of the year prizes so why not have some fun while they still can. Victoria has no concerns about who is having sex with whom, provided The Family, or the Townsends aren't impacted.

Mr. Metcalf departed after saying grace before the meal. "I'm too old for these types of parties." He told her. "You have fun for the both of us."

When she was younger, Victoria had been afraid of the man. He was stern all the time and she felt like he kept a close eye on her whenever they were in the same room. As though he knew her secret. It had given her the creeps. Now, he seems more like the grandfather she never knew. More genial, but with a shrewd side. He'd reassured her after the debacle with Paul that she would be a talented leader, if she didn't back down or take anyone's shit.

"...Thank you all for coming and making this day even more special. Cheers."

Oh, thank God she's done, Victoria thinks, and raises her glass.

Chairs scrape against hard wood floors as guests scramble to get more alcohol. The crowd determined to be adequately satiated before the next speech. Before another word is spoken, wait staff replace the empty bottles in the center of the tables.

Tessa smirks at Victoria and leaves the podium. Her maid-of-honour has to help her maneuver with the train of the sleek, stylish silk wedding dress. Although the top included a wide wrap which hid the bosom, there was a slit in the middle of the front up to above the knee, which Tessa fought with Brigitta to have. She agreed to stick with a modern, yet classic look, but she refused to trap her beautiful brown legs under a mountain of fabric.

As Tessa and her minion pass behind Victoria, she silently curses the woman for putting the podium at her end of the table. For someone who wanted to avoid her being in their wedding photos, she put her in the way for the photographer capturing the speeches. Her cheeks hurt from the plastered-on smile. She massages the crick in her neck from having to look up and sideways as she pretended to pay attention to the speakers.

Brigitta leaves her seat at the Towsend table prominently front and center in the crowd. "Esteemed guests, if you could please take your seats."

The crowd shuffles and those who didn't have time to get served at the bar cling to the new wine bottles.

"Thank you." Mother smiles at her son. "For months, I've been trying to figure out what to say about this perfect couple. Words of wisdom to guide them through the winding road of marriage. No matter what I wrote out, it didn't seem good enough. It was full of clichés and didn't seem to fit the occasion." She finishes her martini and holds her arm out until a petite wait staff replaces it. "Not when my son's place in this family has been stolen from him."

Audible gasps escape the crowd. The room is enraptured by the ill-mannered road the reception has taken. Including Irving McKinnon, who rises and buttons-up his double-breasted suit jacket.

Victoria is shocked Brigitta would risk ruining the perfect wedding, for her perfect boy. Rather than react, she decides to let the woman make a fool of herself. A little icing on the proverbial cake, after a torturous day.

Nicholas stands and pulls Brigitta away from the microphone. Trapping her between him and the wall, but not far enough, as the crowd can hear his whispers. "Mother, we've been over this. You agreed to adhere to father's will and the results of the vote. Let's not make a scene. I think I speak for most of the group, get over it and stop acting like a catty school girl."

Brigitta tries to push Nicholas out of the way, but he's stronger, and keeps her in place.

Victoria get's up and fumbles with the microphone as she tries to figure out how to turn it off. There's no on/off switch and it's mounted to the podium. Tessa's face is ghost white and her mouth is agape like a cod fish. Brigitta has gone off script. Victoria gets some pleasure in that. "Sorry about this everyone. Talk amongst yourselves while we determine if there are any more speeches. Better yet, don't let an open bar go to waste. If someone who works here can turn this bloody thing off, that would be great."

She turns on Nicholas and Brigitta, who are still arguing over whether or not Brigitta can finish her speech. She interrupts their bickering. "No one is finishing anything. I've been civil today. Taken your quips in stride, but if you think you can go off the rails while Irving is here, you better think again."

"She's right," Nicholas adds, "What you're doing is not helpful."

"I have to do something and Irving won't meet with me in private. Maybe now, I have his attention."

Victoria rolls her eyes at the woman's desperation. She grips Brigitta's chin. "It's not only Irving's attention you have and that's the problem."

As if on cue, their leader joins the group, which has grown to include Tessa. "Everything alright here?" he asks.

Victoria releases Brigitta. "Good evening, sir. Yes, everything is fine. Brigitta's going to take her seat, isn't she?"

"Before she does that," Irving says, "Why don't we talk. Privately."

With her tactics working, Brigitta can't hide a small smile. With her alcohol free hand, she straightens her dress. "Come on Nicholas."

"Not Nicholas." He nods to Victoria.

Nicholas' shoulders deflate. Tessa glares at Victoria as the three depart with the crowds' eyes glued to them.

Irving guides them into a temperature-controlled glass room, on the other side of the building's entry. The walls of the room are lined with humidors, boxes of cigars, and high-end liquor. Without instruction, an employee pulls down an intricately carved humidor, with the name "McKinnon" etched into a gold plaque on the side, from the shelf behind them. Placing it on a mahogany bar-top, he steps out and gives the occupants their privacy.

The bustle of the party goes unheard in the sound-proofed room.

Irving offers the women a cigar. Both refuse. He takes his time cutting the end and puffs of smoke float to the ceiling while he ensures the cigar stays lit. Unlike the fluffy clouds, Irving's voice is authoritarian. "Brigitta, out of respect for Nathan, I've given you some leeway after his death to work through your grief. Including, your anger at Victoria's ascension. Things haven't gone as you planned but my decisions are final and I will not have you ruining everything I built because you are hurt that your little boy doesn't get to sit in the big chair."

Brigitta puffs out her chest, "I haven't worked hard for over thirty years so she can reap the rewards. I've supported Nathan during his episodes of madness. Helped train the soldiers, and Nicholas. I've killed for this family and this is the thanks I get?"

"You're right. Your hard work hasn't been for her benefit. It's been for The Family. For me. Let's not forget who you are ultimately working for."

Brigitta mouth moves as though she wants to protest, but no sound comes out.

Irving continues, "In light of everything that's happened, and with the stipulation that this is where the fighting ends, I'll give you one free shot at Victoria. Right here."

"I'm sorry, what?" Victoria asks.

Before Irving can clarify his instructions, Brigitta has her hands wrapped around Victoria's throat and is squeezing as hard as she can.

Victoria's instinct kicks in and she grabs the woman's forearms, just above the elbows and pulls her closer to her. With a swift knee in the gut, Brigitta grunts and releases her hands. Victoria kicks the legs from under the woman and her rival falls to the floor. A puce puddle.

Brigitta scrambles to her feet. "You said I had one shot. She intervened; I should get another one."

"I appreciate your eagerness, but you didn't give me time to stipulate the rules. You've lost the opportunity. Now, there's the matter of how we all move forward from here. Hint, the answer includes working with each other not against each other. Victoria, I think it's time we tell her."

The fine wrinkles on Brigitta's forehead deepen.

Victoria brushes her hair behind her ears and smirks. "Before Nathan's death, he and Irving agreed on what his Will would stipulate."

"No? Nathan and I agreed it would always be Nicholas. That is until you got your little claws into him."

"I'm not the one with claws in anyone." Victoria steps in front of her rival. She's been dying to tell the woman that she's known her secret, but Irving insisted they wait until it's use was most beneficial. "You know I never wanted to return. I had nothing to do with the repercussions from his death. You should have thought about that before you tried to orchestrate the future you wanted."

Brigitta takes a step back and grips the edge of the bar to keep herself upright.

"Did you think we wouldn't find out?"

"How?" The word almost sticks in her mouth.

"The same report that told me about the cyanide in his blood. What was your plan? You knew Nathan would never have relinquished power without a fight. Hell, he kept running everything while losing his mind."

Brigitta eyes dart between the people before her. "After he made a few poor decisions, I called you," she looks to Irving, who eyes her over the rim of his glasses, "I asked you to come for a visit. I wanted you to see Nathan's deterioration for yourself. Once you were on the compound, I was going to prove how competent Nicholas was and request the power structure be changed. But you kept postponing it."

Irving remains silent and continues to cede the power in the room to Victoria.

"So, you kept poisoning him and it got the point that Nicholas felt compelled to take things into his own hands."

"I never wanted my son to kill his father. I just...well, Nathan had been so engrossed with the business that I was tired of being left out. I felt like another pawn in his game. If he had only taken a less active roll and let Nicholas carry the burden none of this would have happened. But he wasn't willing to relinquish power, and were being made to look like fools before The Family."

"The Family didn't have any suspicions about Nathan's deteriorating mental acuity. You, Nicholas and Tessa acted out of your own paranoia of failure."

Brigitta raises an eyebrow.

"Yes, we are aware of Tessa's involvement. The question is, is Nicholas aware of yours?"

Brigitta's eyes widen and she swallows hard.

"I'll take that as a no. Well, that's a bit of a relief as if he'd been deceiving me about that, we'd have a big problem. And he'd never have any power around here."

Panicked, Brigitta speaks, "It was me. Only me. I swear he didn't know." She looks to Irving for acknowledgement her son won't be punished.

The man steps forward. "I've spoken with Nicholas over the past few months and have no reason to believe he knew what you did. I shouldn't have to step in and remind you who is in charge around here. Victoria is my number two. You will listen, and obey her. You will work together for the betterment of the Townsends, and of The Family. Beyond your sheer hatred for her, do you have any reasonable objections to my orders?"

Brigitta straightens her posture and tosses her golden hair over her shoulder. "What happens when The Family finds out who she really is? It's bound to come out eventually. Then what trust will they have in her? In us?"

"Victoria, would you like to respond to that?"

"I'd love to." Hands on her hips, she locks eyes with Brigitta. "We've already told them."

The blood drains from the older woman's face. "You...but..." She collapses on a barstool. "Nicholas?"

"The three of us agreed he wouldn't tell you until your indignation had ceased. Or at least simmered. We didn't want you sharing the news with people outside of the Townsend inner circle, like Tessa. And you still won't tell her."

Brigitta's voice sounds like it's grasping for air, "So, everyone of importance in The Family and on our compound know about...her?"

Victoria whispers in her ear. "You can't win." She steps beside Irving. She may be bound to a different monster, but like the previous one, he was also her new protector.

He removes his glasses, and cleans them with his pocket square. "Brigitta, lets not make this harder than it has to be. There's no need for theatrics, hysterics, or any other acts of disobedience. Be grateful, you're being kept around at all. Tonight's episode has proven that you can't be trusted. Because of that, you will be removed from the inner circle. We'll find other ways for you to contribute to the business."

The veins in Brigitta's neck throb. She goes to speak, but Irving raises his hand and continues, "We could have easily sent you off somewhere, a retirement of sorts, but Victoria suggested you be kept around."

"She...but?"

Victoria knew better than to let an enemy run off and gather their own army. Keeping her close increased the chances of staying alive for the time needed to put Nicholas in the Director's seat. If she had to use the tools at her disposal to get rid of the woman permanently, she would. She hoped it wouldn't come to that, as Nicholas would be devastated.

"Hearing no objections, you may return to the celebration." Irving holds out his arm to guide her out.

Brigitta's red nails clench the handle of the cigar bar's door handle. Victoria can sense the tension coursing through the woman's body. The fight isn't over, but it's been restrained.

When the door opens, the bass from the music reverberates the glass.

The silence returns. Irving turns the humidor towards Victoria, who selects a cigar, runs her nose along it and inhales the woodiness and spices. She's becoming accustomed to the metallic pepper flavour and the memories they conjure of a round tube hanging from Nathan's mouth.

"She won't give up. You know that, right?" Victoria says.

"I doubt it. She's always been a fighter. I have faith you can handle it from here."

"I'm sorry you had to intervene. She'd been mostly good all day. I thought we had avoided having this conversation. I suppose she was waiting until all eyes were on her."

"It's done now. She knows whose side I'm on and hopefully that will put her in her place for a while." He takes a long draw on his cigar. "There's something else we should talk about."

"Have you heard more about the pending raid on the compound?"

He shakes his head as he exhales smoke. "Nothing yet. I'm starting to wonder if my source was misinformed. Continue the diligence though." He ushers her to two large brown leather chairs and taps his cigar on an astray.

They sit and Irving's eyes soften. A little.

Victoria's stomach churns. Something is wrong. "What happened?"

"Nothing. Well, not recently. I want to talk to you about something that happened twenty-one years ago."

Victoria's throat swells and her mouth becomes dry. Her eyes dart between each of his as she can't decide which one to focus on.

"I want to talk to you about your parents."

ACKNOWLEDGEMENTS

This book would not exist without the love and support of you, the reader. The support I've received for my first four novels has pushed me to keep creating. Not to mention the continual requests over the past year to set something in Nova Scotia. Here you go!

There are not enough thank yous for how much a reader's support means to an author, to me. Here's one more – Thank you.

Many thanks go out to the writing community here in my new province. I found my people! When I first started to dig into the writing process during the pandemic, there was no real community that I felt engaged with. Fast forward to 2023, and I was embraced by my library's writing groups, and I haven't looked back. From process to critique, thank you to the members of these groups for your honest and gracious feedback – it really does take a village to finesse writing skills and a story.

A special thank you to Clo Carey Schwager, mentor, writer, group organizer, critique partner, and friend. Without your eyes on this piece, it would not be what it is today. Literally, I removed half of the novel after your feedback. Your expertise and encouragement of writers of all levels is inspiring and I am very grateful that I get to call you my friend.

My writing process involves a lot of time in my head, in my office, and out of town – alone. I would not be able to take the time to bring a book together if it wasn't for my husband, Brian. He keeps me well fed, the pets distracted – sort of, and encourages me to take a weekend, or week, to 'just write'. I am extremely lucky to have such an amazing partner – much love.

My editor, Lisa Klemmensen, the lady who tells me where my comma's go. Your support over these past five books has been invaluable. Your friendship over the past fourteen years, even more meaningful. Thank you for the encouragement to put my work out there.

As always, I would not be where I am today without the love and support of my family. My dad, one of the rocks in my life, whose encouragement to be myself, in life and in writing, has propelled me to keep writing. My mom, the continual promoter of my work to anyone who will listen. Last, but not least, my sister, who exemplifies finding what you want out of life, seeking it, and making it happen.

WANT MORE?

There's three more things to say before you go:

Firstly, if you want to receive early access to my writing, see the behind the scenes of this author's process and life, or be the first to know when a new book is coming out, you can sign up to my monthly newsletter at https://www.nlblandford.com

Secondly, if you enjoyed this book, I'd love to hear from you – nl@nlblandford.com or find me on Instagram https://www.instagram.com/nlblandford/

If you can spare a few minutes, I would be really grateful for a short review on the site from which you purchased the book. If you bought it direct, you could post the review to Goodreads, Storygraph and/or Google. Reviews are invaluable to an author as it helps us gain visibility and provides the social proof we need to keep selling books.

Lastly, a heartfelt thank you for spending your valuable time with these characters.

www.ingramcontent.com/pod-product-compliance
Lightning Source LLC
Chambersburg PA
CBHW050558190726
48283CB00007B/2189